MW01133152

The Siege of Earth
The Ember War Saga Book 7

Richard Fox

ISBN: 1535332182
ISBN-13: 978-1535332187

CHAPTER 1

From the cold void between the stars, Earth's reckoning approached. A dusty gray sphere almost the size of Earth's moon, its surface broken up by circular portholes the size of cities and pitted by micro-meteorite strikes, slowed to a stop near Pluto. The orbits of the moons Hydra and Kerebos altered as the new arrival's gravity threw off the dance maintained around the dwarf planet since long before the birth of humanity.

When Admiral Makarov's Eighth Fleet first encountered the sphere, they named it for an angel of destruction that commanded an army of locusts: Abaddon. The battles that followed in the hours after the discovery claimed the lives of every man and woman in the fleet.

From a distance, Abaddon looked as if wrapped in a symmetrical black web. The web sloughed off the

3

planetoid as the millions of Xaros drones that formed the object's propulsion system uncoupled after their long journey from Barnard's Star. Portholes across the surface opened and millions more drones poured from the interior like wasps evacuating a hive. Drones flew together so closely a person could have walked from one drone to another across the hundreds of miles spanning the entire length.

Inside Abaddon, the conduit connecting the hollowed-out moon to the rest of the Xaros network flared to life. Red plates of armor floating in the center of the command sphere formed into a humanoid shape. Tiny links of chain-mail armor grew between the plates, forming a containment vessel ready to receive the General.

The General's essence flowed into the armor. Bright light glowed beneath the thin eye slits of his facemask.

He floated from the plinth and stretched his mind through his drones, absorbing everything they'd collected on the human defenders.

Workstations flashed to life around the General, showing orbital emplacements around Earth, moons of the outer gas giants, and a sizable fleet over a cold, dusty red planet.

The General looked through the data a second

4

time, examined the waste heat coming off fortifications and double-checked the data his drones had collected the first time they wiped this solar system clean of the humans' polluting presence and what he'd pulled from Torni's mind while she'd been his prisoner.

There were too many ships. The human fleets were an order of magnitude greater than what he'd defeated in the void just beyond Barnard's Star, and that was the last of what had survived when the humans returned and recaptured their home world.

The humans could only breed so quickly. Everything he saw arrayed against him across the solar system was in stark contrast to what he knew the humans had and were capable of producing in the years since their return.

The General's armor burned brighter as anger coursed through him. The conclusion was inescapable: he'd been tricked. The humans were stronger than he thought possible, and he'd burned through much of the potential combat power within Abaddon's mass to reach Earth before the humans could ready their defenses.

He—the one chosen by the Xaros Masters to cleanse this galaxy of its indigenous intelligent life to pave the way for the rest of his kind's glorious arrival—had blundered into a battle not of his design. His drone armadas had annihilated intelligent species through much of the galaxy through a combination of advanced technology and sheer weight of numbers. Had he known the true scope of the humans' defenses he would have brought three transports the size of Abaddon to Earth and been assured an easy victory.

But what he did have…he ran simulations through the computers around him and found his chance of victory almost even with defeat.

He considered leaving his drones to their programming, let them bleed the humans white while he went back to organize another assault force, but to show such contempt for the humans would be a mistake. They were a dangerous foe and he was still unsure what they had removed from the ancient vault hidden deep within the vast nothingness of interstellar space.

No. He would defeat the humans here and now. If Keeper learned of the difficulties he'd encountered while defeating one race of upright mammals that paled in comparison to the might of galactic empires his drones had crushed before reaching the Earth…His position with the peers was tenuous at best. Anything but a simple march across the stars would make him look week.

He would not leave this battle to chance. He broke off a segment of his total force to sow victory. Even if he lost the main fleet to the humans, it wouldn't matter. The entire galaxy was full of his drones, and he would bring that strength to bear quickly and decisively.

A line made up of thousands of drones broke away from the end of the column as the drones left Abaddon. The splinter force made for Pluto.

CHAPTER 2

In their rec room, Hale's Marines crowded around a wall screen filled with the night side of Earth, a live feed from one of the many cameras and telescopes mounted around the *Breitenfeld*. The glare of cities ran through the mountain ranges of Japan, Australia and Korea. Tiny pinpricks of light from cargo shuttles stretched from Earth to orbital platforms and space stations.

Egan clicked a button on a remote and the image changed to the space above the North Pole. Hundreds of warships waited at anchor as dozens of cargo ships cycled into and out of a blocky supply ship.

"OK," Standish said, "none of this was here when we left, right?"

"There must be millions of people down there."

Bailey stood on her tiptoes to peer over Orozco's shoulder. "Crikey, the lights are on in Darwin."

"We must have done the time warp again," Standish said.

"We did. Malal put us in stasis for a couple years until he and Torni could fix the jump engines," Yarrow said. "Didn't you and Bailey get all freaked out when you saw Eighth Fleet on Hawaii? Same explanation. All those lights…got to be proccies."

"How could Ibarra have made so many?" Orozco stroked his chin.

"I guess it depends on how many tubes he has," Yarrow said, "and how fast he can make more tubes. It takes nine days to grow a proccie, right?"

"Little birdie told me there were fifty thousand tubes left after the Toth came for a visit," Standish said. "By 'little birdie' I mean one of Admiral Garret's aides who could not hold his liquor."

"And if Ibarra's been making even more tubes at, say, ten percent a growth period…" Yarrow tapped on his forearm screen and frowned. "That can't be right."

"I didn't join the Marines to do math, new guy. Spit it out," Standish said.

"It's like we're bacteria. The growth curve is exponential," Yarrow said.

"Meaning?" Orozco crossed his massive arms across his chest.

"'Exponential' a big English word you don't know?" Standish gave the Spaniard a quick poke to the ribs. Orozco laid a meaty hand on the back of Standish's neck. "Because I sure don't know what it means. Help a brother out, Yarrow."

"Everything depends on how fast Ibarra could build tubes. Look at that fleet." Yarrow nodded at the ships anchored over the North Pole. "Two supercarriers, half a dozen strike carriers like the *Breitenfeld*. Enough guns to slag everything from Moscow to Warsaw in an afternoon. You think building a tube would be hard for Ibarra?"

"If the solar system's full of proccie bad assess, then why was Admiral Garret's staff walking around on eggshells when the big man showed up?" Bailey asked.

"Doesn't help that our ship's on commo blackout, does it?" Standish looked at Egan, the team's communications specialist. "If only someone we knew could access the telemetry channels back to Titan Station and tap into the restricted data feeds."

Standish leaned toward Egan. "If only he'd tap into the smoke line and let our Ubis synch up with the cloud servers."

Egan backed away. "How do you know about that? I mean, I don't know what you're talking about."

"The smoke line is real?" Orozco asked.

"There's no such thing." Egan shook his head.

"Really, Egan? After all we've been through, you're going to play this game with us?" Standish asked.

"You son of a...fine." Egan flicked his fingertips across his forearm screen and started tapping. "There's a way around the blackout. It's supposed to be a trade secret," he said, flashing Standish a dirty look. "Commo guys have had secret channels since the early days of radio, gives us a way to talk to each other when we need to. Don't go broadcasting this all over the ship. Word'll get back that it was *me* that spilled the beans and then I'm in a world of hurt."

"Synching." Bailey's eyes lit up as she looked at her screen.

"Hey, we're getting paid again! Four years of back pay just hit my account." A smile spread across Standish's face.

"Wait...I've got almost nothing in my account." Yarrow tapped his screen several times. "A garnishment? What the hell? This some sort of proccie tax?"

"I got paid everything," said Egan, a procedurally generated human being, just like Yarrow, "even my flight

11

bonus."

"This is bullshit!" Yarrow kicked a waste bin across the room.

"Settle down, new guy." Standish gave him a pat on the shoulder. "Not like we can buy anything right now. Plus, I'll spot you a few bucks. Three points a month. You pay at least ten percent of what you owe every three weeks or I break a finger."

"Piss off, Standish." Yarrow pulled away and swiped across his screen several times. He tapped his screen, then froze in place.

"Combat pay and everything," Bailey said. "We go on shore leave again and I am going to get so shit-faced that...why is Yarrow so pale?"

Standish snapped his fingers next to Yarrow's ear. The medic didn't respond.

"New guy," Standish said, waving his hand in front of Yarrow's face. "Earth to new guy. What's the deal?" Standish peered over Yarrow's arm. "Look at that—it's your girl, Lilith...and she had a baby. She had a baby?"

Yarrow sank down onto a bench, his mouth trembling.

"Yarrow..." Orozco shook his head slowly. "You dog."

"She says I have a daughter." Yarrow looked up.

"Found out she was pregnant after we left for the mission with Malal. They're in Phoenix…she needed money so she put in for child support and there are hundreds of messages from her. And pictures. And my little girl is named Jessica." His eyes rolled up and he slumped to the side.

Egan caught him before he could fall over.

"Who wants to tell Gunney Cortaro about this?" Standish asked.

"We tell him and he'll want to know how we found out," Bailey said. "Maybe we keep this our little secret for a bit. Doesn't mean we can't celebrate. You have cigars, Standish?"

"What, are you crazy? Of course I have cigars. And booze." Standish gave Yarrow a none-too-gentle slap on the cheek. "But I think new guy's going to need a lot more than liver abuse to get through this."

CHAPTER 3

A Destrier flew through the red haze of a Martian dust storm. Floodlights diffused through the blowing dust creating a glare beneath the heavy transport as it slowed over a landing pad.

More dust kicked up as the ship's thrusters brought it to a halt against the expanse of black stone. The ship's landing gear settled down, compressing against the Destrier's bulk as the thrusters died away.

The fore ramp lowered and the Iron Hearts set foot on the red planet. Technicians and mechanics unlimbered equipment from the cargo bay as the three armor soldiers made their way to a diminutive figure waiting at a roadway leading to an open sally port built into the side of Olympus Mons.

"Hello!" said the man in a lightly armored space

suit as he ran up to the Iron Hearts. "I am Mr. Dinkins, Adjutants Core, at your service." He flipped the cover off a tablet and removed a stylus from a pocket attached to his breastplate.

"I'll need your full names, serial numbers and dates of your last mandatory training—" Dinkins looked up and saw the Iron Hearts walking toward the mountain. He scampered after the armor, struggling to keep up with the gait of the fifteen-foot-tall suits.

"Hello? Can you hear me? This Martian atmosphere is so thin," Dinkins said, waving to Kallen.

The armor continued.

"Yes, sorry. I simply must have this information before you go any farther." Dinkins tapped his slate against Kallen's leg.

She stopped.

"Thank you. I need your last—" He garbled his last words as Kallen grabbed him by the ankles and lifted him into the air. She dangled him, upside down, in front of her helm.

"Carius," she said.

Pens and mechanical pencils fell off Dinkins as he swung gently in Kallen's grasp.

"Unhand me! This is most—" he squealed as Kallen dropped him. She grabbed him by the ankles again before his skull could reach the ground.

"Carius," she said again.

"He's inside! Bay three-seven!" Dinkins bent at the waist and grabbed Kallen's finger. She released his ankles and the adjutant held on by his fingertips. Kallen lowered her hand and flicked him away.

By the time Dinkins found his tablet, the Iron Hearts were at the entrance to the cavern cut into the biggest mountain in the solar system.

The sally port could have fit five armor soldiers abreast. Heavy doors with rock facades and layers of quadrium and reinforced metal hung from massive hinges. Inside, six-wheeled trucks armed with gauss rotary cannons lined the walls. Suited mechanics and Marines in ochre power armor loaded boxes of bullets onto the trucks while others performed last-minute maintenance on the vehicles.

The hangar buzzed with activity...until the Iron Hearts walked past. The room fell quiet, many pointing at the armor and whispering to each other.

"You think they take their admin crap that seriously on Mars?" Bodel said over their private channel.

"Maybe they've never seen armor before," Kallen said.

"Can't be. There are coffin units in the next

16

hallway," Elias said, "and we know Carius is here."

"I don't like being stared at," Bodel said. The soldier had been moody, shy even since he was injured defending the Dotok world of Takeni. He'd suffered a stroke, one that left him with a half-slack face and a weakness through the right half of his body.

"There's nothing subtle about us in armor. Let's find Carius," Kallen said.

An access tunnel connected to the back of the hangar curved away in a gentle arc. The center was busy with motor traffic shuttling supplies and personnel. The Iron Hearts strode along the outer edge.

"They were busy while we were away," Bodel said.

"You think this highway goes all the way around Olympus?" Kallen asked.

A trio of armor soldiers walked toward the Iron Hearts. Elias slammed a fist against his chest in salute as they passed. The lead armor returned the courtesy.

"Vladislav's Hussars," Elias said.

"Haven't seen armor since the Smoking Snakes." Bodel's helm twisted around and looked over the rotary cannons attached to the Hussars' backs opposite their rail cannons. "Would be nice to catch up with the others. Find out about their new toys."

The Iron Hearts crossed the highway and stopped

at a set of tall doors labeled BAY 37.

The doors swung open and the Iron Hearts stepped into an air lock. Once an Earth-normal atmosphere surrounded them, the inner doors opened.

Workstations showing Mars from orbit and segments of the surface were manned by tired-looking men and women from the different military branches. None batted an eye at the Iron Hearts' arrival. A suit of armor held tight in a coffin stood at the end of the bay next to a platform that reached up to the armor's chest.

A man in plain fatigues and with long white hair that hung loose off his shoulders stood in front of a screen, his arms clasped behind his back. The glint of neural plugs in the base of the old man's skull twinkled in the low light.

Elias went to the platform, snapped his heels together and struck his fist against his heart.

"Colonel Carius," Elias said.

The man picked up a cane leaning against the big screen and turned around. He leaned against the cane and returned Elias' salute. Elias' gaze went to the cane, polished metal taken from the commanding officer of the Chinese People's Army Armored Corps after the Battle of Aurukun. General Zhi hadn't complained—not that he could have after Carius ripped him clean out of his armor.

18

Elias felt his face pull into a smile. That had been a good day.

"Iron Hearts," Carius' flint-gray eyes looked over the three soldiers, "glad to have you back in the fold. You've all served with honor, distinction…and some controversy."

"That paper pusher upset my humors," Kallen said. "I didn't hurt him."

"Don't be cute with me, Desi. I'm talking about what happened on the *Breitenfeld*." Carius waved his cane at her like an admonishing finger. "I got Captain Valdar's complete report and his recommendation that I take away your spurs. Oddly enough, while I was rereading it, all references to something called 'Malal' erased themselves. I think Ibarra's little pet doesn't want word about this 'Malal' getting around.

"But, with no statement to instigate any kind of punishment, there's nothing I can do to you. I would have told him to shove his recommendation up his ass anyway. I don't care how famous he is—no one tells me how to lead my troops." Carius turned and stabbed a button with the tip of his cane. Mars appeared on the big screen.

"Destroying that monster was the right thing to do. We don't regret it," Elias said, "and if Valdar wants my armor, he can come and take it."

Carius chuckled, dry as dead leaves.

"I always liked you three. Even before you became the reason we have so many new bean heads," Carius said. "What did they tell you about Mars?"

"'Be on the shuttle at 0900 and get the hell off my ship,'" Bodel said.

"Welcome to Fortress Mars." Carius stabbed another button and dots appeared across the Martian surface, all spaced almost equally from each other. One of the dots rose from the surface and spread across the screen: a cross section of a massive gun barrel buried deep in the soil. A series of concentric rings extended from the end of the barrel to the surface.

"Macro cannons," Carius said. "Ibarra took the rail gun and decided to push it to the very limits of physical science. Each of these cannons can fire a round big enough to crack a Xaros leviathan or rip through a few square miles of drones. The impeller rings can bend the munitions a few degrees…gives each cannon more sky to shoot. Mars is geologically dead, which is the only way any of this would work. We try it on Earth and one little quake would wreck the calibrations."

"How do we get the Xaros to stand still long enough for us to hit them?" Kallen asked.

"You notice that massive fleet over the North

Pole on your way in? Admiral Garret's going to grab the Xaros by the nose and let the cannons pound them to dust," Carius said. "We've got macro cannons all over the planet and can put effective fires on the entire sky from about a thousand kilometers on up. Phobos and Deimos have a cannon each, but we shoot it and those moons will go flying off into space, or into the planet."

"And if they try to bypass? Or attack Mars?" Bodel asked.

"They try to skirt around and the cannons will beat them to death the entire trip to Earth. They try to outrun the big guns and they'll just die tired. They come to Mars and Garret will pound them to dust from orbit. This is Fortress Mars, not a vacation spot. No civilians or collateral damage to worry about. Every structure is deep enough to survive a bombardment—so I'm told." Carius gave a dismissive shrug.

"Now…to the armors' part of the fight." Carius hit another key and Mars rotated to show an area full of shallow canyons. A macro cannon emplacement named Nerio blinked several times. "We're providing near security for each of the cannons. Anything gets through the fleet, the air defense artillery, and the Eagle fighter squadrons assigned to each cannon and it will be dealt with by us armor and the cavalry squadrons you walked past on the way in here."

"We are the last, last, last…last line of defense," Bodel smirked.

Carius stabbed the tip of his cane into the platform and the Iron Hearts stiffened.

"This is where we decide the battle, Hans," Carius said. "The cannons will keep the Xaros away from Earth. Mars is a bone-dry shit pot so I don't mind tossing kinetic strike munitions at her. We try to have this same fight on Earth and we'll kick up so much crap it'll make the nuclear winter of '32 look like a day on Waikiki. Not a single civilian on this planet, Earth has children. The future."

"I understand my failing and will not repeat it," Bodel said, repeating the only acceptable response to a correction from armor training at Fort Knox.

"The big brains on Garret's staff looked at putting us on the fleet, ship internal security or auxiliary rail cannon support." Carius spat on the ground. "We are the force of decision. Not some 'auxiliary' bullshit. The ships are crammed full of doughboys armed with pneumatic hammers and pissed-off dispositions. They've got that covered. That Mars is mostly empty is a plus, and a minus. We can't concentrate our forces in one point, have to spread out so the cannons are always a threat. Lots of space to cover. Lots of avenues of attack from orbit to the cannons.

"But Mars," Carius said, raising a finger, "we are armor. No fear of the atmosphere. We are mobile. We are deadly. You three are assigned to Nerio cannon with a troop of bean heads. Keep the Xaros away from the cannon and see that the big guns never tire."

"A troop?" Elias asked. "Where did you find twelve new recruits and the time to get them through selection? Proccies can't take the plugs."

Carius smirked.

"Your troop isn't human."

****

The Nerio cemetery held space for twelve suits of armor. The hydraulic lifts, tool benches and repair frames were the same as the *Breitenfeld,* but the walls were bare rock instead of the dull gray bulkheads that Elias was used to staring at.

Elias stood in the repair frame, a metal cage used by technicians to lift armor plates, weapons and heavy battery packs onto his armor.

A tech in a lifter suit carried a pike taller than a man between hydraulic pincers from its transport case to the cage. She set it into a foot-wide cradle attached to a corner bar and the cradle tightened around the pike. The cradle raised the bar with a hiss of compressing air and stopped next to Elias' right arm where his chief armorer waited for it on a scaffold.

"Brand new," Chief Aguilar said, "made from composite steel fashioned over a graphene lattice. Aegis shell might take a hit or two from the Xaros."

The Iron Hearts had inherited Aguilar and his Brazilian crew after the death of the Smoking Snakes. The Iron Hearts lost most of their own techs when the *Breitenfeld* took damage over Takeni. Their lone original technician, Sanders, had managed to pick up enough Portuguese to integrate—mostly cuss words and proper names for tools.

"New aegis armor," Aguilar said, "new high-energy capacitors and batteries, new pintle cannons. You're going to smell like factory grease when the Xaros show up."

"I need to hit the range. My synch rating is bottoming out," Elias said.

"Always happens with new gear." Aguilar shoved his hands into an oversized pair of gloves, reached into thin air and closed his hands around an unseen rod. Haptic feedback sensors in the gloves stopped his grip and the hydraulics in the cell synched with his gloves. Aguilar lifted his hands and the cradle with the pike mimicked his action.

Aguilar set the pike into Elias' forearm housing. He took his hands out of the gloves and picked up a data slate.

"How's the fit?" he asked.

"Lighter than the last one. Hard to trust it's an improvement," Elias said.

"You'll manage," Aguilar said. "I've got something else for you." He took a data drive the size of his thumb out of a pocket. "I got the director's cut of that movie."

"Movie?"

"*The Last Stand on Takeni*. You haven't seen it?"

Elias turned his helm to Aguilar.

"They made some puff piece about the Dotok rescue. You and the rest are in it. Even my *Cobras Fumantes*. That fight with the walker wasn't anything like how it really went down but the rest is sort of accurate." Aguilar tapped the drive against the slate and the movie uploaded to Elias' system.

"You want me to tell the range your re-fit is going to take longer?" Aguilar asked.

Elias stepped out of the cage and stalked toward the door.

"Sweat saves blood. I'm going to the range now."

CHAPTER 4

A hologram of Pluto and Abaddon floated over the tank in the *Breitenfeld*'s command center. The ship's senior officers watched as drones billowed out of Abaddon and abandoned the vessel used to bring them from one star to another.

"There's something not right," said Ensign Geller, the ship's navigator. "Abaddon is almost as big as Luna, heck of a lot bigger than Pluto. Its gravity should have slapped Pluto's moons out of orbit. Heck, Pluto and Abaddon should be forming into a new planetary system right now."

"Then what does that tell us, Ensign?" Executive Officer Ericcson asked.

"It's doesn't have any significant gravity…because it's hollow?" The ensign tapped a finger against his chin.

"Which is in line with the assessment from Ibarra and his probe." Captain Valdar reached into the tank and zoomed in to the surface of Pluto. "This thing had propulsion rings, same as Ceres and other planets occupied by the Xaros. Admiral Makarov and her fleet managed to destroy them, which is why the drone mass heading for Earth is so small."

"Small?" Commander Utrecht's eyebrows popped up. "There must be tens of millions of drones coming for us."

"If the Xaros had converted the entire mass of that planetoid to drones, we would face drones in the hundreds of millions," Valdar said. "Eighth Fleet managed to drop graviton mines on Abaddon's path, forcing them to burn mass that could have been transmuted into drones. The minelayers sent back telemetry data for six months before the last of the crew…ceased broadcasting.

"While we were sitting in the void waiting for our jump engines to come back online, Earth prepared for this invasion. We should have had a few more years to prep. Ibarra's plan was for the Xaros we defeated at the Crucible to broadcast that only a few of our ships survived the battle, and they'd return with a force large enough to crush the survivors. The Xaros don't know about the proccies, didn't know about the armada we'd build in the time it took them to travel here from Barnard's Star."

"But they're here early, aren't they?" Lieutenant Hale asked.

"There's the rub," Valdar said. "We don't know if it was when the Xaros saw our ship at Anthalas, Takeni, or when they took Torni prisoner, but they figured out we were still around and decided to step off from their jump gate on Barnard's Star before the message from the drones we destroyed made it back to them. No more connecting the dots. This is where we are and, we're moving on. Explaining time dilation gives me nose bleeds."

"I can do it, sir." Geller held up his index fingers. "You see, when the Xaros sent a message from Earth, it had to travel—"

Valdar slapped a palm against the side of the tank and Geller shut up.

"Even with the losses inflicted by Eighth Fleet and the burn rate across the void, the Xaros are here in overwhelming force," Valdar said. "Admiral Garret has the majority of our fleet in orbit around Mars. He thinks he can stop them there, save Earth and the civilians from collateral damage."

"So when do we leave for Mars?" Durand asked. "No ship has more experience fighting the Xaros than us."

"We don't," Valdar said, pointing to Pluto,

"watch." He touched the holo and it swung around, revealing the dark side of Pluto and Charon. Red lines washed over Pluto as the image switched to infrared. A perfectly circular hole lay at the base of Pluto's ice mountains. Drones and tinkling specs shuttled from the hole to an artificial satellite high above Pluto's surface. The satellite looked like a frayed ring.

"They're building a new Crucible," Ericcson said.

"That's right," Valdar said. "They're mining through Pluto's crust for materials. There are several shafts around this main dig site, and it is days away from completion. It's not as big as the Crucible over Ceres, but if the Xaros can open a gate to one of their garrison worlds…billions more drones could come through and then we don't stand a chance."

"What are we waiting for?" Hale asked. "There's a fleet over the North Pole. Send it through our Crucible and blow the hell out of what they're building."

"We do that and Earth is vulnerable," Valdar said. "What we send through won't make it back to Earth before the Xaros. The drones can outrun us from Mars to Earth, too. Garret is confident he can stop them on Mars, but he's not the 'all eggs in one basket' kind of strategic thinker. Enough drones get to Earth to overwhelm the orbitals and there's no fleet to stop them? They will slaughter every last man, woman, and child on Earth. They complete the new Crucible? Millions more drones come through and the fight is unwinnable. Same outcome."

"We have a lot of ways to lose this fight," Utrecht said.

"The plan is for the *Breitenfeld* and a small task force to jump through our Crucible and destroy what the Xaros are building, then return to Earth using our jump engines. We fail and the reserve fleet does the job, leaving Earth vulnerable," Valdar said.

"It's not enough to wreck their construction site," Hale said. "They've got to have something massive digging that hole and converting omnium. We don't take that out and they'll just build another Crucible."

"Correct. We're taking on more strike Marines to augment you and your team," Valdar said. "Which reminds me…XO?"

"Attention to orders!" Ericcson shouted, snapping everyone but Valdar to attention.

The captain took a small knife from his belt and flicked it open. He cut into Hale's lieutenant rank patch and ripped away a corner.

Ericcson cleared her throat. "The Atlantic Union emergency council, acting upon the recommendation of Fleet Admiral Garret, has placed special trust and confidence in the patriotism and integrity of Lieutenant Kenneth A. Hale."

Valdar ripped Hale's rank off and flung it aside.

"In view of these special qualities, and his demonstrated potential to serve in the higher grade, Lieutenant Hale is hereby promoted to the rank of captain, Atlantic Union Marine Corps, effective immediately," Ericcson said.

Valdar took out a pair of silver bars rank insignia and pressed the metal pins into the uniform where Hale's old rank used to be. Valdar put his palm against the rank and raised an eyebrow.

Hale stared back at him, impassive.

Valdar lifted his hand and slammed it against the rank, driving the pins into Hale's chest. Hale didn't even blink.

"Well done, son." Valdar shook the new captain's hand. The rest of the bridge broke into applause. Valdar stepped back so the rest of the crew could file through to congratulate Hale. No one else tried to beat Hale's rank into his chest.

A rare smile crossed Valdar's face. Promoting his godson was one of the few happy moments he'd experienced since the Xaros invasion. Valdar's wife and their children were dead. His connection with Hale was the only familial tie he had left in the world.

Despite the honor and attention from the crew, Hale didn't look happy. He kept his gaze away from the ship's captain.

Something's wrong, Valdar thought.

****

Valdar held the door to his ready room open for Hale as the two entered the captain's only place of sanctity on the entire ship. Hale noted that the room was clean, the bedsheets tight enough that they looked fused to the mattress and there was no smell of neglected food trays.

Hale stopped next to a wall where Valdar had a collage of family photos tacked to the bulkhead. One picture had both the Valdar and Hale families taken during a lake trip when Hale was just a boy. Everyone in that photo but Hale, his brother Jared, and Valdar was dead. Jared…he'd probably never see him again.

"Shame we missed seeing him off," Valdar said. "Jared will do well on Terra Nova. His passion was always for construction, plenty of chance at that on the new colony."

"At least he's safe, sir," Hale said, adding an honorific he rarely used when in private with Valdar.

Valdar's mustache twitched and he flopped down in a cracked leather chair.

"What's eating you, son?" Valdar asked.

Hale touched the captain's rank on his chest.

"I don't deserve this. Captain Acera, God rest his soul, he commanded a team for three full years before pinning on captain. Went to advanced recon school, forward air controller training…couldn't Ibarra create a more qualified officer in one of his proccie tubes and send him here instead?"

"You heard Ericcson, 'demonstrated potential.' You've got that in spades. Hell, you've got a slew of Purple Hearts and other awards in the pipeline. Bureaucracy is slow at best—during wartime it's molasses moving uphill in winter. You weren't this hesitant when you took over the defenses of an entire Dotok city. What's really eating you?"

Hale chewed on his bottom lip. "When I was with Stacey on that vault…she said something to me. Something that didn't make sense."

Valdar leaned forward and rested his arms atop the desk.

"It was about the Toth, when I was on Europa negotiating with one of their damned overlords." Hale's lips pulled into a sneer. "Stacey said we were never going to hand over the proccies. I was just a delaying tactic until she could bring help or Ibarra could get another fleet crewed."

Valdar turned his head aside.

"But…" continued Hale as he walked up to Valdar's desk, "you told me to sign the treaty that would have done just that—given up every proccie on Earth, handed over all the tech used to make them. All my instructions from Earth came through *you*, Uncle Isaac. I can't make this work in my head. Either Stacey was lying to me…or you were."

"Ken…I thought they were abominations."

"No!" Hale slammed a hand against Valdar's desk. "The proccies are just as human as you and me. Yarrow dragged my bleeding body off the battlefield and stitched me back together. Rohen led the Toth away from the rest of my team so we could get off of Nibiru. Every last sailor that died in Eighth Fleet to give Earth a fighting chance was a proccie."

"I know that!" Valdar snapped to his feet. "I stood next to Makarov on my flight deck, picking through dead bodies, and that's when I realized I couldn't tell the difference between the proccies and the true born. I was wrong. Wrong to see them differently. Wrong to try to get rid of them."

"Do you know what the Toth would have done with them?" Hale asked. "I've seen it with my own eyes, seen them feeding off us. I saw the blocks on Nibiru where they auction off living beings like cattle! That's what you wanted for them." The Marine turned away.

"What you did was treason. Why didn't you turn yourself in after the Toth were defeated?" Hale asked. "Was it because all the True Born terrorists were dead? You thought you could get away with it?"

"Ibarra knew," Valdar said. "He knew I was involved with the True Born before we even went to Europa. Ibarra played me like a damned fiddle. I think that's how he got the bomb onto the *Naga* and gave us a fighting chance against that thing. After that, he forced me to keep quiet, gave him some leverage over me."

"So you went from making a deal with one devil to another," Hale said.

"He gave me a shot at redemption. So long as our mission to kill Mentiq was a success, he'd keep what I'd done away from Garret. It all worked out, son. All's well that ends—"

"You used me." Hale jabbed a finger at Valdar. "You lied to me. I trusted you and you twisted that bond to make me do your dirty work." Hale's hand fell to his side. "You're my godfather, supposed to be my father if anything ever happened to Dad. I know it's not the same when I'm grown…but why would you do that to me?"

"Ken, the whole world's been turned inside out. Our families are gone. The world we knew is over. Then Ibarra comes up with this plot to replace everyone and I…I couldn't accept that."

"Jared's gone, and I don't think I'll ever see him again." Hale's shoulders slumped. "You were all I had left, and you threw it away."

"Ken, don't talk like that. I should never have done that to you—I know it. The way I saw things…I didn't know what—"

Hale turned around and stood at attention. "My new Marines are waiting for me. Will there be anything else, sir?"

"Ken, hear me out."

"Will there be anything else, sir?"

Valdar dropped his knuckles onto his desk. "Dismissed."

Hale saluted and left the room.

Valdar stood at his desk for a minute then sank into his chair. He pressed his hands to his face and fought back tears.

CHAPTER 5

The cell was nothing more than a metal slate for a bed, a toilet, and a force field across bars.

Torni sat on the slate, staring at a cold plate of food on the floor near the bars. Her shell rippled with fractals and checkerboard patterns, all swirling as her mind worked. She didn't breathe, didn't blink; Xaros drones didn't bother with such biologic concerns.

The doors to the prison block opened and a middle-aged woman with mixed Asian and Caucasian features entered. She shooed away the lone guard on duty with a flick of her fingers and then lowered the force field on Torni's cell.

Torni looked up and didn't return the woman's predatory smile.

"You have a visitor," the woman said. She wiped

her hands together several times and produced a small ball in a flair of sleight of hand. She tossed the ball to Torni and it stopped of its own accord just outside the bars.

The ball floated into the cell and a hologram of Marc Ibarra formed around the holo sphere. The old man looked around, his gaze stopping on the untouched food.

"They just don't understand, do they?" Ibarra asked.

"Shall I leave, boss?" the woman asked. Ibarra waved a dismissive hand at her.

"That's Shannon. She works here. We haven't met, have we?"

Torni leaned back slightly.

"Is it the cell? It's the cell." Ibarra rolled his eyes. "When I told Admiral Garret that we had a POW returning, his surprise went right up to eleven when I mentioned you were in a drone shell. He insisted on some security measures...then there was that misunderstanding with Malal and the armor on the *Breitenfeld*. Thanks, by the way, for not letting him be destroyed. We're on enough shit lists with the wider galactic alliance against the Xaros."

"Why are you here?" Torni asked.

"To talk! Be neighborly. You are on the Crucible after all and it's not like I get out much. Plus, we have a lot in common." Ibarra smiled.

"I am a Xaros drone. You are a hologram with no mute button."

"And we're both dead," Ibarra beamed. "I'm sorry…that came out way too cheerful. I died. Soon as the fleet entered temporal stasis right before the first Xaros invasion hit, there wasn't any point in me hanging around. So the Qa'Resh probe took in a copy of my mind. Kept a 'me' going. Does this sound a bit familiar?"

"Like what the Xaros did to me. Just not voluntarily."

"And here we are. An 'Ibarra' and a 'Torni,' the first humans to ever transcend the bonds of death."

"No. You're acting like we're still who we used to be. I'm not human anymore. Neither are you." Torni eyed the holo sphere in the center of Ibarra's chest.

"Certainly there's some…" he said as he wiggled his fingers in the air, "tactile differences. But I feel the same, think the same, same winning personality."

Torni huffed.

"But you…are so much more than you used to be," Ibarra said. "I saw what you did to the *Breitenfeld*, such beautiful craftsmanship with her aegis armor. My shipwrights are in awe of the repairs you made."

"Malal's instructions, my efforts. Where is he?" Torni asked.

"Elsewhere in the Crucible. We're keeping him under wraps. The general public has enough to worry about with the Xaros here. Word gets out we've got a soul-eating star god cooling his heels up here with me and there goes the whole day."

Smoke rose from Torni's arms. Embers burned over her shell, smoldering as a swath of her shell became pitted.

"He mentioned this." Ibarra stepped back. "You were close to a Xaros construct when it died. The kill command is still active...obviously."

"It's always there." Torni held a hand out to the food tray and it flew into her hand. She crushed it between her hands. White light seeped from between her fingers and her shell flowed over the damaged areas. A second later, she was as good as new.

"The command is always scratching against my mind," Torni said. "I lose focus, get angry...it'll take a piece of me. Malal taught me to fight it, but sometimes I slip."

"I'm sorry," Ibarra said.

"On Malal's vault, I could pick up Xaros communications. Not words, just impressions and desires. I feel something now. There's something powerful, overriding much of their programming. Something I've felt

40

before."

"The General," Ibarra said.

Torni's shell went black.

"We expected him to come. Which may prove useful," Ibarra said.

"What? If he's here, then you've got better things to do than chitchat with me."

"Hardly. First, I must thank you. Even without saving the *Breitenfeld* and returning Malal to us in a timely manner, you did a great service to the entire war effort and I'm not talking about what you did on Takeni."

"I was their prisoner. I willingly cooperated and gave up sensitive information about the Qa'Resh, the Crucible, our fleet. I am a traitor and I am right where I deserve to be—in a cell," Torni said.

"Oh, don't be all doom and gloom! You probably saved us all by cooperating."

"Come again?"

"See, my girl, the thing about interrogations is that no matter the method, no matter how perfect the questions, a subject can never give up what she or she doesn't know." Ibarra hooked a thumb at Shannon. "I learned that from the best.

"You told the Xaros that our fleet was beat to hell after the Battle of the Crucible. Then, the General encounters Eighth Fleet in deep space, whose numbers and strength were a bit stronger than what survived the Crucible. Eighth Fleet…was lost, and all the information available to the General was that…" Ibarra raised an eyebrow to Torni.

"He destroyed the last of our fleet in deep space," Torni said.

"And this last part is important. You never knew anything about the proccies before your physical death, did you?"

"The what-ies?"

"Exactly! You never learned about our re-population plan with the procedurally generated human beings. Nine-day wonders. Tube kids. 'Blasted abominations' according to some. The General thought Earth was defenseless as a newborn babe in the woods. He didn't know we had years to get stronger, build fleets and fortify mountain cities.

"What I wouldn't have given to see his face when he looked across the system and saw that we were almost ready for him," Ibarra said.

"Almost?"

"We planned on having more time, but when the Xaros got a good look at the *Breitenfeld* on Anthalas and then Takeni, they knew their invasion of Earth hadn't gone as planned. The General sent Abaddon over sooner than we'd anticipated. At least Eighth Fleet's sacrifice bought us some more time."

"Are we going to lose?"

Ibarra pressed his lips together and his head wobbled from side to side.

"The math isn't in our favor, but we're working to change the equation. Which brings me to why I'm here besides idle chitchat," Ibarra said. "We need your special skills. Our omnium reactor is churning out aegis armor and quadrium shells as fast as we can push it, but it's not really the tool to make something elegant."

Ibarra held up a hand and the schematic for a complex piece of machinery floated above his palm.

"I don't know if I can make that," she said.

"You'll have the finest tutors known to man and aliens." Ibarra closed his hand and he passed through the bars of her cell. "Come on. No time to waste."

Torni went to the cell door, put two fingers against a bar and cut through it with a tiny disintegration beam. She ran her touch over the bars and kicked down her improvised doorway.

Shannon had her back to the wall, a hand inside her jacket.

"Something tells me you could have left that cell

43

anytime you wanted," Shannon said.

"I didn't have a reason before now." Torni's shell rippled from the top of her head to the tip of her feet, leaving her in fatigues and her original appearance.

CHAPTER 6

Hale looked over the cue cards in his hand and felt his stomach knot up.

Captains don't get nerves, he thought.

He could hear muffled conversation from around the corner where his full-strength company of strike Marines waited for him. The *Breitenfeld*'s Marine complement took casualties when they set foot on Earth to recover Ibarra and his probe. Losses on Takeni coupled with entire teams reassigned and not replaced before the mission to Nibiru left the ship with a single full-sized team—Hale's—and a few support personnel. Strike Marine companies were smaller than line infantry companies, but the idea of commanding fifty Marines instead of five was a big pill for Hale to swallow.

"Sir?" Cortaro said from behind. "Your Marines

are ready."

Cortaro stepped in front of Hale and looked at the new captain's rank. "Looks good on you, sir."

"Same to you, Top," Hale said. With a full company to command, Hale needed a first sergeant as his top NCO.

"Just don't ever think I'm one of those 'in the rear with the gear' first sergeants and we'll get along just fine, sir," Cortaro said.

"The thought never crossed my mind. You got them into berthing. Any feel for the new teams yet?" Hale asked.

"Their records are watertight. They're all annotated as being 'cohort trained.' I asked around, turns out that means they're all proccies who remember each other from their tubes. Means we've got fully integrated and trained teams, not a bunch of warm bodies thrown against a manning roster," Cortaro said.

"Why'd you ask around, instead of asking them directly?" Hale asked.

"A first sergeant knows everything, sir. Nothing escapes our attention or wrath."

"Right. I suppose the company commander's supposed to know it all too."

"If I know it, you'll know it. Same as when we had

just the team. You lead the team. I'll run the team."
Cortaro slapped Hale on the shoulder.

"Anything else I should know?"

"They're tense—more than just new-unit jitters. I
don't think it's the mission either. Heard a couple of them
mentioning a movie when they thought I was out of
earshot. That, and Yarrow's been acting weird."

"Fair enough, let's get going," Hale said.

Cortaro went around the corner and called the
room to attention.

Hale followed once the sound of scuffling feet
faded away. He kept his head up, chest out and looked his
new Marines in the eye as he went to a wooden podium in
the middle of the briefing room, a pair of screens at his
flanks.

"As you were," Hale said. The new Marines sat
down like there were magnets in their seats; his old team
took a half second longer. All had note pads and pens
ready. Hale picked out four lieutenants, three men and a
woman that looked barely out of their teens.

Are they so young or am I so old? he thought.

Steuben was in the back of the room. The
Karigole warrior gave Hale a slow nod, and Hale felt much
of his anxiety wash away.

"Welcome to the *Breitenfeld*," Hale said. "I am lieu-

Captain Hale." He tapped his cue cards on the side of his podium. "You know what? We don't have a lot of time before this mission kicks off, so I'm going to get right down to brass tacks." Hale touched a button on the podium and the mine entrance on Pluto appeared on the screen to his left.

"The Xaros are building a Crucible, which we're designating as objective Grinder, around Pluto. It is our mission to land on the planet, figure out what they're using to dig up raw materials for the device and mark it for orbital bombardment or sabotage the device ourselves," Hale said. "The *Breit* will jump in on the opposite side of the planet and cover our insertion as they assault Grinder. We're not going straight into the pit. We'll secure these shafts leading out of the Norgay Montes and work our way inside. Intell says the shafts are out-gassing the same material as the pit and should be connected."

Hale gripped the side of his podium. "In a perfect world, we'd have months to plan this operation. Rehearsal landings. A better idea of what the Xaros have in there. Most of this war has been on the fly so we are going to do what Marines have done since the days of sail. Adapt and overcome. Our mission is to destroy the Xaros mine works, stop them from completing the Grinder and get back to Earth and join the line before the rest of the Xaros fleet can reach our planet."

"Sir," said the lone female officer as she stood, "Lieutenant Jacobs, Crimson team, what about Abaddon? Have the Xaros kept a reserve force inside that thing?"

"The Xaros don't keep a reserve," Steuben said from the back of the room. Marines twisted around to look at the new speaker. "They always mass their strength to overwhelm opponents—a viable strategy. Most solar systems rarely have more than one habitable world to defend."

"They brought millions of drones to our system," Jacobs said. "Why bother building another jump gate if they've got the combat power to wipe us out?"

"Maybe they're not as confident as they used to be." Another lieutenant stood up. "Sir, Lieutenant Bronx, Amber team. Eighth Fleet slowed them down, hurt them pretty bad. They get here and see the solar system bristling with weapons and defenses. Maybe they don't think they'll win so they're building an insurance policy."

"Sound thinking, Bronx," Hale said. "High command put investigating Abaddon as a secondary objective…" Hale looked at a screen showing the moon-sized object and shook his head. "If it's not empty, the Xaros will come pouring out of there the moment we arrive and the mission will be scrubbed."

Hale glanced at his watch. "We're on a compressed schedule. All enlisted Marines report to First Sergeant Cortaro at the simulation range. Officers and Mr. Steuben see me after this. Dismissed."

****

Standish hefted his new rifle against his shoulder and looked down the holographic sites to a Xaros drone floating down the firing range. The plasma rifle was shorter and lighter than the gauss weapon he'd carried since his first day in the Marine Corps, forcing him to adjust his firing stance.

The range was full of strike Marine teams, each firing on floating targets or throwing antiarmor grenades at hanging bull's-eyes.

"Here goes nothing," he muttered. He pulled the trigger and a bolt of energy slammed into the drone, breaking off stalks and crushing the shell. Standish held the rifle at arm's length and frowned at it.

"That can't be right," he said. "There's no recoil. Hey, Oro, this plastic toy set right for the sim?"

Orozco leveled his new heavy plasma repeater at a smaller drone walker construct, the same kind that had chased Standish through the streets of Phoenix, and fired.

Bolts the size of Standish's fist stitched up the constructs torso.

Orozco looked at the weapon, then to Standish. "There's no recoil."

"That's what I'm trying to—like you'd even know. Hey—" Standish waved to one of the new arrivals at the next firing station, "you. Yes, you." Standish waved him over.

The Marine, a private first class with WEISS stenciled on his armor, hurried over, keeping his plasma rifle pointed up and down range. Weiss' eyes darted from Standish to Orozco, his breathing quick and shallow.

"You've fired these on a live range, right? What's the deal with the recoil?" Standish asked.

"No recoil, Lance Corporal…Standish?" Weiss cocked his head to the side. "You're alive?"

"Well, of course I'm alive. Why wouldn't I be?" Standish asked.

"Sergeant Orozco? *The* Orozco? I can't believe it's really you," Weiss said.

"Hold on. Back up to me not being alive," Standish said.

"Well…you're not in the movie. Where's Vincenti?" Weiss asked.

"Vincenti's KIA, been that way since we got

Ibarra's ghost out of Euskal Tower," Standish said. "Back up. Again. What movie?"

"*The Last Stand on Takeni.* You mean you haven't seen it?" Weiss asked. "It came out a year ago. Your entire team's in it. They used some new holo tech to make all the actors look just like you. Biggest movie in decades. I think everyone's seen it at least two or three times."

"What?" Standish sputtered.

"They based it on holo recordings, after-action reports, Dotty testimony. I get all choked up every time Sergeant Torni says good-bye to Vincenti. I ain't too proud to admit it," Weiss said.

"Excuse me, Sergeant Orozco?" A Marine from Weiss' team came over and offered a marker to the Spaniard. "Would you sign my armor?"

Standish grabbed Weiss by his chest plate and shook him. "You mean to tell me that there's a movie about *my* exploits and I'm not fucking in it?"

"Oh wow, Standish," the other Marine said, "I guess those rumors were true."

Orozco wrapped an arm around Standish's waist and pulled him off Weiss.

"Rumors!" Standish yelled.

"Something about one of Hale's team members being a disciplinary problem. The director didn't want any controversy so he recast…you, Lance Corporal," Weiss said. "Everyone knows the movie's just propaganda to keep spirits up before Abaddon arrived, but it was still entertaining as hell."

Deep chuckles erupted from Orozco's barrel chest.

"What's all this grab ass going on?" Egan and Bailey came over to the group. "And why is Standish crying?"

Standish buried his head in Orozco's shoulder. "I'm not in my own movie!"

"What movie?" Bailey

"We're famous," Orozco said and gave Standish a reassuring pat on the head.

Weiss slapped his teammate on the chest and pointed at Bailey's rail rifle. "Dude, there's Bloke. I tried to make sniper because of you, but I washed out of selection. Can I hold it?"

"Not if you want to keep your whole arm attached to your body," Bailey snapped. "I'll let you keep looking at it if you give me a copy of this movie Standish is crying about."

Weiss flipped up his forearm screen and tapped a gloved finger against a data node. He held up a glowing fingertip then touched it to Bailey's screen. Orchestral music blared as the movie began.

"This injustice will not stand," Standish said. "I'm going to find out who cut me out of my own movie and—and there will be a very strongly worded letter! Did the Dotok make a statue? Tell me I at least got my own statue."

"What is this happy horseshit?" Cortaro's voice thundered across the range. Marines snapped back to their firing positions.

****

Hale sat in one of the briefing room chairs, one hand rubbing his temples.

"Continue, Lieutenant Mathias," he said to a dark-skinned officer.

"The movie ends with you and Un'qu on the *Breitenfeld*'s deck, looking out at *The Canticle of Reason*," Mathias said.

"OK, that never happened," Hale said. "I was in sick bay bleeding all over—you know what? It doesn't matter. You've all seen it?"

His lieutenants nodded.

"You've seen it?" he asked Steuben.

"The human playing me moved without grace or

54

military bearing. I was insulted, but Admiral Garret forbade me from challenging the actor to an honor duel," Steuben said. "During training, I constantly had to correct the record as to what happened on Takeni. I still do not understand the human concept of 'artistic license.'"

"We're going to move on," Hale said. "The ship weighs anchor in less than twenty hours. I want all of you to conduct final pre-combat inspections and checks by 0200 ship time. I will do my inspections at 0600 and before we load the drop pods. See that your Marines get a couple hours of sleep. We won't have that luxury after we hit Pluto."

"Sir…" A wiry young man named Uli flashed his forearm screen to Hale. Several red alert icons filled his mail feed. "I know this seems trivial, but personnel is blowing up my inbox demanding updates on initial counseling and—"

Hale took Uli by the arm, touched his screen and erased every email.

"Focus on the mission. Some mushroom of a paper pusher in a cubicle under Camelback Mountain can wait," Hale said. He let Uli go and looked at his lieutenants. "Go. See to your Marines. Meet me back here after chow and we'll go over the drop plan again. Steuben, a minute if you please."

The lieutenants saluted and left the room.

"My god, was I ever that young?" Hale asked.

"They are all procedurals. I am certain you are more than several months old," Steuben said.

"I mean bright-eyed and bushy-tailed...naïve," Hale said.

"They've not gone through the change yet, but they will," Steuben said. "When a Karigole centurion forms, their families hold a funeral for the warriors before they ever see battle. Those who go to war never return as the same person. War reveals one's true nature."

"Would veterans be welcomed back?"

"Always. We had rituals and festivals to mark the adjustment period where the families learned to accept the new person," Steuben said.

"How's your village? Your people adjusting to Earth?"

"There have been some...difficulties. Lafayette is still banished. Getting them to relocate to the Kilimanjaro bunkers was a chore. The geth'aar are all pregnant, and geth'aar tend to be especially cranky when they're carrying strong babies."

"And how's that been?"

"I am glad there's a new battle to take me away from them."

Hale's screen beeped. He glanced at it and sighed.

"There are a million things requiring my attention before we weigh anchor. I never thought I'd miss being a lieutenant. Which reminds me. I need your help, Steuben. I want you to be the company executive officer for this mission. The new teams know you. I know you. It's a good fit," Hale said.

"And what would my role be?"

"You'll be second-in-command. I go down and you take over the mission."

Steuben tapped his clawed fingertips against the armor on his legs.

"I am several hundred years older than you are. I fought campaigns before your nation even existed and I am to be your subordinate?" Steuben asked.

"It would look that way on paper, easier for the rest of the company to understand your role. In reality I don't think I could ever order you around," Hale said.

"You saved my people from the Toth. That is a debt I can never repay. I will be your executive officer."

"Great. Another part of the job is doing everything the company commander doesn't have time to do...or want to do. So I need you on the flight deck inspecting the drop pods while I go figure out why our supply of antiarmor grenades went to the wrong ship and get them back where they belong." Hale gave Steuben a pat on the shoulder and stood up.

"When will the responsibility for the tasks you find undesirable ever end?" Steuben asked.

"Never. Get to it, XO."

****

Egan walked through a passageway, whistling a slow tune as he glanced over his shoulder. A lone sailor shared the space with him. Egan slowed next to a bolted door and waited for the sailor to step around the corner.

The commo tech took out a black key card given to him by Standish and swiped it across the bolted door's access panel. The bolts snapped open and the door swung loose on its hinges.

"Damn, didn't think that would work," Egan said. He touched a microphone on his throat and said, "Get over here."

Egan glanced into the open door. Humming stacks of electrical equipment filled the space, leaving barely enough room for two men to stand in. Yarrow raced around the corner and stepped into the confined space with Egan.

Egan flipped a panel open, revealing a keypad and

screen. He slid Standish's black card through the reader and a cursor popped onto the screen.

Yarrow, pale and sweaty, reached for the pad. His fingers hovered over the buttons.

"Here," Egan said, sliding the card into Yarrow's pocket. "You get caught with that and I know nothing. Standish also says he knows nothing. You want some help, buddy?"

"No, I've got this." Yarrow's fingers trembled.

Egan looked at the phone number on Yarrow's forearm screen and entered the number for him.

"Thanks." Yarrow wiped his face and ran fingers over his shaved head. The word DIALING appeared on the screen. Yarrow glanced at Egan. "You mind?"

"Right. I'll be on lookout. You hear three knocks on the bulkhead that means trouble's coming." Egan let himself out and closed the door.

The screen wavered, then showed Lilith squinting into the camera. Her hair was a mess, but her face held the same natural beauty he remembered.

"You better have a very good reason for calling me right now," she said.

"Lilith, can you see me?" Yarrow asked.

She leaned closer to the camera, then her eyes opened wide. "Jason? Is that really you? I heard the

Breitenfeld was back but they said your ship is on a blackout. Are you…here? In Phoenix?"

"No, still in orbit, but not for long. We're going—that's not why I called."

Lilith rubbed a hand across her face and looked at him through her fingers. "And why did you call?"

"We have a baby? I didn't find out until yesterday. I mean…how…"

"You don't know how?"

"I know how!" Yarrow winced as his words echoed through the tiny chamber. Two knocks sounded against the walls. "What happened? Where is she?"

"I found out I was pregnant a few weeks after you left. It turns out that I have a number of antibodies from Nibiru that negated the birth control shot I got. I am a computer scientist, not a biologist." Lilith looked away from the camera and said something in Akkadian.

"Lil, are you two safe? Your email said something about a bunker in Phoenix—"

"Daddy?" a child said.

Lilith angled her camera down and a little girl with blond hair and a round face rubbed her eyes.

Yarrow's mouth dropped open.

"That's Daddy?" the girl asked.

"Yes, Mary, he's back from his long trip," Lilith

said.

"She…she's…"

"She looks just like you, don't you think?" Lilith asked.

"Yeah…" Yarrow touched the screen.

"Now hear this," boomed through the ship and into the commo room. "Now here this. Make ready for jump. All hands secure stations and prep for combat conditions."

"Ah, not now," Yarrow said.

"You have to go?" Lilith ducked down next to Mary, who was staring intently at her father.

"Yes, they're going to suck all the air out of the ship and—" Three knocks came from the door. "I'll come to Phoenix as soon as I can. You two, stay safe there, promise me."

"Where are you going, Daddy?"

"I have to go stop the monsters, OK?" The screen filled with static. "I love you two!" Yarrow didn't hear their reply as the video feed washed out.

Egan cracked the door. "Let's go. If we don't get to the armory in three minutes, Top will eat us alive."

Yarrow wiped the back of his hand across his eyes.

"You see them?" Egan asked.

"Yeah. Thanks, brother."

CHAPTER 7

Fleet Admiral Garret tossed a baseball over his head and caught it with a snap of flesh on leather. He set the ball on his nineteenth-century oak desk and spun it. The blur of stitching against the off-white leather captivated him for a moment as it meandered toward the edge. His hand trembled as he reached to catch it. The ball hit his fingers and fell to the deck with a thump.

"Damn it," Garret said. He glanced at a drawer where he kept a flask of vodka, tempted to take one last swig before the grand dance began.

No. No more of that, he thought.

He popped open a pill bottle and took out two tablets almost as big as his pinky nail. He dry swallowed them both and winced as a bitter aftertaste washed up his throat. Human warriors had relied on stimulants for thousands of years. Roman gladiators took small doses of strychnine, the soldiers of the Second World War relied on amphetamine "energy pills," American servicemen and women of this century made do with caffeine and cigarettes until the Ibarra Corporation patented the Sustain pills Garret had just taken.

Each Sustain would keep him alert, free from hunger and thirst, and away from the latrine for twenty-four hours, although prolonged use was forbidden and illegal. As the supreme commander of all Earth forces, he could care less about doctor's orders while humanity's fate rested in his hands.

I slept yesterday...didn't I?

As Garret stood and slid his hands into armored void gloves, he glanced at a clock mounted next to the door and counted down from five.

There was a knock on the door as his count ended.

"Enter."

The door slid aside, revealing the head of Garret's Ranger bodyguard detail, Marcella. Lights reflected off the Ranger's obsidian-black armor, the power armor adding to Marcella's already impressive bulk to the point where he could barely fit through the doorway. The major had been confused for a doughboy on more than one occasion, which Marcella didn't seem to mind.

"Sir," the word came from Marcella's throat speakers with a click, "data packet from Earth just came in. Marked for you."

"It's time. Let's get this done." Garret scooped his helmet off his desk. He stopped next to a tattered flag cased next to the doorway, void-black cloth with an embroidered dragon twisted into the shape of an 8. Admiral Makarov's flag was one of the few artifacts recovered from the *Midway*. Garret thought of her and her fleet's total sacrifice to delay the Xaros.

He kissed his fingertips and touched the glass as he left his ready room.

Just a few steps across the passageway, the *Charlemagne's* bridge snapped to attention as he entered. He gave a brief grunt and the bridge returned to their duties. Garret went straight to a wide holo table surrounded by his senior staff. Holograms of the other admirals in his fleet and one general snapped into being around the table.

Mars snapped into the air over the table. Pulsating red dots on the surface marked the macro cannon emplacements, and nearly two dozen fleets orbited the dusty world.

"All fleets report ready condition bravo, sir," said Admiral Dorral, his chief of staff. "On board security augmentees deliveries will be complete to all ships in nineteen hours."

Garret had redirected the system's procedural development farm's computer power to creating doughboys several days ago. It took nine days for a proccie farm to produce another soldier, sailor or technician for the fight against the Xaros; a still gestating human was worth precisely zero in the forthcoming battle. The latest generation of doughboys took twenty minutes to produce a new soldier, and the single-minded biological constructs were ideal for shipboard defense.

"What about the data packet from Ibarra?" Garret asked.

Dorral tapped a keyboard and Mars sank toward the table and melded into a holo of the entire solar system. Garret's eyes flit over the ready status of macro cannons on Ganymede and Calisto, transfer fleets bringing new cruisers from the Mercury yards to Earth, orbital emplacements around Titan and rail gun emplacements dotting Iapetus.

Earth and Luna were a riot of data, too much for Garret to take in at a glance.

A red ring circled Pluto and a much larger planetoid, a new arrival to the solar system…Abaddon.

A hologram of Marc Ibarra's head and shoulders

formed in the center of the table.

"Mars command, this is Ibarra. Shame we have to deal with this time lag, but those are the laws of physics. Here are the brass tacks." The holo zoomed in on Pluto where a thick red line snaked out of Abaddon and traveled toward the sun. "From what our passive collection systems picked up on Pluto before they were destroyed, it looks like we're facing a mass of over one hundred million drones."

Ibarra's recording paused as those around the operation's table took in the number. No one showed any sign of panic or surprise—all were too well trained as commanders to ever make such a misstep—but Garret felt their tension even behind his own mask of command.

One hundred million…the worst-case scenario they'd planned on since the defeat of Eighth Fleet was for only half as many drones.

"Not optimal…at all," Ibarra said. "There is the evacuation protocol that we've discussed—"

Garret slashed his fingertips across his throat and Dorral paused Ibarra's recording.

"We stay and we fight," Garret said. "There are too many civilians on Earth to evacuate through the Crucible before the Xaros can reach our home. We run and the Xaros will find us. We've spent years fortifying

Mars and Earth, building a fleet stronger than I'd ever dreamed possible. The enemy is here, at our gates, but we will break them."

Dorral continued the recording.

"—but I didn't spend the last sixty-five years getting the planet ready for this moment so that I could just throw my hands up in the air now," Ibarra said.

"The Bastion probe has data on all known Xaros assaults on inhabited star systems. We know their tactics," Ibarra said. "The Xaros always attack the highest concentration of military force first, then wipe out outlying settlements at their leisure. Mars, your fleets are obvious, mobile. Earth's defenses are static and the Home Fleet is hidden. Mars will be our anvil, but the Crucible is the hammer. One of them, anyway."

Ibarra raised a hand and snapped his holographic fingers without any sound. A schematic of a device made up of several round shields, each the size of a Mule transport, appeared over the tank.

"Graviton bombs. If the Xaros hold to form and make straight for Mars, then there's only one least-time course they'll take. The Alliance probe and I will send graviton bombs through the Crucible and into the Xaros maniple. The drones are fast and tough, but we've yet to encounter one that can outrun a short-lived singularity.

Still, the effective range on these devices is only a few kilometers, and the Xaros have plenty of room to maneuver in the void. Each bomb will transmit telemetry data on the maniple, which will make subsequent strikes more accurate. The probe is one hell of a computer, and we'll do the best we can to punch them in the face the entire way to Mars.

"Our ambassador on Bastion is working to secure military assistance from our allies, but as we've agreed, we won't bring them into play as a knockout punch until we've got the Xaros by the nose. Show our hand too early and they may change tactics, go to ground and start replicating more drones where we can't touch them. Assaulting a Xaros position will be bloody—we learned that at the Battle of the Crucible—and fighting the Xaros in open space isn't to our advantage. We've got defenses. Let's use them.

"Which leaves our macro cannon phalanx. Fleet Admiral Garret has release authority on them. I'm waiting for your decision," Ibarra said.

Dorral stopped the recording.

"Macro batteries in the outer solar system can commence bombardment as soon as they receive our order," said an admiral at the far end of the table. "But with the time it takes a message to reach the cannons, and how far the Xaros will have moved from their last-known position between then and when the munition hits…"

"They'll be pounding vacuum," Garret said. While the macro cannon shells traveled at a decent single percentage of the speed of light, the Xaros would detect the launch and have time to maneuver out of the way. Garret crossed his arms and tapped a finger against his armor.

"General Krupp," said Garret and the lone holo army officer snapped to attention. "All Mars macro cannons will begin immediate area-of-effect bombardment on the center mass of projected Xaros positions. We'll receive telemetry data from the graviton mines before Ibarra does—don't wait for him to paint a better target picture. Phobos and Deimos batteries will load munitions but are not to fire."

"Yes, sir. I'll have rounds in the void within ten minutes. The big guns will never tire." Krupp turned away from the holo table and spoke to someone Garret couldn't see.

"I want to fight them here, on Mars," Garret said. "All fleets will join the line beyond Phobos' orbit as the enemy approaches. We will bring the outer system batteries to bear once we've engaged the Xaros."

"Sir," Dorral said, clearing her throat, "relying on

70

a macro cannon shell from so far away…if the firing solution is off by anything we run the risk of hitting Mars…and us."

"'God fights on the side with the best artillery,'" Garret said. "Let's have faith that He is with us."

CHAPTER 8

The range was a cave the size of a basketball court. A wide rubber mat filled the rear half while the firing range took up most of the rest. Suits of armor stood shoulder to shoulder against the wall, their breastplates open, pilot cradles empty. The unarmored soldiers clustered around the holo wall where Xaros targets flew in a deep illusion of the Martian surface, watching as two soldiers in armor marked with runes engaged targets.

Bodel and Kallen, in armor, watched the other soldiers use their forearm cannons and shoulder-mounted rotary guns to tear through a swarm of drones coming over a hilltop.

Elias turned a corner to enter the range. Anger flared in his chest as none of the soldiers but Kallen noted his arrival.

No awareness, he thought.

He walked up to the firing line and stepped into the holo envelope. The range linked up with his suit. As soon as the synch was complete, his suit would provide recoil the same as if he was firing live ammunition. The progress bar filled slowly.

Elias twisted his helm around and looked over the seven unarmored pilots.

They were all Dotok. Their blunted beak mouths hung open as they all looked up at Elias with eyes wide against their broad faces. Something nagged at Elias as he scanned their faces and matched his roster to the English name patches sewn to their uniforms.

Hair. They all still had thick strands of dark hair coming off their scalps. Traditionally, a soldier shaved his head the day they had the surgery to install the neural plugs at the base of their skull that linked to the armor. Those newly minted—and completely bald—soldiers earned the nickname "bean heads."

Elias turned his attention back to the range. He swung the rotary cannon up from his back and felt it snap into the shoulder mount. He felt a pinch against his flesh-and-blood shoulder, a psychosynaptic reaction to a change in his suit.

"Range. Calibration." Elias raised his forearm

cannon and waited for the holo field to shift to known-distance targets, bull's-eyes every few tens of meters. A reticule popped up on his vision. As he moved his gaze around, the rotary cannon moved to match. He raised his forearm cannon and tested moving the two reticules around each other.

"Firing line," he said to the armor next to him. "Time trial. Engage all targets. Count down from five."

The range popped the count down over his vision.

His weapons activated and Elias tore through the targets, sweeping the rotary gun up one side, his forearm cannon up the other. When the last target exploded, Elias' completion time flashed up in the holo range. Three point two seconds. The other armor finished in a little over eight seconds. Murmurs of surprise came from the other Dotok pilots.

"Range. Cease fire." Elias lowered his weapons. "You two didn't use simultaneous fire. Why?"

"The neural load is dangerously high," the nearer suit said, the voice female. "We try to fire both weapons at the same time and we risk a redline."

Elias' hands clenched into fists.

"'Try,'" Elias let the word hang in the air. "Is the Dotok nervous system inferior to a human's?"

"Not at all, sir," the other armor said, this one

sounding young and male. "Our synch rates are almost twenty percent better than—"

"Then why aren't you pushing yourselves?"

"It's…risky," the female said.

Kallen started toward her, but Bodel put a hand up and stopped her.

"If you're not willing to push yourself in training, you will not push yourself in battle," Elias said.

"We score higher than all the human pilots on every test," the younger one said.

Elias pointed to two unsuited Dotok. "Armor up. Now. All four of you against me on the mat."

Elias went to the far end of the fighting mat, pacing back and forth as the other two Dotok loaded into their wombs and plugged into their armor. The four Dotok armor hesitated at their edge of the arena.

"Rules?" one of the newly chosen asked.

"Range, set threat condition black," Elias said. A green icon popped against his vision. The suit would let the armor push to the limits of their capabilities, but stop them from inflicting any serious injury. There were safer settings, but Elias had never used them.

The four Dotok stepped onto the mat and set into a fighting stance.

The female looked at her fellow combatants and

asked, "When do we—"

Elias charged forward and punched her in the abdomen. The sound of steel on steel rang like a bell across the room. Elias dug his fingers around the edge of her armor plates and hurled her against the Dotok armor standing next to her, sending them both to the ground in a jumble of limbs.

Elias' torso whirled around on its hip actuators and smacked the back of his fist into the shoulder of a lunging Dotok. Elias sidestepped the disrupted charge and drove his spike into the attacker's back. The spike bounced off the armor, Elias' strength limited by the rules of the match.

"Killing blow," sounded through the room. The Dotok flattened against the floor, the armor locked.

The still-standing Dotok leaped into the air, spike extended and poised to strike as he descended on Elias. Elias activated the aegis shield on his forearm and segments of the shield unfolded into a kite shape in a split second.

Elias knocked the Dotok's strike aside with the shield and thrust his own spike up and into the falling armor. Elias' spike collapsed into the housing, saving the Dotok pilot from being impaled.

"Killing blow."

Elias ducked forward and kicked a leg back, catching the female Dotok in the chest. She stumbled back and caught the tip of Elias' spike beneath her armpit.

"Killing blow."

Elias grabbed her deactivated armor by the throat as it fell and threw it at his final opponent. The last Dotok caught her and came to a stop. Elias bashed his shoulder into the pair and sent them flying back.

Elias raised a foot over the prone Dotok and slammed his heel toward the alien's chest. Elias' suit overrode his command and shifted his heel to the side and into the ground hard enough to break through the flooring.

"Killing blow."

Elias' shield and spike retracted into their housings.

"Pathetic," Elias said. "You think test scores matter. You think your rank against each other matters. It does not. You all lack a killer's instinct and I do not know if I can find it inside you. Get up and get off my mat. The next four of you, suit up."

The two armor soldiers that stoked his ire got to their feet as the simulation released them. Elias read the English letter names on their chests: Caas. Ar'ri.

No, can't be, he thought. He knew those names,

Dotok children he'd met on New Abhaile, the Dotok city on Takeni where the world's population sought refuge. He remembered carrying them in his arms to an evacuation center and promising to protect them from the monsters assaulting the city.

Now the two would fight beside him in the coming battle.

No different. I wouldn't have done anything different, Elias thought. *The Xaros will not show mercy, neither must I.*

****

Kallen's womb lowered from the inside of her armor and popped open. Bodel caught her and gently removed the plugs from her skull. He lifted her emaciated frame into a waiting wheelchair and wrapped a shawl over her shoulders. Kallen's head lolled to the side.

"How is she?" Elias asked.

"Passed out again." Bodel touched two fingers to the side of her throat and frowned. "Heart rate's a bit erratic...but getting stronger. She could have taken another neural booster, even a hit of adrenaline to stay awake. She's getting worse, Elias."

Kallen had been diagnosed with Batten's Disease, a neurological disorder that had afflicted many armor soldiers in the past. The symptoms were easy to identify and the disease was reversible in its earliest stages. But Kallen was a quadriplegic, had been since she was a little girl. There had been no warning for her as the disease progressed. According to the doctors on Earth, she was well into the terminal phase.

"We knew this would happen," Elias said.

Bodel gently pushed her head back and ran a towel through her hair.

"Doesn't make this any easier for me." He gave Elias a dirty look. "Shouldn't be for you either."

"It isn't, Hans. We promised to keep her in armor for as long as possible. It's what she wants."

"It will be me—don't you get that? It will be me that takes her out of her armor the last time. That has to take care of her body. I've been doing this for her for so long…but it'll be soon. She'll be just like this, but she's won't wake up. It has to be me…but I don't want to do it."

Kallen's eyes fluttered. She opened and closed a bone-dry mouth and brought her head up. Bodel placed a straw against her lips. She took a long sip of electrolyte water and gave Bodel a smile.

"Hans, have you been crying?" she asked.

"No." Bodel stepped behind her wheelchair

before she could get a better look at him.

"Elias, you didn't kill any of our bean heads, did you?" she asked.

"I sent them back here with their tail between their legs. There was some improvement," Elias said.

"If you could get out of your armor, I think Aguilar would have kicked your ass for all the repair work he and his techs have to do," Bodel said.

"I regret nothing," Elias deadpanned.

The door to the cemetery opened and two Dotok came inside. Elias zoomed in on their coveralls to read their nametapes. Caas and Ar'ri.

The two came up on the catwalk running at the stored armor's waist height.

Caas' beak clicked several times, glancing between Kallen's open armor and the woman in the wheelchair.

"Forgive us," Caas said. "We are looking for the Iron Hearts."

"You've got us," Bodel said.

Ar'ri looked around his sister's shoulder at the two. His head cocked from side to side.

"Truly?" he asked.

"We are armor," Elias said, his voice thundering from his speakers, causing the two Dotok to jump as if the catwalk had suddenly electrified.

"Elias?" Caas recovered and put a hand to her chest, then bowed slightly.

"We came to thank you and to beg forgiveness," Ar'ri said.

"For?" Kallen asked.

"You three are the reason we volunteered for the armored corps," Caas said. "We thought we'd serve on the *Vorpal* or as pilots once we were old enough to serve. But when word came that we could be like you...we had to try."

"The human recruiters were very happy to see us," Ar'ri said. "It seems Dotok can more easily integrate with the armor's neural links and we do not suffer from clouds row phobia. Closet foopia. The word. After so many generations aboard starships, we are used to tight spaces."

"Recruiters are always happy to see anyone who can help make their quotas," Bodel said.

"You are not pleased to see us?" Caas asked.

"You were children the last time we saw you. Now you're...grown," Elias said.

"Outside your armor..." Ar'ri hesitated, "you are not what we expected."

"And what did you envision?" Kallen asked.

"We knew some Marines. Mr. Standy, Torni,

Orozco. They are—" Caas' foot scratched at the catwalk.

"Not cripples," Kallen said. "Tell me why Elias would have murdered you on that mat if the computer hadn't saved you."

"Our training was deficient," Caas said quickly.

"No." Bodel shook his head and wiped a bit of spittle from the slack half of his mouth. "He was pushing you."

"Your body doesn't matter in the armor," Kallen said. "Your mind is the killer, the armor the extension of your will. In the armor you are more. Faster. Stronger. Able to withstand harsh environments and take down the hardest targets. We don't wear the armor because we are weak. We are armor because we are strong enough to push ourselves further and harder than anyone else."

"Few soldiers could ever make it through selection," Bodel said. "Armor was expensive, difficult to build and maintain. We were never weapons that could be mass-produced. But the few of us that fought made the difference in every battle."

"We aren't worthy." Caas' shoulders slumped. She backed up and turned away.

"Who are you?" Elias asked.

"Trooper Caas," she said.

"No." Elias leaned out of his coffin. A panel on

82

his breastplate popped open. Elias' true eyes opened slowly. "Who are you?"

"Armor," Ar'ri said.

"I am armor," Caas said slowly.

Elias touched a finger to her sternum. "No one wants the armor, no one gets their plugs, unless they've got iron in here. You understand?"

"Yes, sir," Caas said.

"You came in here to apologize for something?" Bodel asked.

"For our poor performance," Ar'ri said.

"You won't be sorry against the Xaros. You'll be dead," Kallen said.

"You bean heads have six hours to shit, shower and shave before the next training cycle," Elias said. "Wait—why do you all still have your hair? Carius wouldn't let tradition slip just because you're not human."

The two Dotok spoke to each other in their own language for a moment.

"We don't have hair," Caas said. She went to Bodel and turned her head to the side and let him get a closer look at the thick strands coming off her scalp. "Dotok do not…leak…through their skin to reduce body heat. Blood cycles through our dendrites to cool. If these were removed, we would overheat and die."

"But we would most certainly bleed to death and die before we overheat," Ar'ri said. He looked up at Elias.

"I'll let it slide," Elias said.

CHAPTER 9

Klaxons wailed across the *Breitenfeld*'s bridge announcing combat conditions. Captain Valdar strapped himself into his command chair and took a helmet out from under the seat. He looked over his crew. His gaze went to Ensign Geller, the navigator, then he got out of his chair.

"All decks report ready for combat conditions," Commander Ericcson said from beside the holo table. "Shall I set for zero atmo...Captain?"

Valdar leaned over Geller's seat and put a heavy hand on the young officer's shoulder.

Geller's head snapped up to look at the ship's master and commander, his eyes wide and face pale.

"Sir?"

Valdar lifted an air line off Geller's chair and

tapped the nozzle against the navigator's faceplate. Geller's hand went to the back of his helmet and felt the empty spot where the auxiliary air hose should have jacked into his suit.

"Your suit can keep your air going for three hours," Valdar said. "Do you know how long this battle will last?"

Geller shook his head.

"Do you want to be in the middle of steering my ship and find that you're out of air?"

Geller shook his head.

"That's why you check your lines." Valdar snapped the nozzle into the back of Geller's helmet. His faceplate flexed slightly as air rushed in. Valdar gave the top of Geller's head a double pat and went back to his command chair.

"XO, void the ship," Valdar said as he donned his helmet and connected his auxiliary lines. His void suit flexed against falling air pressure as the bridge's atmosphere was sucked into storage tanks. Fighting in a ship full of flammable oxygen—ready to explosively decompress when exposed to vacuum—was not a smart choice during void combat. Damage during a battle might rip a sailor's suit and spill their air, but that risk was better than losing most of the ship and crew to one hull rupture.

He swung a data slate up from an armrest and ran his touch down the line of all the ships under his command, opening a channel to the captains.

"Task Force 37, this is *Breitenfeld*. Our mission is to destroy the Grinder, stop the Xaros from bringing in reinforcements, and get back to Earth and join the line. Update me with your combat readiness and the Crucible will open a wormhole on my mark."

Ship icons went from red to green up and down the board...except for the *Centaur*, one of his two *Manticore*-class vessels armed with salvaged Toth energy cannons.

The face of Commander Davies, commander of the *Centaur*, came up on Valdar's screen.

"Sir, my ventral energy cannons are having fits. Engineering has a work-around. We'll be locked and loaded in...six minutes," he said.

"We're waiting on you," Valdar said. He opened a different IR channel. "Gall, how are things on the hull?"

"Itching to get going," she said. *"I've had to explain to some of my newer pilots your habit of kicking us off the ship every time you get the chance. The two Dotok think you don't like us anymore."* She and the rest of the *Breitenfeld*'s complement of fighters and bombers were magnetically locked to the outside of the ship's hull to make room for what high

command deemed "mission critical equipment." Durand had a lengthy rebuttal on just how critical her fighters were, which Valdar opted not to share with their higher headquarters for fear of the damage it would do to the French pilot's future.

"Hale, drop pod status," Valdar said.

"All systems go." Hale's response was hurried. Valdar had kept his distance from Hale after their conversation in his ready room. Both had men and women to lead and a battle to plan. Valdar promised himself he'd make things right with his godson once Earth was safe. If they lost this battle, then Hale's feelings toward Valdar wouldn't matter.

"XO, what's happening on my flight deck?" the captain asked.

"Missile pods one through four are on rails and ready to deploy. Chief MacDougall promises they'll be clear and ready for flight ops within ten minutes of pushing the last pod out the door. Missileers are at their stations below decks, ready to go," she said.

During the Toth incursion, the *Breitenfeld* had used her jump engines to deploy guided missile pods and devastate the Toth armada. Given his ship's unique capabilities, Valdar wasn't surprised he'd been tasked to replicate the maneuver. He hadn't anticipated the target being in orbit around Pluto or commanding an assault fleet at the same time, but war was full of surprises.

The *Centaur*'s icon flashed green.

"Main power to rail cannons and point defense turrets," Valdar said.

"Aye, Captain," said Commander Utrecht, the ship's gunnery officer.

"Crucible, this is Valdar. We're ready to go."

"Forming your wormhole now," Marc Ibarra said, *"good hunting."*

Valdar opened a channel to every sailor and Marine in his task force.

"This is Captain Valdar. My ship has a custom before battle, one connected to the proud lineage of her name. I will remind you that as we go into battle, God is with us. *Gott mit uns.*"

A white disc spread from the center of the Crucible and engulfed Valdar's task force.

Valdar's hands gripped his armrests as the blinding light pounded his skull.

"Sir!" Geller called out. "There are some fluctuations in the wormhole. Our exit point is off by…about three thousand kilometers."

Valdar's teeth clenched. Once, just once, he wanted the damn jump drive to work perfectly.

"Where are we—"

The *Breitenfeld* broke through the wormhole and into real space. They were over Pluto. The dwarf planet's wide swath of glaciers looked ruddy, almost smoke-stained. Valdar picked out the Grinder in the distance and just above the horizon.

Off to port, a ripple of light appeared out of nothing and danced across a cylindrical object the size of a frigate. Valdar's heart sank as more ripples appeared ahead of his ship, each revealing a Xaros warship.

"It's an ambush!" Valdar shouted as he opened a channel to his ships' captains with one hand and pointed to Utrecht with the other. The gunnery officer needed no further instructions. The *Breitenfeld's* rail cannon batteries slewed toward the nearest Xaros ship.

A crimson beam lashed out and hit the *Breitenfeld* amidships, disintegrating an Eagle before it could release from the hull.

"All ships! Charge through the ambush, weapons free!" Valdar shouted.

His bridge crew were in action before he finished his sentence. Geller pressed the ship forward with engines blazing. Ericcson overrode the Eagles' mag locks and cut the squadrons free from their grip on the *Breitenfeld*.

Rail guns flashed bright enough to leave an

afterimage against Valdar's eyes as they fired. The nearest Xaros ship cracked in half from the impact and tumbled toward Pluto, burning all the way down.

There were at least a dozen Xaros construct ships, none larger than a frigate, but all were pounding his ships with the cannons running through the center of each alien vessel.

A flash of jaundiced light broke over the starboard side of his ship.

"*Tyre* just went critical," Ericcson said. "*Hutchinson* and *Erebus* both reporting heavy damage."

"Two enemy vessels just fractured," Utrecht said, "broke into drones…they're going for the drop ships."

Part of Valdar wanted to scream and find out why Hale and his Marines had been let go into the middle of the battle, but the answer to that question wouldn't do anything to help them survive the descent.

"Gall, break off and cover the pods. We'll make do with point defense," Valdar said.

"*—good shooting, Manfred…Roger, Captain. We're breaking off but that will leave my bombers unprotected,*" Durand said.

Valdar found a trio of Condors on his screen making a hasty attack on a Xaros ship dead ahead of the *Breitenfeld*. They were tens of seconds away from torpedo range...and taking fire from Xaros drones.

"Recall the bombers soon as their missiles are loose," Valdar said. Regret squeezed at his chest as he said the words. He'd just signed death warrants for those three Condors, but Hale's mission on the surface was mission critical, the Condors surviving their attack run...less so.

The ship lurched to the side, swinging Valdar against his restraints as the *Breitenfeld* made a high-energy turn. A Xaros ship flew beneath the ship's keel. There was a flash from the ventral rail cannon and Valdar felt a bone-rattling kick through his seat.

"Target destroyed!" Utrecht announced. A grimace went across his face. "Ventral battery is off-line. The buffers weren't designed for a perpendicular shot off the hull."

Charon swung into view and the ship rocketed toward the moon. Smaller ships from the task force raced ahead of the strike cruiser.

Arrowheads of white energy shot over the *Breitenfeld*'s bow.

"*Centaur* is firing," Ericcson said, "but she's falling behind."

"Helm. Slow and take us to starboard enough for the ventral cannons to cover the *Centaur*," Valdar said.

The ship's prow shifted to the right and the two

rail cannon batteries twisted so far Valdar could almost see down their barrels.

"Enemy ships are breaking off—" the flash of rail cannons forced Ericcson to turn her face away as she continued "—retreating back to the Grinder."

"No, we're the ones retreating," Valdar said. "They don't have to destroy us all, just keep us off the jump gate until it's complete."

He looked at his data pad. Two of his ships were gone, the rest damaged. Only his ship was relatively unscathed despite the pounding she'd taken.

Must thank Torni for the upgrades, he thought.

"Breitenfeld," Durand said, her transmission laced with static, *"drop pods…attack…least one."*

Valdar released his restraints and went to the holo table where a larger picture of the battle raging over Pluto's surface came to life. The drop pods streaked toward Pluto, none on course to land where they were supposed to. Dozens of drones fought with half as many Eagles around the pods.

"Shall I send the corvettes back?" Ericcson asked. "The *Scipio* and the *Barca* could reach them soon."

"No." Valdar shook his head as another drop pod flashed amber. A red X appeared over the icon a moment later, destroyed. "They can't make a difference now. Get the task force to Charon and keep the moon between us and the Grinder."

Valdar touched the Xaros jump gate in the holo tank and dragged it closer to him. Three-quarters of the linked spike circumference was complete. Drones swarmed over the unfinished edges, transmuting omnium into the basalt-like material that made up the spikes, bringing the two ends closer and closer together.

Construction was nearly complete, and Valdar didn't have long to stop them.

****

The drop pod bucked beneath Hale hard enough to slam the back of his helmet against his seat. His visor display and gauntlet screen erupted with warning icons and dozens of panicked voices talking over each other through the IR.

"Bridge, this is Roughneck 6, status report?" Hale asked.

"*—are clear. They're going for the drop pods. Release! Release!*" Durand's shout carried through his helmet. "*They are sitting ducks!*"

"Egan! Why are we still attached to the *Breit?*"

"Not sure, sir." Egan sat near the apex of the drop

pod in a pilot's chair, the only one with access to a window. Egan did a double take and leaned against the view port. "Bandits coming right for us!"

"Bridge! Why are—" The dorsal rail cannon battery thundered, shaking Hale and his team against their restraints like peas in a can. Hale tried to get his senses back and felt his body weight shift against different parts of his restraints.

"Egan?"

"We're released," Egan said, struggling with the controls as red flashes of light came through the windows, "but the engines are off-line."

"Egan! I am too young and beautiful to die!" Standish yelled.

"Shut up!" Egan roared back. The drop pod lurched to the side and Hale felt a strong vibration through his acceleration seat as the engines came online.

"All teams, this is Roughneck 6. We are on the way to the drop zone. Report status in sequence," Hale said through the IR.

"Crimson has release!"

"Gold has release!"

"Slate…damage…dead stick. I repeat dead—" The lieutenant's words ended in a wash of static.

"Damn it. Egan, do you have vis on Slate's pod?"

A scarlet beam stabbed through the hull and gouged a line through the deck just inches from Hale's feet. The drop pod's electricity cut out, plunging the team into near darkness. Light from Egan's cockpit wobbled across the pod as it lost control.

"I've lost engines," Egan said. "I blow the ejection seats or we're all dead."

"Do it!" Hale shouted.

"Brace!" Egan opened a yellow and black panel and grabbed the neon-green handle within.

Hale pressed his head against the back of his seat and grabbed his chest restraints. There was a flash as explosive charges blew his seat out of the drop pod. Hale tumbled over and over, catching alternating glimpses of the icy plains of Pluto and the *Breitenfeld* and her task force locked in a knife fight with Xaros ships.

He grabbed release pins on each of his shoulder restraints and pulled. One came free, but the other slipped out of his grasp. The left half of his body sprang away from the seat, jamming his right arm against the harness. Centrifugal force pulled his free arm away. He strained to reach the other pin, but even his pseudo-muscles in his power armor couldn't overcome the force of his mad spin through Pluto's thin atmosphere.

Hale jerked his right shoulder and found some

wiggle room. He jerked again and came free of the chair. He kept rolling end over end, the thin layer of nitrogen and methane over the dwarf planet's surface doing nothing to buffer his fall. He keyed the thrusters in his boots every time he saw Pluto's surface and twisted his body to plunge headfirst once his tumble eased.

Hale looked around. Gauss point defense batteries across the *Breitenfeld* and her task force ripped through the void. Rounds flashed as they hit drones or raked across the sides of Xaros construct ships.

Burning streaks descended across Pluto's brief horizon. Hale didn't know if they were disintegrating drones or dying fighter craft. He looked to the surface and saw a puff of ice and snow as something impacted against a glacier.

"Here goes," he swung his feet to the surface and fired the thrusters attached to his boots. He felt his stomach sink and blood rush from his head as g-forces played across his body. As he tried to gauge his descent with how hard he was about to hit Pluto, he wished he'd had a few more days to rehearse this emergency landing.

Hale hit like a falling dart. Ice shattered and a fine layer of dust and snow covered his visor. Hale felt pressure against his entire body, but no pain. He raised an arm, shifting daggers of broken ice the size of his hands across his helmet. He wiped his visor clear and saw the still-raging void battle high above.

He pushed himself onto his knees and felt for the plasma rifle on his back. He breathed a sigh of relief when his hand closed around the handle. He looked around. Low mounds of rolling ice stretched across much of the horizon, but the Norgay Montes were to his north.

Another Marine landed ahead of him. Hale pressed off the ice, taking long, loping strides through the gravity barely a twentieth of Earth's. He kept an eye to the sky, aware that his gray armor made him an easy target against the pale white ice.

He leapt over a lump of ice the size of a bus and found Egan struggling out of his impact crater.

"Everyone got clear of the pod," Egan said. "This was *not* how we were supposed to get down here."

"What about the other teams? Did they make it down in one piece?"

"No idea. I was too busy trying to fly a falling stone, then trying to do the descent math in my head before my ejection seat could kill me." Egan drew his rifle. "Blast must have fried the seat's thrusters. Damn lowest bidder."

"Sir!" Standish and Yarrow waved to them from the edge of the depression. "We've got a beacon from the landing zone. At least one team is where they're supposed to be."

"Thank God for small favors," Hale said. "Any sign of Cortaro or Bailey?"

Yarrow touched the side of his helmet and nodded.

"I've got line of sight and IR to them both. Cortaro is not happy with us standing out in the open," Yarrow said.

"Let's get moving." Hale bounded up the hill.

The Marines formed into a wedge formation and ran toward the beacon, picking up Cortaro and Bailey on the way.

"Just so everyone knows," Standish said, "there's a master release button in the center of the Y-harness."

"Why are you telling us this now, Standish?" Egan asked.

"Oh, no reason."

Hale didn't have to look at Standish to know he was winking at him.

****

Hale crested a hill made of ice and stone and saw a round mineshaft big enough to swallow a Destrier transport in the side of a cliff.

He keyed his IR. "This is Roughneck 6. Anyone copy?"

"6, Crimson leader, I've got you. We're just inside the opening. Plenty of room for you," Lieutenant Jacobs said. "Mind the drop pod. We've got it under camo twenty-five meters from the entrance."

"Roger, inbound." Hale made for the opening, his team behind him. He got to the shaft and jumped over the outer edge. The shaft wall looked like the surface of the ocean—perfectly still waves a few inches high descending into a deep abyss.

Five Marines from Crimson huddled against the edge of the shaft, their attention on the horizon. A black body bag lay off to the side.

"Xaros hit Fredericks," Jacobs said. "His armor stopped most of the beam, but it cracked his suit. He suffocated before we even hit the surface." Her gaze stuck on the dead Marine.

"What's the status on your equipment? Any other casualties?" Hale asked.

Jacobs didn't answer.

Hale grabbed her by the shoulder and turned her to face him.

"Look at me and focus," he said. "Fredericks is

gone. You can't do anything about that now. Mission. Lead your Marines that are still alive."

"Right, sir, sorry. Pod came down intact. We got all the special equipment out. No one else is hurt," she said.

"What about the other pods? Gold is supposed to meet us here. You hear from Mathias or Bronx from landing zone bravo?"

"I saw…I saw one drop pod explode. I don't know which," she said.

Ice gripped Hale's heart at the news. An entire team of trained and ready strike Marines—his Marines—gone in an instant, gone before they could even get into the fight. And there was a fair chance Steuben was on that doomed pod. No matter the gamut of emotions running through Hale's mind, he was the company commander. They still had a mission to accomplish.

Hale looked at Cortaro. "Get an IR relay set up. We're heading down as soon as it's set up."

A flash of light broke across the sky. One of the frigates slumped out of the formation around the *Breitenfeld*, its engines sputtering. It nosed down and corkscrewed toward the planet's surface. The ship crashed into a distant mountain face, the sound of a muted explosion echoing through the wisp-thin atmosphere.

"They're breaking through! Look!" Jacobs pointed to the *Breitenfeld* as the ship unloaded a broadside on a Xaros cruiser and blew it into burning fragments. The strike carrier and her escorts sprang through the gap in the Xaros lines.

The *Breitenfeld*'s guns slewed around and fired. Quadrium shells burst to life, tendrils of electricity leapfrogging through the Xaros ships. The stricken enemy vessels went off-line.

Hale thought Captain Valdar would have kept his guns on the Xaros as they slowly succumbed to Pluto's gravity. Instead, the *Breitenfeld* and her surviving escorts sped away on burning engines. They vanished over the horizon within seconds.

"Where are they going?" Jacobs asked.

"I don't know, but Valdar must have a plan," Hale said. He looked at Egan and said, "Can we still contact them?"

"Not unless they left buoys, sir." Egan took a sheet of optic camouflage from the case and unfurled it over a small satellite dish propped up on the lip of the tunnel. He poked the antenna through a small hole. "But when they're back in line of sight, we'll have comms."

"Maybe he's scrubbed the mission," Jacobs said. "Should we wait here?"

"The *Breitenfeld* doesn't give up, lieutenant. This fight is far from over. Get your Marines up and ready." Hale turned and looked down the mineshaft that extended deep into the abyss. "We're going in."

****

Hale marched through the tunnel, relying on his visor's IR filters to see anything. The tunnel entrance was a faint dot behind them. The two teams of Marines moved in stacked wedges, Crimson squad in the lead.

There'd been no word from the teams with Steuben from landing zone bravo. Steuben and the Marines with him knew the mission; they'd follow him through the tunnel once they found it. If they were still alive. The longer Hale went without any contact from them, the more certain he became that they were lost.

Should have ordered the drop pod release sooner, he thought. *No, I should have gone with the low-orbit, low-opening jump instead of the pods. Would have been safe in the* Breit *until Durand cleared out the drones. Some company commander I'm turning out to be.*

Cortaro raised a fist, bringing the teams to a halt. He knelt down next to a sparkling lump of material jutting from the wavy ground.

"Sir," Cortaro said, "look at this."

Hale motioned for Crimson squad to continue on while his team stayed put. Taking long steps in the weak gravity, he got to Cortaro's side.

"What is it?"

"This…" Cortaro cocked his fist to the side twice and a Ka-Bar blade sprang out of its forearm housing. He poked the tip into the twinkling material and knocked a bit free. He scraped up the material with the edge of his blade and brought it up to his visor. "This is quadrium ore. My cousin Emmanuel worked for Ibarra Mining, was going to get me a job there when I hit my twenty years of service and retired. He told me about a drone survey of Pluto from years and years ago. Said the ice out here has a hell of a lot more quadrium than Earth's oceans or Europa."

"If this is so valuable, why didn't Ibarra mine it out before the Xaros ever arrived?" Hale asked.

"Look around, sir. We're pretty damn deep. Quadrium wasn't worth much before the war, and it would cost a fortune to get this far under the surface. Plus, the Chinese had a research station out here. They weren't real open to non-Chinese mining interests on anything they'd planted their flag on."

"We brought back that omnium reactor from Anthalas," Yarrow said. "That made all the q-shells we'd

104

ever need. Why would Ibarra muck around in the ass end of the solar system?"

"Better question is why are the Xaros digging for quadrium, if that's even why they're down here," Hale said.

"Sir…" Jacobs bounded over. "We found something weird a little farther ahead."

"The perfect tunnel dug through the surface isn't weird enough?" Standish asked.

Hale pointed a finger at Standish and the Marine stopped talking.

"Show me," Hale said.

He followed Jacobs down the tunnel another hundred yards until it ended against a marble-smooth wall of rock. Silicate crystals glinted beneath the polished surface. Quadrium ore dust hung around them, swirling in thick eddies as the Marine officers approached the wall.

"Not this," Jacobs said, pointing to the edge of the tunnel. An arched hole in the tunnel twice the size of a Marine opened to a tunnel with rough rock walls. Jacobs went to the hole and picked up a pebble in each hand. She reached over the threshold to the tunnel and dropped both pebbles. The rock inside the passageway fell significantly faster than the rock released in the tunnel.

A Marine ran around a corner and stopped at the edge of the doorway. His visor was up, face exposed. His mouth moved, but Hale heard nothing.

Jacobs tapped her helmet.

The Marine lowered his visor.

"Sorry, ma'am, forgot you're in vacuum. Atmo in here is at sea-level pressure, Earth standard gravity mixture of oxygen, nitrogen and carbon dioxide in the air. Temp's good too," he said.

"Just like the Crucible," Standish said. "Void one side of a wall, atmo on the other."

"Got eyes on enemy troops," came through the IR from one of the Crimson Marines.

"How many drones?" Hale stepped over the threshold and felt weight return to his body. He stumbled against the rough-hewn wall, scraping his pauldrons against the rock.

"This way, sir," the Marines said. "We set up an observation post."

"Not drones, Captain. Humanoid. Working on some kind of a truck."

"Moving." Hale looked back and saw Egan setting up an IR receiver at the passage entrance. The more times they changed direction in the mines, the harder it would be to keep comms with the *Breitenfeld*.

The passage wound its way through several yards of broken rock before Hale noticed light spilling across tan

106

stone. The Marine ahead of him went onto his hands and knees and crawled forward, and Hale followed suit.

The hallway opened up to a cavern. Glowing orbs floated through the air, casting a uniform light across everything. Quadrium ore glinted across the cavern's walls and ceiling. A waist-high wall of rock led from the opening to a stairway cut into raw stone that zigzagged down to the base of the cavern.

Crimson's sniper waved Hale over. The Marine raised the detached optics from his rail rifle over the lip of the wall. Video feed came up on Hale's visor.

Two figures in dark armor made up of sharp angles lifted glowing cubes of omnium from a pile in the center of the cavern onto a hover sled.

"What do you think, sir?" Jacobs asked.

"That's omnium…last time we saw this was in Phoenix. Xaros normally have their drones converting mass," Hale said. There was something familiar about the armored figures, both of whom had their backs to Hale.

A chill went down Hale's spine.

"Jacobs," Hale said, grabbing her arm, "ambush. No q-shells. Aim for center mass. Knock 'em down. We're not going to get much intell if you blow them into mush."

"Yes, sir." Jacobs gave a few curt commands. She counted down from five with her fingers then she and her team stood up and aimed their plasma rifles. Two rifles fired almost simultaneously.

"Targets down," Jacobs said.

"With me." Hale took to the stairs, his weapon trained on the two bodies lying next to the sled, smoking holes in their backs. Jacobs followed close behind.

She pointed to a semicircle tunnel branching away from the cavern and ordered her Marines down to cover the approach.

Hale got to the first body and gave it a swift kick in the lower back. The strike of armor on armor sounded like clashing metal. No reaction. Same result with the second body. Hale put his foot against a corpse and pushed it onto its back.

The thing had once been human. A man's face was visible beneath a see-through crystal half-helm, his mouth and chin slack, eyes staring into oblivion. The irregular armor covered the back of his head and the rest of his body.

"What are they? What happened to them?" Jacobs asked.

"Banshees, human banshees," Hale said. "The Xaros found a Dotok colony fleet in the void, turned them into slave soldiers and set them loose on Takeni. I spent a lot of time debriefing that fight with the intell squirrels.

They think the Xaros did it because they didn't have enough drones on hand. They convert mass to drones, hard to find much in interstellar space."

"But where'd they find them?" Jacobs asked.

"Pluto was unmanned…Eighth Fleet. The Xaros must have taken prisoners, turned them," Hale said.

"We can still save them. Can't we?"

Hale shook his head. "Banshees were hardwired to the Xaros network. Dr. Accorso tried to free one, killed it in the process. Treat these as hostile."

"But, sir…these are human beings. We can't just…kill them," Jacobs said.

Hale tapped his screen and opened a private IR channel to Jacobs. She stiffened and raised her chin.

"Listen to me, Lieutenant. I was there on Takeni. Fought the Dotok the Xaros changed into monsters. There was no mercy from the banshees. They killed every man, woman and child they got their claws on. There is no coming back from this. We have hours, a day if we're lucky, before the Xaros finish their gate and Earth is lost," Hale said. "The mission is all that matters right now. You get me?"

"Got you, sir. Just…" she hesitated, pointing her muzzle at one of the bodies, "first time I've killed a…person."

"Captain," Cortaro said aloud, his visor open, "I've got an idea."

"Let's hear it."

"That quadrium survey my cousin told me about, the one that mapped out all the deposits in this mountain range, it should still be on file somewhere. Might give us a map of where the Xaros are digging," Cortaro said.

"But the *Breit*'s still out of contact," Hale said.

"It'll take seven minutes to get a message back to Earth," Egan said from the top of the stairs. He held up the end of a line snaking back to the tunnel. "I'm bouncing off the relay sat way up over Uranus."

"Who on Earth would even have that data?" Hale asked.

"Marc Ibarra," Cortaro said. "We've got the freq to the Crucible. Let's ask him."

CHAPTER 10

A small red needle appeared in the holo tank, another graviton bomb delivered through the Crucible into the invading armada of Xaros drones as they crossed through Saturn's orbit.

"Augustus cannon firing," Dorral said from across the table.

Garret acknowledged with a tap of his finger. The hypervelocity round tracked away from Mars and sped toward the approaching foe.

It would be another hour before the telemetry data from the latest graviton mine reached Mars and General Krupp and his team could refine their targeting data. Garret would have delayed Augustus' launch, but Mars' rotation would have turned the cannon away if he'd waited another ten minutes.

But as soon as Mars' rotation took Augustus off the firing line, it brought Nerio to the fore. Mars had enough cannons scattered over the surface to always have six guns that could engage targets in the distant solar system. As the enemy drew closer, the number of effective weapons would fall as the angles of attack shrank.

Since the Crucible sent the first graviton bomb through a wormhole, their picture of the Xaros armada had improved with each attack as the probe processed data off each explosion. The initial attacks were like lunging for an enemy in pitch blackness—they had a good idea where to strike, but hit nothing at first. As soon as a mine connected with a substantial number of drones, the defenders gained a handhold on their foe.

The probability of inflicting damage rose with each new attack. The Xaros were fast, nimble, and had begun to spread out as the graviton mines destroyed more and more of them. Mars' cannons took their toll, but Garret wouldn't know how much of the Xaros force had been whittled away until they were almost on top of Mars.

The red smear of the approaching Xaros blinked as new data came in. The Xaros mass forked apart like a snake's tongue. There was a rustle of unease from the officers around Garret.

"Give me course projections."

Dashed lines ticked away from the two tips and traveled toward the center of the solar system. One track led to Mars, the other to Earth.

"That's…unusual." Dorral tugged at her bottom lip. "Xaros attack methodology always uses their numbers to overwhelm a target. They've never split up like this before, even in the face of a defense in the depth like we're putting up."

"Something made a command decision. It's here." Garret tapped his fist against the table's railing. "The leadership entity *Breitenfeld* encountered on Takeni, the same one that Makarov faced in the void."

"This changes things," Dorral said. "Even with the Xaros just within the orbit of Saturn, they're faster than us. They'll reach Earth before our fleets here can."

Garret looked at the fragmentary data in the holo tank and made quick calculations.

"The Xaros are sending enough drones to overwhelm Earth's defenses…and enough to keep us tied down on Mars. We're being played." Garret reached into the holo field and touched his thumb and middle finger together. The holo zoomed out to show the entire solar system.

"Send a priority message to the *Breitenfeld*," Garret said. "Have her jump to Mars once the Grinder is destroyed. No delay. We'll use her jump drives to shuttle ships of the line back to Earth. That could make all the difference."

"Aye, sir." Dorral turned away and went to a commo station.

Garret opened a frequency and Krupp's holo appeared next to him.

"Sir?" the general asked.

"We need to end the battle over Mars faster than we'd anticipated. Here's what I want you to do."

As Garret laid out his plan, blood drained from Krupp's face.

****

Red warning lights flashed as the *Charlemagne* withdrew air from the bridge. Garret felt his helmet flex as vacuum tugged at his faceplate.

His fleets formed a slight concave shield between Mars and the approaching Xaros fleet. Tens of millions of drones crept toward the red planet, slowing as they entered the outer fringe of the planet's gravity well.

Garret waved his hand across the combined fleet. Twenty *Midway*-class supercarriers, hundreds of battle cruisers armed with rail cannon batteries, fifty *Manticore*-

114

class frigates boasting salvaged Toth energy cannons, and over a thousand more ships of the line made up the rest of his grand fleet. Then the fighters, tens of thousands of fighters filled the space between the warships like dust in the air around a stampede.

It was too much for one man to manage, he knew that. Each fleet admiral had autonomy to carry out his orders however he or she saw fit. The memory of designing the temperament and skill of each admiral before they came out of the proccie tubes churned his stomach, but if each could fight as well as Makarov, this day might end in victory.

"Enemy front-line trace will cross engagement line black in…five minutes," Dorral said.

"How long until Phobos rises?"

"Thirty-five minutes," Dorral said with a wince.

"We'll make do." He dragged the holo around to focus on the Xaros. The miles-thick line of drone icons spread out like blood over an invisible globe, all just beyond the effective engagement of his fleet's weapons.

They've learned, he thought. *Good thing we still have a few surprises waiting.*

The Xaros swarm was a mass of single drones, difficult targets for the rail guns on most of his ships. The enemy meant to flood his ships with a deluge of drones. A

115

single Xaros could cut through a ship's aegis armor and wreak havoc. He'd seen the damage firsthand when walking through the *Midway*'s dead halls.

Garret opened a channel to General Krupp. "Ground command, I doubt we can stop them all. Prep your local security forces. They'll come for the cannons."

"Of course," Krupp said, "not like there's anything else down here for them to visit. I've got three cannons ready and able to support you. Rest are either out of the engagement envelope or firing on the force heading to Earth."

Garret closed the channel and brought his trembling fingers to a pulsating red button. He swallowed hard and pressed it to open IR-beam communication to every ship protecting Mars.

"Combined fleet, this is Garret. Mars is our fortress. Our enemy will break against our iron will and die beneath our guns. Let's give these Xaros bastards a proper welcome. All fleets, begin attack pattern theta. Garret out."

He felt a slight vibration through the deck as the *Charlemagne's* few rail guns fired.

The trace of rail gun shells zipped away from the fleet and struck out at the outer edge of the Xaros swarm. Quadrium rounds exploded into jagged bolts of deep blue lightning that coursed through the drones, knocking them off-line and rendering them into little more than a lump of metal traveling on a simple vector. Flechette rounds fired from rail cannons tore through the drones like a close-range blast from a shotgun.

Revetments carved from mountains surrounding the macro cannons slid aside and rail cannons rose from their hiding places to join the assault on the Xaros.

The spread of the Xaros slowed. A few hundred drones managed to skirt through the assault, fewer than combat models in the past few years predicted. Garret refused to let his hopes rise.

The top of the Xaros-made dome moved toward the line of human ships like the tip of a knife pushing against a cloth. The edge of the alien force retreated toward the base of the spike emerging from the mass.

"The drones are combining." Dorral zoomed in on the spike. Red lines danced over the spike's surface as a single massive construct emerged, a dagger pointed at Garret's fleet and into the heart of Mars. Makarov had described battling a leviathan-class vessel, but this was larger by an order of magnitude.

"Krupp," Garret said, reaching into the holo and double-tapping the new Xaros creation, "we're not going to have another chance like this. Fire target Durandal." A timer appeared next to the leviathan, counting down the seconds until Phobos cleared the far side of Mars.

Red spots of light grew up and down the Xaros' spike.

"All fleets execute honeycomb maneuver—" Garret called up firing solutions from the macro cannons on Mars, hating himself for every second he wasted, "—Echo. Ninth Fleet, drag your heels a bit until we have launch and stay out of the line of fire."

The defending fleets moved away from each other slowly, spreading into a lattice to deny the Xaros a concentrated target.

"Give me three point targets on the leviathan," Garret said to the gunnery officers next to Dorral. "Do we have eyes on any seams in the hull?"

A gunner cocked her head to the side.

"The whole structure is covered in ravines hundreds of meters deep." A close-up of the spike flashed into the holo. Deep fissures glowed red, like the spike was covered in cracked obsidian and filled with lava.

"Plenty of potential weak points. Sending three now," she said.

Garret touched the three white target reticules that appeared on the spike.

"All fleets, fire at will. Hold back bomber wings until further notice." Garret looked to the timer and tapped his fingers against the table railing.

Something's not right, he thought.

Beams of ruby-colored energy stabbed away from the spike, ripping through the thin line of ships. Garret lost ten ships in the blink of an eye, all smaller frigates and destroyers that lacked enough aegis armor plating to withstand much more than a blow from a Xaros construct made up of a few dozen drones.

The fleet struck back, launching concentrated rail cannon fire against Garret's assigned targets. Point defense fire erupted around the point targets like sparks off a live wire.

The timer flashed as Phobos rose from behind Mars. Ready icons popped up next to Deimos, the outer moon looming over the battle.

"Here we go." Garret's hands gripped the railing.

Phobos held nine macro cannons quarried through its rocky body and hidden beneath dusty firing ports. All nine revealed themselves at once and brought their capacitors online. The six cannons hidden in Deimos did the same. The moon batteries were designed to fire one at a time in support of the Mars-based weapons, but Garret needed an assassin's mace for this battle.

Garret said a silent prayer for the crews that volunteered to remain with their guns. They had a chance to survive—a very slim chance.

"Rounds away!" a gunnery officer shouted.

Flight paths stabbed through the holo tracing the incoming macro cannon rounds fired from the two moons and several cannons on Mars. All the projected paths led to the great spike.

The fire mission Garret and Krupp devised brought devastation down on the Xaros construct from multiple directions and with enough firepower to crack Earth's moon wide open.

Garret didn't breathe as the giant shells raced toward the spike…and hit home.

A cheer broke through the bridge as the spike burst into jagged fragments the size of the *Charlemagne*. The remains sizzled with internal fire along their broken edges.

Garret stared intently at a fragment tumbling end over end. He felt a brush of fear against his heart as the fragment slowed down…and the smoldering embers within the broken pieces died down.

Dozens of fragments came to a halt, a few hundred kilometers away and almost parallel to his fleet.

"No…" Garret's throat tightened as he struggled to comprehend the new fight he and his sailors were about to face. "All ships! Engage the fragments immediately. The enemy is still in this fight."

Several of the larger jagged remnants shattered…releasing tens of thousands of drones that swarmed toward the human fleet. The rest of the pieces shifted into constructs the size of battleships, forming cavernous assault cannons through their middle.

"They weren't really joined together when we hit them with the macro cannons," Garret said and punched the railing. "They suckered me in and caught us all flat-footed."

"Sir! Phobos…it's broken apart!" Dorral said. Garret's hands squeezed into fists as the expanding mass of rock and shattered metal that had been the inner moon began their final descent toward Mars. All the crew were dead. Garret knew the risks. It was his decision and they'd died accomplishing little against the Xaros.

But there was nothing he could do for the dead.

The *Charlemagne* rocked beneath him as a Xaros beam cut across the prow.

The holo table was a riot of clashing ships, thousands and thousands of fighters and drones in a dogfight larger than any other in human history.

This is my battle. Time to fight it.

CHAPTER 11

Elias kept his back to the wall of the small, enclosed bunker. The other Iron Hearts were braced against the sides. A screen on the wall counted down to zero and the ground shook like someone had dropped a battleship on Mars a few miles away.

"I'm liking these macro cannons," Kallen said. "Would be nice to see the end result."

"I'm sure Garret will put together a highlight reel once it's all said and done," Bodel said. "The man loves his propaganda."

"He sounds jealous. 'Bodel' didn't have any lines in the movie," Kallen said.

"You sound snippy. They didn't make a limited-edition action figure of you," Bodel said to her.

"Just because I'm a girl and they don't make a

little plastic me for the kids?" Kallen's voice rose an octave. "I played with action figures when I was a little girl. I had to hack my family's 3-D printer to make an Athena after I saw that *Olympus* movie. I find the Ibarra Corp douche that made that decision and I'll crush his damn head."

"At least you're taking it well," Elias said.

The screen on the wall beeped several times.

"Fire mission," Elias said, reading from a message displayed inside his womb, "battle cruiser coming in from the southeast. Green platoon will fire with us. Displace to bunker Golf-19 after rounds complete. Follow me."

Elias grabbed a thick metal handle bolted to the rock and heaved a sliding door aside. Red sand swept past the exit.

Elias ran through the door, his heavy footfalls crushing the jagged edges of black rocks as he went to a small mesa. He vaulted over the edge and found a patch of solid rock. He raised his right foot and dropped the anchor running up his lower leg into the rock.

His rail gun lifted up from his shoulder and locked down next to his helm. He turned to the southeast and easily found the incoming target. The Xaros construct burned through the Martian atmosphere like a comet, trailing fire miles behind it.

"Locked," Bodel said from several yards away. Kallen flashed him a thumbs-up.

"Green, status report," Elias said into the IR.

"Two locked," Caas said, *"third broke his anchor point and is—"*

"We have thirty seconds until we fire and no time for excuses," Elias said.

"Three locked," Caas sent back a moment later.

The vibration of his charging rail gun coursed through his womb. A target reticule appeared just in front of the Xaros ship and Elias lined up his shot. Firing a bullet that could reach orbit meant little in the way of adjusting for gravity and atmospheric effects to the trajectory, especially not when the target was coming right for them.

"Drones! Drones coming in low and fast," said Zuli, the third member of the Dotok green platoon.

"Hold your anchor," Elias said. Threat icons appeared over distant drones cresting over the top of a canyon. They'd be on the armor in seconds. "Fire in three...two...mark."

Rail cannons fired in a ripple from the Iron Hearts and the Dotok armor. Elias didn't bother to see if the shots connected as he swung his rail gun off his shoulder and brought his rotary cannon to bear. The multi-barreled weapon spun to life and spat white-hot tungsten bullets toward the dozens of drones bearing down on them, with more coming over the canyon walls every second.

Elias withdrew his anchor back into the leg housing and sidestepped toward a rocky outcrop that could provide some cover.

The combined fire of six rotary cannons ripped through the approaching drones, blunting their advance like a levy against a flash flood. He picked off any drones that made it through with his forearm cannons.

Elias' shoulder cannon ceased firing, but kept spinning. Error icons flashed, alerting him to a broken belt in the ammo housing. He cursed, increased the rate of fire on his forearm cannon and ran toward Kallen.

The stream of drones over the ridge ceased, leaving more than fifty still heading for the armor. The drones veered up as one, flying straight into the sky.

"I'm stuck!" Zuli shouted. *"My anchor won't release!"*

The drones' path curved into a dive then split into two paths, one heading toward each group of armor.

Elias took aimed shots at the drones flying straight for them as Kallen opened a panel on the back of Elias' armor, tore away a kink in the ammo belt, and reloaded the weapon. She slapped him on the back once she closed the access panel.

Stalks lit up across the swarm of drones. The Iron Hearts deployed their shields and bunched together, their weapons firing through gaps in their wall. A beam struck Elias' shield and slashed across Kallen's. Black smoke rose from the impact, but the shield held.

Elias fired off two rounds and shattered a drone. Five drones were seconds away from hitting the wall.

"Ready…break!" Elias jumped aside from Kallen. He reached out and snagged a charging drone by its stalks and slammed it into the side of the bunker. The drone cracked the bunker wall and tugged at Elias' grip. He swung the drone overhead and bashed it into the ground. He raised his right heel, released the tip of his anchor out of his heel and impaled the drone.

Red and orange pyrite exploded out of the impact.

Elias looked to Bodel and saw the soldier's cannons leveled right at him. Elias instantly ducked. Bodel's cannons destroyed a drone that had been mere feet behind Elias.

"Clear," Kallen said.

A roar filled the air. Elias looked up and saw the cruiser, dying, broken into burning fragments coming down on Mars. He quickly guessed as to the wreckage's path, as it may or may not have fully disintegrated before it hit, and was sure it wouldn't hit the Nerio macro cannon.

Gauss shells shot over the ridge between Green platoon and the Iron Hearts.

"Let's go." Elias took off running to the battle still raging between the Dotok armor and the drones. Fire subsided to nothing as he rounded the corner. A dozen broken drones lay in the Martian soil…and one suit of armor. Its chest had been ripped open, arms bent at the elbow to the sky, as if reaching for something. One knee was bent, and Elias could see the anchor spike extending from the heel into the ground.

Caas and Ar'ri stood over the fallen armor.

Caas looked at Elias and waved her hand at Zuli. "He didn't…didn't blow his emergency release. Just was stuck there. We stayed…stayed with him."

Elias went to the armor. Zuli's womb was ripped open. He stared into the sky with still eyes, steam rising from the fluid that had been part of his womb. Elias popped up a shoulder panel on Zuli's armor and removed an identity chip.

"Take his ammo, battery packs," Elias said. He stepped back from the body and tried to connect to the local defense network. The lines were full of garbled transmissions and panicked updates.

"What? We can't do that," Ar'ri said. "The articles on his body at the moment of death—"

Bodel grabbed him by the chest.

"He's dead. He can do nothing for you now but offer his gear. Take it and you might not end up like him."

Caas lifted Zuli's body and unsnapped an ammo canister. She tossed it to her brother. "They're right, Ar'ri. We will atone at a shrine when this is over. Zuli will forgive us." She stood up. One hand held Zuli's rail gun clip, the other his spare battery stack.

"Red platoon is off-line," Elias said. "Outrider companies in their sector are in contact."

A distant macro cannon shell ripped through the atmosphere, leaving distended clouds and a line of fire in its wake. The flash of Xaros beams and exploding ships carried through the thin atmosphere high over their heads.

"Iron Hearts will go to Red sector," Elias said. "You two get to bunker Golf-19. We go off-line, fall back to the Nerio cannon. Let's move."

Kallen waited for Elias and Bodel to run ahead of her. She fell back a few dozen yards and kept pace as they ran. A red icon pulsed against her vision, warning her of damage to her lower back. She hadn't felt the drone stalk that pierced her armor and the womb beneath it. Her armor had resealed itself around the puncture and saved her from the Martian atmosphere, but the suit warned her of damage to her body.

Kallen opened her eyes. The fluids in her tank swam with red eddies. She was bleeding. Elias and Bodel wouldn't know—she'd cut off her vital reading from her suit's telemetry reports as soon as her heart rate spiked at the beginning of the battle. Kallen dosed herself with an adrenaline spike and kept running.

Beside them, she thought. *It must be beside them.*

****

Paar raised his forearm cannons and knocked two drones off an antiair turret before they could kill the crew inside. He looked up and brought his rotary cannon to bear on a half-dozen drones screaming down on him and the other two Dotok armor soldiers of Green platoon. Ale'ti joined her rotary cannon to his, destroying the drones in a vicious crossfire.

"Nik'to, you want to help?" Paar asked.

Nik'to backed toward his platoon mates, scanning the skies.

"I'm getting some weird interference on the IR," Nik'to said.

"Atmo on this dust ball isn't helping," Paar said. "Every time the dust kicks up we have to link to a tower to get anything."

"Dust storms aren't as bad as what we had on Takeni, and at least we can see the whole sky," Nik'to said. He cocked his head to the sky and saw a sliver of light burning through the pink haze of blowing dust.

"What's that?"

The light impacted against the Martian soil like a lightning bolt. Paar backed away, trying to sort through his helm's optics to see what was within the haze of dust and searing heat.

A blast of light shot out of the haze and hit Ale'ti in the chest. The beam pushed Ale'ti off-balance then ripped right through her.

Paar and Nik'to opened fire. When Nik'to's cannons fell silent, Paar looked over and saw his friend's mangled armor lying before the General.

Paar saw a horror described in Dotok religions, an ancient demon that came to collect the souls of the living. He shot the General twice, but both rounds bounced off an energy shield and whistled through the air as they tumbled away.

The General raised a hand over his head and flashed toward Paar, chopping his arm down on his cannons and slicing them to pieces. The General snatched Paar by the actuators and machinery just beneath his helm and raised him into the air.

Paar brought his rotary cannon down and fired as fast as the cannons would spin. Rounds bounced off the General's shield and ricocheted off Paar's armor. Bullets ripped through the shield and sparked off the red plates covering the General's photonic body.

The General slammed Paar to the ground, rattling the Dotok against his womb. Damage icons went berserk across his vision as his helm, rotary cannon and limbs were ripped away before he could move.

Paar found himself trapped within his armor, darkness pressing all around him.

Five burning points of light came through his breastplate. The General ripped the front of Paar's armor away, exposing the womb within. Paar couldn't move. He could only stare in horror as the General cut through the womb with a clawed fingertip and flicked the severed portion aside.

The fluid around Paar bubbled as it boiled away in the thin Martian atmosphere. Paar struggled to move, but his link to his armor shunted all his commands to missing limbs.

The General reached for Paar, but hesitated. This wasn't a human, not like the pilots he'd killed inside other armored suits elsewhere on the red planet. Still, the species was known to him, a space-faring race his drones had encountered between the stars and chased to a barely habitable world where he'd encountered the human armor soldiers.

The General ripped the Dotok out of the womb, its limbs twitching and mouth gasping in the thin atmosphere. He passed a scan field through Paar's brain and shifted through recent memories…there. The human that had managed to hurt him was nearby and it had a name: Elias.

The General tossed Paar aside to die and shot into the sky.

****

Elias ran past a jeep crashed against a boulder, the driver and gunner dead in their seats.

Antiair turrets blazed around Nerio's cannon's opening. Packs of drones attempted to assault the towers, only to be knocked down by concentrated fire.

"Not like them," Kallen said, her words clipped as if she was almost out of breath. "They usually mass together."

The sound of metal on metal broke through the air. Elias looked to the sound. Several drones circled just over a draw in the mountains surrounding Nerio.

"That's gate four," Bodel said.

Elias took a running leap and climbed half the hillside with a single bound. He came over the crest and opened up with his rotary cannon, annihilating the circling drones.

A walker construct the size of a three-story house pounded against the aegis-reinforced doors to the gate. Both arms were fused into giant clubs that it bashed against the gate. One door was already bent against the hinges, the second badly dented. The blasted remains of Red platoon littered the roadway leading to the gate.

Elias skidded down the side of the ravine, one hand balancing him against the slope, the other holding up his cannons. Elias fired a burst of gauss cannon shells into the walker's knee. Black fragments of obsidian-colored armor sprang out of the impacts. The walker's leg buckled and it stumbled back from the gate.

Elias unsheathed his pike and hit the ground. He sprinted toward the construct and leaped into the air. The walker swung a massive arm at Elias, who flipped his heels over his head and gained an extra foot of height with the acrobatics and a push from his anti-grav linings. He landed on the walker's arm and stabbed the pike into its arm. The spike burst through the opposite side of the arm with a crack.

The walker's other arm morphed into a cannon, a deadly red beam already forming at its core.

Elias wrenched the pike to the side and cracked the walker's arm like a rotted log.

The walker swung its cannon arm toward Elias. Sparks and hunks of armor flew off the cannon as Bodel and Kallen pounded it with fire.

Elias pressed his heels against the cracked arm and tried to wrench it away, but the Xaros' metal reformed around the puncture, trapping him in place. Elias strained against the hold, then released the pike from the housing and flew back, smacking against the side of the ravine.

Dust and rocks showered around him. The walker punched its broken cannon arm straight at Elias. The Iron Heart lurched out of the depression in the soft soil and felt the walker's arm swipe through the air as it pounded the ravine.

Elias fell at the walker's feet and rolled to the side before it could stomp the life out of him. Elias thrust his forearm cannons against the thing's knee and blew a gaping hole into the joint.

The walker stumbled to its side. Elias saw a sudden shadow in the corner of his eye and caught the walker's other leg against his entire body. The kick hit Elias like he'd stepped in front of a freight train. He hit the ground hard and bounced twice before coming to a sudden stop against the damaged gate.

His vision swam. His armor was alive with damage warnings. He pushed himself to his knees and raised his cannons.

Kallen was on top of the walker, one hand gripping the edge of a gauss bullet hole while the other plunged her pike into the Xaros' head and shoulders over and over again.

Bodel hung onto the Xaros' chest, his cannon arm jammed between the walker's plates and firing point-blank.

The walked lifted an arm over its head and knocked Kallen flying.

"Desi!" Elias got to his feet.

Bodel tugged at the walker's cracked armor plate and ripped it away, exposing glowing pyrite beneath. He let go and fell to the ground just before the Xaros beat at his chest and almost crushed the Iron Heart.

Elias fired his forearm cannons and hit the walker in its exposed core. Red cracks broke across the construct's surface. It leaned back, propping itself up on an arm, then froze in place. Armor plates fell into the red soil with muted thumps as it broke apart.

"Bodel?" Elias stumbled toward him, his balance still shaky after the kick.

"Fine," Bodel said as he stood. "I'm fine."

They saw Kallen lying on her side. One arm pushed her body up, then she collapsed into the bloodred soil.

"Kallen?" Elias ran to her, Bodel a step behind.

He rolled her onto her back. One arm had been crushed; sparks and hydraulic fluid poured out of the fragmented armor. Her helm had a deep dent against the side and her breastplate was malformed.

None of the damage came through to Elias' suit.

He pushed her helm to the side and clicked a button just beneath her chin to reset her telemetry settings. A flood of data came to him. Kallen's heartbeat was slow, her blood pressure dangerously low. The fluid in her womb was full of blood.

"Desi...what did you do?" Elias asked.

"I feel cold," she said.

"You're bleeding out." Bodel knelt next to her and touched the side of her breastplate. He was about to lift it away when her good hand pushed his arms aside.

"This is it, Iron Hearts." Her helm swung to the side as her damaged optics stared up at Elias. "Need to...see you."

Elias flipped the view port down on her chest and grabbed her good hand. Bodel put his palm over their hands.

Kallen looked up from the slit, her pupils wide and unfocused. She looked at Bodel, then Elias, then sank away.

"Just hold on," Bodel said. "We can get you inside, to an aid station."

"No. This will be over before you can get my tank out. This is how I wanted it. I love you, Hans, but this is the end. Love you…Elias. You fight. Keep…fighting."

Her heart stopped beating.

Elias laid her hand across her chest. Wind skirted between the three, blowing a thin shroud of dust over Kallen's armor.

"Elias…"

"Get her ammo. Batteries. The fight's moving into the cannon." Elias stood up, made the sign of the cross, and went back to the gate. He scooped up his pike from the last remnants of the walker and snapped it back into the housing.

At the damaged outer doors, he wrenched aside a loose piece of metal and made an opening big enough for his armor to squeeze through. The inner doors were undamaged.

Bodel was still at Kallen's side.

"Hans. Hans, battle calls."

Bodel took Kallen's ammo pack and her spare battery. He trotted over to Elias and handed over the ammo.

"She was the best of us," Bodel said.

"I know. We'll come back for her when this fight is over. Now keep moving."

****

Elias and Bodel made their way through a hallway scarred by gauss rounds and Xaros beams. Dead Marines and doughboys lay every few yards and Elias took care where he stepped.

The sound of fighting echoed around them, shouts and the zap of alien weapons growing stronger as they neared an intersection. Elias clanked around the corner and found a haphazard barricade of aegis plates. Marines and doughboys fired over the top.

"Friendlies coming through," Elias boomed. A Marine sergeant saw Elias' helm and waved him over. He ran to the armor before they could reach the barricade.

"Boy am I glad to see you guys," the sergeant said. His breastplate was heat warped from a Xaros beam and Elias couldn't make out his name. "Got the entrance to cannon control on the other side of the barricade. Damn

Xaros have been trying to get through there for the last ten minutes but we fight them off every time they push. We're low on ammo, was about to switch to harsh language before you showed up."

"Where are they?" Elias asked.

"Next cross-hall over. What do you want us to do?"

"Move your men back and stay behind us," Bodel said. The armor went to the edge of the barricade and waited for the defenders to fall back.

Elias waited until the thrum of Xaros drones grew louder, then charged through aegis plates, knocking them aside like they were twigs. Elias destroyed a drone attempting to cut through the control room doors and ran forward. He swung one leg in front of him and slid to a stop in front of the next cross-hall.

A dozen drones floated in the air. His rotary cannons snapped up next to his face and ripped through the drones. Bodel came in a heartbeat behind him and added his cannon to the fire. With no room to maneuver, the drones didn't last long.

"Clear," Bodel said.

"You wrecked our fighting position," the sergeant said, kicking at one of the plates.

"Rebuild it around the control room doors," Elias

said. "We'll help."

Hydraulic whines emanated from the control room door. One side popped loose. The door shifted slightly, like someone was trying and failing to open it. Elias grabbed the edge and swung it aside slowly.

A small, plump woman in a tech's environment suit stuck her head through the door. She pointed a finger at Elias.

"I need you," she said, shifting her finger to Bodel, "and I need you. The rest of you, don't let the Xaros in."

"What do you think we've been doing out here, Mable?" the sergeant said as he grabbed a doughboy and pushed him toward an aegis plate to pick up.

Elias gauged the door, then got down on his side. "We'll have to crawl in."

"Fine, just hurry up." Mable retreated to the control room as Elias pulled himself through, like a grown man trying to fit through a doggy door.

"OK." Mable reached in and waved her hands at Elias to get him to hurry up. "I don't know how much you know about magnetic induction coils, but the number twelve inferometer shit the bed eight minutes ago and we've got a fire mission in the queue."

Elias got his legs through the doorway. The

control room was full of enough technicians, holo screens and operations tables that it made the bridge of the *Breitenfeld* look like a lazy street corner. Reinforced glass wrapped around the outer section of the control room. The Nerio cannon lay beyond—a long barrel the size of a frigate covered by induction coils rested in a great cavern. Frames with giant cranes crossed over the cannon. Giant actuators shifted the cannon to the side at the rate of a few feet per minute.

One of the frames was bent at the corner, blackened.

Elias got to his feet and stared at Mable, who had her hands on her hips. Elias shrugged.

"Drones got into the chamber and fragged the number three crane before the doughboys managed to nail it. They also managed to clip inferometer twelve, which wasn't an issue until we did the pre-charge and saw it go tits up," Mable said.

"You needed something?" Elias asked.

"Naturally crane three services inferometer twelve, god damn Murphy's Law. I need you and the other one to get out there and replace the inferometer so we can shoot. I'll guide you from here." Mable pointed to an access door leading to a set of stairs that ran to the bottom of the cannon.

"Spare's already broken out. Whatever you do, don't touch the live coils." She reached up and slapped Elias on his metal rear end. "Good luck."

Elias grumbled and crawled through the next door. Once through, he jumped out and let Mars' lesser gravity take him to the bottom of the cavern. The rest of the facility was under Earth standard grav. Working in Mars' natural environment made sense to him from an engineering point of view—less effort to move large heavy things.

He thumped against the bare stone floor and found an induction coil the size of a small car with a pile of packing material next to it.

Bodel landed next to him and surveyed the weapon.

"Ideas?" Bodel asked.

"Gross weight on the packaging is a lot less than us," Elias said. "The cranes can carry that thing. The frame should hold us both and the coil…probably."

"Just one of us take it up?" Bodel asked.

There was a muted slap against the glass wall above their heads.

"You two want to get your thumbs out of your asses and get moving?" Mable asked over IR.

"I'm not sure if she has a death wish or is just

unusually brave," Bodel said.

"You go up first." Elias went to the induction coil and grabbed it by a thick metal handle attached to one end. He lifted it up with one arm and tested the weight. "I'll carry it."

The struts leading up the side of the damaged crane were several feet apart, just wide enough for Elias to use as a ladder. He climbed up with one arm, holding the coil behind him with the other. The ascent was slow, but steady.

"Admiral Garret just called and asked why he has to wait so long for fire support," Mable said.

Elias growled into the IR.

Bodel waited for him at the top of the cross frame; the top bar was just wide enough for him to stand on it.

"Ready." Bodel held his arms out. Elias swung the coil up and Bodel grabbed the handle on the other side. The two lowered the coil very gently to rest on the top of the frame.

"You move the coil. I'll get the crane," Elias said. He looked down at the broken crane and realized just how high he was. Elias' hands slapped against the side of the frame.

"Elias?" Bodel asked.

"Moving." Elias crawled onto the top of the frame and reached down to the crane, but his hands were a few inches too short to touch. He snapped out his pike and pushed the crane along the runner bar. The crane jiggled against the bar, testifying to broken parts within.

"You need to go forward another fifty meters," Mable said.

"At least the broken part isn't clear on the other side of the barrel," Bodel said.

Elias guided the crane forward until their guide ordered them to halt.

"OK, you see that black smoking induction coil directly beneath you? Get down there and remove it. Don't touch the coils next to it or the world ends in a giant white flash."

"Brace the crane." Elias retracted his pike and leaned down. He felt a brief wave of vertigo, then fell forward. He grabbed the thick cables running from the crane to the swaying hook below and held on for dear life. The hook extended a few yards down, nowhere near enough to reach the damaged coil. Elias looked at the hook, then to the crane, and gave the crane a punch against the side.

The rollers inside the crane came loose and the hook plummeted toward the gun below.

"Um…Elias?" Bodel said.

The hook stopped over the broken coil, swaying from side to side.

"I knew it wasn't long enough to go all the way down," Bodel said.

Elias lessened his hold and slid down the cables. He stopped on top of the hook and reached down to the damaged coil.

"The system's meant to be interchangeable. Find the four clamps and get that thing out of there," Mable said. *"Also, don't touch anything else. Because electrocution."*

Elias unsnapped the clamps, breaking through warped metal and blackened carbon. He grasped the coil by the carry handle and lifted it up. The coil came loose with a tug and he pulled it clear as he stood.

"Now you have to climb all the way back up with that broken part." Mable let out a long sigh.

Elias swung the coil back, then forth, moving his perch on the hook farther and farther each time. His swing brought him close to the control room, and he hurled the coil away.

"What the hell are you—" Mable ducked away as the coil flew across the cavern and smashed into the wall just beneath the control room floor. *"Or that. Fine. That was just fine."*

Elias leaned away from the direction of his swing

and killed the momentum.

"I'm looking in the cradle," Elias said. "Not sure if what I see is good or bad."

"Are the Faston tabs and field coils still viable?"

Elias looked up at Mable.

"Do you see glowing blue things on the long end of the cradle?"

"Yes."

"Are they covered in shit or are they clean?"

"Clean."

"Good to go. Get the replacement in there so I can save the admiral's ass."

Elias looked up at his fellow Iron Heart. "Drop it."

"Drop it?"

"Drop it. I'll catch it." Elias held his hand up.

Bodel lay down on the cross bar with the coil extended to Elias, scooted forward a few inches and let it go.

Elias ignored Mable's panicked screams and watched the coil fall toward him. Mars' gravity brought it to him at a rate less than half of what it would have been on Earth. The metal frame creaked as the coil fell. The damaged joints on the other end buckled and dropped Elias and his hook several feet before it came to a stop.

Elias reached to the handle and found he was swinging. He shifted his weight to the side and tried to get beneath the coil. He stretched up…and missed by a fraction of an inch. He whirled around and almost lunged off the hook. He got a grip and lifted it straight up. The bottom handle whipped down and dipped into the empty space where the last coil had been. The cables twisted around, then unwound.

Elias held the coil up like a kettlebell as the momentum to his swing faded away.

"I'll admit it," Mable said. "I peed a little."

"Maybe we're too heavy," Bodel said.

"Now you say that." Elias bent at the knees and set one end of the coil in the cradle. The rest of the machinery snugly fell into place and Elias clamped it tight. An electric hum and snaps sounded from under Elias.

"Now what?" Elias asked.

"Now get your asses away from the barrel. My firing window closes in two hundred seconds and I'm sending this round before it closes," Mable said.

Elias grabbed a cable and shimmied up one side to the crane.

"Pull the hook up behind you. There are rubber stops but I wouldn't trust them to keep an arc off you," Mable said.

Bodel fished up the other cable with his pike and

pulled the line to him.

"You could have given us some warning," Bodel said.

"I don't fire and the Twentieth Fleet dies to a Xaros leviathan, then Mars falls and all of us die. Or I fire and risk killing you two. There is no decision," Mable said.

"I can't fault that logic," Elias said.

He got to the top of the cross bar and helped reel in the hook.

"Ten seconds!"

Bodel did a double take at the control room. "What happened to—"

"Target moved. Hold on tight!"

The coils beneath the Iron Hearts lit up. Electricity arced between the cross beam and the armor. Elias felt his teeth humming and squeezed his arms and legs around the metal.

There was a crack of thunder as the cannon fired and the cross beam wobbled beneath them. The hum faded away…but the cross beam started leaning toward the base of the cannon.

"Elias, think we're in trouble," Bodel said.

"Jump for it." Elias stood up on the beam and tried to balance as it tipped over with a groan. Elias risked a glimpse at Bodel and saw him with a footing just as unsteady as his. The beam crashed down on the next lower beam.

Elias leaped away and activated his maneuver thrusters. He looked down and saw row after row of induction coils pass beneath him as he lost altitude. He crossed over dirt, dipped his shoulder forward and rolled over the sand and gravel. He skidded to a halt inches from the wall.

Bodel bumped off the wall and fell on his ass.

"Smooth." Elias reached to him.

"Piss off." Bodel took Elias' hand and stood up.

"Good news, you didn't break anything else with your little stunt," Mable said. *"There's an access door to your right. Someone from Green platoon says they need your help."*

"I really do not like her," Bodel said.

Elias knocked the back of his knuckles against Bodel's chest.

"We need to keep moving," Elias said.

CHAPTER 12

A cube of omnium took up the center of the round workshop. Empty workbenches, with backless chairs tucked beneath, stretched around the outer wall, broken up by a single doorway.

Torni held a hand over the cube and drew omnium into the air.

Lafayette, standing on the opposite side of the cube, held up a wide data pad with a diagram for a piece of machinery that looked like a cross between an old vinyl record player and a ramjet engine.

"Part number one, attempt fifteen," Lafayette said into a beeping recorder on his arm.

Torni glanced at the diagram then focused on the omnium swirling just beyond her fingertips. The ghostly substance twisted against itself, colors rippling up and down as it morphed into a shape to match Lafayette's diagram.

Torni smiled and guided the part to a workbench where Malal sat with his feet dangling over the edge, hands laid loose at his side. His chin was down, eyes closed.

"Well?" Torni asked.

Malal opened an eye, then leaned forward and sniffed at the part.

"Your mid-coupling is three degrees off axis. Do it again," Malal said.

Torni squeezed her hand into a first and crushed the part. It melted into omnium and she tossed it back into the cube.

"This is bullshit," she said. "The tolerances on this thing are impossible. I'm better off making more q-shells or aegis plates."

Malal returned to his meditation without comment.

"No one has ever constructed a device like this, Ms. Torni," Lafayette said. "The underlying design is borne out by observation, but the physics governing its function are someone theoretical."

"What?"

"It will work. We just have to make it perfectly," Lafayette said.

"Explain again why this is worth the time and effort." Torni pressed two fingers against her temple. Her fingertips sank into her head. She winced and pulled her hand back. Her shell returned to normal with a quick shake.

"The details…do you still feel the connection to the Xaros General?" Lafayette asked.

"He's out there."

"Is he aware of you?"

Torni cocked her head to the side. "I don't…I don't know."

"If he is, and I tell you our purpose, it could compromise the device's effect," Lafayette said. "This *is* important. Admiral Garret is leading the fleets over Mars to slow the Xaros advance because Ibarra and I convinced him that this will work. Thousands and thousands of your fellows are fighting to give you the time to make this work, Torni."

Torni's face screwed into a frown. She held fingers up next to Malal's ear and snapped them several times.

"Malal. Malal, what am I doing wrong?" she asked.

"I find your attempts to gain my attention vexing," Malal said.

"Answer me and I'll leave you alone."

Malal's eyes half opened. "Your mind is fractured and of your own volition. Humans evolved to be humans, in human bodies. It is why your damnable armor soldiers fight in humanoid suits and not in something more elegant or effective. You fight against your natural form and that distraction follows through your efforts."

"*This* is my natural form." Torni touched her chest.

"Once." Malal closed his eyes.

Torni looked at Lafayette.

"Stand back." Torni looked down at her hands. Smoke rose from her fingertips, then they stretched into stalks. Torni's body flashed to shifting patterns and morphed into an oblong drone's body with several stalks breaking loose from the surface.

Lafayette backed into a bench and dropped his data slate.

"What?" Torni's voice came from the drone.

"My autonomous nervous system is creating an involuntary reaction," Lafayette said.

"You're afraid." Torni's stalks went to the omnium cube and drew the substance into the air again.

"It was a mistake to keep that atavistic feature, I believe." Lafayette picked up his data slate and held it up for Torni.

"Malal, is there anything else I should do?" Torni asked.

"There is a magnetic field coming from a surveillance device in the ceiling. It will slow our progress if it remains functional," Malal said.

Torni moved a stalk across her shell and stabbed the ceiling where she felt the field.

In another part of the Crucible, Marc Ibarra broke into a string of profanity.

****

Torni's stalks played over the surface of an orange crystal glowing from within. More stalks touched the crystal, then moved with blurred speed as they carved golden lines of circuitry. Torni held up the crystal, examining the scrimshaw.

"Acceptable," Malal said. "Place it in the device."

The work of many days had resulted in a device almost the size of a coffin. Torni set the crystal into a waiting cradle. Clamps snapped down and the device drew the final component inside its housing.

"Now what?" Torni asked.

"Now we make another one. We'll need a

resupply, of course," Lafayette said, gesturing to the omnium mass in the center of room. The cube had been reduced to a few inches of material during the fabrication of the device Torni still didn't understand.

The door to the workshop opened—not by sliding or swinging—they crumbled from a centerline and bled into the frame. Shannon walked in and froze when she saw Torni in her drone form.

"It's her," Lafayette said, "and it's quite alright."

Shannon's eye twitched. "The probe needs to speak with Malal."

Malal slumped forward, his knees buckling almost to the point of collapse when he hit the ground. His body stayed upright and he locked in place, as if a rod of iron had suddenly gone through his spine. He followed Shannon out of the room, his arms tacked to his side.

The doors closed behind him.

"He is most disconcerting," Lafayette said.

Torni shifted back to her human form and Lafayette sighed in relief.

"I spent years with him waiting for the *Breitenfeld*'s jump engines to recharge," Torni said. "He treated me like a house plant. Spoke to me only when he had direct repairs, or to give instruction on transmuting another substance. Otherwise, he acted like I wasn't even there. It was…lonely."

"How did you cope? Humans seem to be very social creatures. Your sense of self still seems rooted in that despite your condition," Lafayette said.

"Yes, my 'condition.' The ship needed a lot of repair work—that kept me busy. I even spent a month in the void to grab an asteroid and ferry it back for raw materials. Stacey would return from time to time. Kept me supplied with books and vids. Then we finally made it home and I think, 'I can see my Marines again. Let them see me as they remembered, not as the thing they're fighting.'"

Lafayette's arm jerked to the side and buzzed.

"Him again." Lafayette turned his palm to the center to the room and a hologram formed out of a projector in his wrist.

"Done? Progress? Did I pick the wrong week to quit drinking?" Ibarra asked.

"The device is complete," Lafayette said. "I estimate we can complete the next unit in seventy-two percent of the time."

"I'll send up another cube. Well done, but get the next unit done in half the time." Ibarra touched two fingers to his temple in a mock salute and faded away.

"Ibarra, wait," Torni said. Ibarra's hologram grew

stronger.

"These proccies of yours, tell me about them," she said. Her thumbs rubbed against her forefingers and she chewed on her bottom lip.

"There are over a billion now, almost all in the military," Ibarra said, his face growing serious. "The answer to your question is 'no.' I can't make you a new body."

"Why not? Are you just saying that to keep me working away as some sort of…Santa's elf?"

"The procedurally generated minds grow within the bodies as they gestate. I try to make a full-grown body without the mind and it's nothing but a vegetable. The brains won't take a fully formed consciousness at the end of the process," Ibarra said.

The hologram touched its face.

"You think I like this?" Ibarra asked. "Being a ghost trapped inside a machine. I know what you want, my dear. I want it too." He looked at Lafayette and his cyborg body. "We must adapt to what we are, not what we want. The omnium will be here shortly." Ibarra vanished.

Torni's chin lowered to her chest.

"You fear they won't accept you as you are now?" Lafayette said.

"They thought I was dead. The Torni they knew *is*

157

dead. I'm just a copy." She looked at her hands and let them revert to swirling patterns. "My last moments downloaded into a Xaros matrix. If I was flesh and blood…it would be different. Better."

"Your team helped rescue the last of my people from the Toth. Did you know this? There is a Karigole village in Africa. Men, women, geth'aar, children and adolescents. But I cannot see them, take part in the customs and celebrations of my culture. I am a pariah because of my form." Lafayette tapped metal fingers against his chest with a *clink*.

"It is easy to despair," he said. "The last hundred Karigole warriors took an oath to avenge our loss against the Toth. It gave us purpose. Reason. Once that oath was fulfilled and our people were free…they rejected me. I still love them, just as I think you still love your Marines. This work will save the Karigole. Save all of humanity. Do not despair."

Lafayette went to Torni, took her arm, and hugged it against his chest.

"What are you doing?" Torni asked.

"Hugging. A gesture of empathy and kindness, correct?"

"Not like…come here." Torni took her arm away and gave Lafayette a brief hug around his shoulders.

The doors opened and an omnium cube floated into the room on a robot-driven grav-dolly.

"Time to get back to work. Have a good game." Lafayette slapped Torni on the rear end.

CHAPTER 13

Acceleration pressed Durand against her seat. Compression pads tightened around her thighs and her abdomen, keeping blood in her head where she needed it. Her Eagle shot over Charon's surface, a barren expanse of ugly rock and ice. She glanced up and saw the distant Grinder in orbit over Pluto, light from the drones building it winking against the star field.

"Keep your eyes peeled, boys and girls," she said. "Let's complete this pass and drop the buoy."

"Gall, this is Lancer," said the Condor pilot she and two other fighters accompanied on their high-speed orbit. "Relays one and two are down. Should be done in another three minutes."

"Why are the Xaros just sitting out there?" asked Manfred, one of her Dotok pilots. "It's not like them to just let us limp away after a fight."

"What's our purpose out here?" Durand asked.

"To blow that damned thing up before it opens a portal to the underworld and floods our new home with death and destruction," said Lothar, Manfred's brother.

"What do you think the Xaros defenders' purpose is?" Durand asked.

"To...not let us do that?" Manfred quipped.

"To protect the Grinder until it's done," Durand said. "They come after us and they're vulnerable to another strike from Earth through our Crucible. It takes light almost six hours to get from Pluto to Earth," she said, looking at the timer on her dashboard, "which means Earth either just saw our last fight or they're listening to Captain Valdar explain what happened."

"Relay three down," Lancer said.

"And we have to wait six more hours for instructions to reach us from Earth," Lothar said. "Or we wait for them to send reinforcements through...which could come at any time now."

"Welcome to life at the edge of the solar system," Durand said, "where the speed of light is just too slow to get things done."

She tapped into the camera feed from a relay and zoomed in on the Grinder. The gap in the ring was smaller than when they'd first arrived. When Valdar first briefed the mission, he said intelligence estimated the jump gate wouldn't be done for days. At the rate the Xaros were working, they looked like they'd be done in a few hours.

"Relay four down. The task force has eyes on the Grinder. Ready to burn home," Lancer said.

"Maintain speed," Durand said. "We flash the afterburners and they'll know we're up to something."

Durand ignored the grumbles from the pilots, all of whom had been in their cockpits for the last twelve hours and were eager to land on the *Breitenfeld* for some much needed rest. She felt sweat trickling down her body and a heat rash forming around her joints. Such were the realities of life as a void fighter pilot. There was danger, glamour, mediocre bonus pay and the persistent funk of one's own body odor.

The flight flew across Charon and came upon the task force…where Durand did *not* see the missile pods in the void around the *Breitenfeld* as she'd expected.

"Ahh…this is bullshit," Durand said. She opened a channel to the ship's flight tower. "Blue flight reports mission accomplished. We are running on fumes. Where the hell are we supposed to land if those big blocks of missiles are still on the flight deck?"

"This is Valdar. There's a FARP on the port side

between point defense cannons three and four. Cycle through there for new batteries and ammo."

Durand choked down some choice words. Conducting resupply on a forward arming and refueling point while in the void was never easy. Trying to land on the pinhead's worth of space between the two gauss turret batteries would make the task even harder. She directed Lothar and Manfred down first.

"Captain, I think there's something you wish to tell me?" Durand asked.

"We received a transmission from Phoenix," Valdar said. "More of those cloaked Xaros ships hit the planet and did a number on the Luna fortifications and the home fleet is decisively engaged. There's no help coming."

"How did we fall for the trick the Toth tried to pull on us?" Durand asked. She'd been in space over Europa when the Toth's *Naga* de-cloaked after a broadcast from the Crucible disrupted their cloaking field. The Toth had attempted to sneak the dreadnought to Earth during negotiations. Only a lucky observation by Stacey Ibarra had deduced that the Toth had come to the solar system with far more than could be seen.

"Different cloaking technology," Valdar said. "Lepton pulse didn't disrupt it. Xaros have never used cloaking tech before and high command's assumption that they wouldn't use it now came back to bite us in the rear. The Crucible's worked out a counter, which doesn't help everyone who died on Luna."

"I'm not going to worry about Earth's problems right now, especially when we've got plenty of our own," she said. "Do you see the Grinder?"

"I do…even if I started screaming for reinforcements, there's no way Earth would get the message and send us help in time," Valdar said.

"I look at what the Xaros have, what we have, and all I can think of is the Battle of Agincourt…and we're the French," Durand said.

She brought her Eagle over the FARP and locked her gaze on a crewman standing on the hull, holding two lit cones over his head. The crewman directed her down, signaling minute adjustments to her descent. Her landing gear hit the hull and crewmen slapped magnetic chocks against them to lock her fighter in place.

Durand felt her seat rock slightly as batteries, thruster pods and gauss magazines were swapped out. What she wouldn't have given for an ice-cold soda right then and there.

"We're not going to go charging through their guns if we can help it," Valdar said. "Not the *Breitenfeld*, at any rate. Our working theory is that the Grinder is able to affect wormhole formation even if it isn't complete, just like our Crucible. That's why we came back into real space in the wrong spot and directly under the Xaros guns."

"This sounds like another assumption," Durand said, "which is the mother of all fuckups, if I am to believe the things you Americans say."

"Have you ever heard of an American named Muhammed Ali? He had a move called the rope-a-dope," Valdar said. "We're going to take a chance and see if we can use that move out here."

"I don't know what you're talking about, but I don't like the sound of it," Durand said.

****

Durand flipped her fighter upside down and keyed a maneuver thruster on the edge of a wing, pushing her over the top of a line of Eagles. She looked up and into the cockpits of her pilots, looking each in the eye as one final readiness check before the battle.

She passed last over Glue, her second-in-command. The Chinese pilot looked tired, but focused as ever. Durand maneuvered back to the other end of the line. The rest of the task force, minus the *Breitenfeld*, was arrayed into a loose cone. The *Centaur* with her gleaming energy cannons sat at the tip, while heavier ships fell into rings behind the *Centaur* with corvettes at the base of the cone. The *Breitenfeld* hung in the distance, well behind the formation.

Durand and her fighters hovered over the *Vimy Ridge*; her remaining bombers were on the other side.

"Task Force 37," Valdar said, "we've got one shot at this. If the Xaros get the Grinder up and operational, they will flood our solar system with drones. If this ship's maneuver fails, we will ram the construct."

Durand swallowed hard. If Valdar was willing to send the *Breitenfeld* on a suicide run, then the captain didn't expect anything less from the rest of the task force. France did not have a tradition of kamikaze attacks, but if she had to turn her fighter into a human-guided missile, she would do it. Probably.

"*Centaur*, begin your attack," Valdar said.

The lead ship's engines flared to life and she accelerated forward. Durand cut ahead of her fighters and led them around Charon. The task force picked up speed and left the *Breitenfeld* behind.

The task force cleared the horizon and rose away from their close orbit of Pluto's largest moon and angled toward the Grinder.

"Pull it up," Durand said and banked higher, clear

of the line of fire between the ships and their target.

The *Centaur*'s energy cannons let off a ripple of energy blasts that streaked toward the Grinder. A loose coil of burning points of light closed the gap to the Xaros jump gate in seconds.

The defending constructs snapped away from their position around the Grinder and made for the attacking human ships. The *Centaur*'s attacks smashed into Xaros ships well short of their intended target. The Xaros pulled damaged ships away from the leading edge of their swarm.

"They'll take hits, but not lose any part of their line," Glue said. "I hate how smart these things are."

Rail cannons from every other ship but the *Centaur* fired. Red beams from Xaros point defense stabbed out and destroyed most of the shells before they could connect. Two Xaros ships fell back, cracked and burning.

The *Centaur* opened fire again.

Durand's hand tightened against her control stick. She hated watching a fight, but her Eagle would make about as much of a difference as a sparrow between two fighting elephants if she tried to get between the two fleets.

The disintegration beams stabbed through space and hit the *Centaur*, leaving deep dents as it burned through the aegis armor. One beam struck a Toth energy crystal, shattering it into a cloud of tiny shards.

The ship rolled on its side, a substance like white smoke trailing from the shattered cannon.

One of the corvettes, the *Scipio*, swooped down and put itself between the *Centaur* and the focused fire from the Xaros. A scarlet beam raked across the corvette's rail cannon and cut into the starboard engines. The *Scipio* spun out of control, taking another hit that tore through the shuttle bay door.

One of the Xaros ships began to spin on its axis as lumps of its hull flew off and morphed into drones.

"Here we go!" Durand shouted and brought her fighter about to intercept the new targets. "Take them out before they can reach the ships. The *Breit* should be here in—" a white portal opened several miles above the Grinder and collapsed, leaving the strike carrier in its wake "now. She's here right now."

Durand flew straight at an incoming drone and fired the gauss cannon slung beneath her fighter. The bullets ripped the drone apart and Durand flew through the debris. Burning stalks bounced off her canopy.

Four cubes slid out of the *Breitenfeld*'s flight deck. Missiles slid out of the cubes and streaked toward the Grinder, each IR guided by a sailor inside the ship.

Durand snapped her Eagle to the side and got on

the tail of a drone as it made a mad dash back to the Grinder. She destroyed it with a blast of gauss bullets and dove back to the dogfight…which had turned into a chase as the Eagles pursued drones fleeing back to protect the jump gate.

"Xaros ships are breaking off!" announced Nag, another of her Chinese pilots.

Guided missiles struck the Grinder. The denethrite explosive warheads broke thorns off and sent them spinning through the void where they disintegrated seconds later. The Grinder broke in half under the onslaught of more missiles.

Rail cannons from the task force kept firing, catching the Xaros as they tried to maneuver back to the dying jump gate.

Guided missiles kept coming from the pods, now steering toward the Xaros ships. The *Breitenfeld* and her task force had the Xaros in a deadly crossfire. The rest of the battle was over within minutes.

"All ships, pull in tight around the Breitenfeld. *We will jump out as soon as we've recovered the* Scipio's *life pods,"* Valdar said.

"Wait, what about Hale and the Marines on Pluto?" Durand asked.

"Negative contact," Valdar said. Durand could have

sworn she heard a tremor in the captain's words. *"Admiral Garret wants our ships back in the fight as soon as possible. We're to jump to Mars immediately. This isn't my decision, Gall. The situation on Mars is in doubt."*

Durand looked down at Pluto, watching as slag spewed from the giant mineshaft running beneath the Norgay Montes. She had no idea if any of the Marines were even alive. She hated the idea of leaving the Marines behind…but there was more at stake than just their lives.

"Manfred, Lothar, stay with me out here until the life boats are recovered." Durand said to her squadron, "The rest of you get back on the *Breit* and get ready to fight again."

CHAPTER 14

Egan felt his gauntlet vibrate. A data packet arrived, streaming through IR relays from the Crucible to the display on his forearm.

"Got it, sir!" Egan swiped images showing cross sections of Pluto's crust and blotchy engineering schematics that he had no idea how to interpret. "Definitely got something…"

Hale looked over Egan's shoulder at the images.

"What do they mean?" Hale asked.

"Hell if I know. I only set up an IR channel from the distant edge of the solar system through five different relays and established a discrete packet cipher with Ibarra's probe to get this data. Guess I forgot to tell him to send us something a grunt could figure out," Egan said.

"*Ay dios mio.*" Cortaro ran a line from his gauntlet

to Egan's and copied the data. He looked over the pics for a few moments then pointed to the wide opening on the right side of the cavern. "There's a quadrium vein the size of Standish's mouth through there. Other side looks like it leads to another of the smaller shafts we came through…which connects to drop zone bravo."

"If the other teams survived, they'll come through here," Hale said.

"How will they know which way to go?" Jacobs asked.

"There's the trail of our dead." Hale nodded at the two corpses.

"I've got it," Cortaro said. "Standish, tag that wall."

Standish, crouched next to the tunnel leading to the large quadrium vein, drew his Ka-Bar and began carving into the rock.

"Between me and Crimson's commo tech," Egan said, "we've got five more relays. Not sure how far we can get before we're out of comms with the surface. Pluto's rotation is so slow we can stay in touch with Earth for days."

"Leave a team behind?" Jacobs asked. "Maybe two Marines to stay in contact."

"No, we'll need every rifle if we come across a

mass of turned humans. We're staying together," Hale said. He went to the sled loaded up with omnium cubes and gave it a gentle push. It floated away easily, remaining perfectly level.

"I've got an idea."

Standish looked up from his work, the words GOTT MIT cut into the rock. He leaned toward Orozco. The big Marine had his plasma cannon aimed down the dark tunnel. "You hear that, Oro? Captain's got an idea. He's had the rank for barely two days and he's already talking like old Captain Acera during field ops. I swear they really do sprinkle pixie dust on officers to make them lose their damn minds."

"We had Lieutenant Hale so well trained," Orozco said. "Got us *almost* killed a couple times. *Almost* never got lost. You think Cortaro can keep the good-idea fairy away from him?"

"Not since he became a goddamn movie star," Standish said through grit teeth. He opened his visor and blew dust out of the word UNS.

"Heh, so I was going through all my email, right?" Orozco gave Standish a punch on the shoulder. "The 'us' in the movie—well, not you—look just like us. No actors. So I've got thousands—thousands!—of letters from beautiful babies saying they just can't wait for me to get

173

back to Earth. They sent pics. Video clips. It's amazing. Don't worry, Standish. I'll ask if they have any ugly friends for you."

"Well, aren't you just one heck of a pal?" Standish slapped his visor down over his face.

****

A wraith pointed the spike protruding from beneath her wrist at a glittering rock wall. A short blue beam snapped from the spike and traced a line through the quadrium ore. The ore dissolved into glowing smoke and traveled down the spike and across the wraith's chest and along her other arm. The smoke coiled around an omnium cube floating above several other wraiths. The cube expanded slowly as the smoke from the wraiths curled around it.

A hover sled drifted behind the work party. It bumped against another waiting sled, sending the two drifting apart like billiard balls. One of the sleds hit a wraith carrying an omnium cube, knocking him to the dirt. The sled spun around, dumping cubes over the side.

Instruction queries alerted the Xaros drone overseeing the dig site to the disruption. The drone flew from its perch in the ceiling and redirected wraiths to deal with the disruption. The wraiths had limited capabilities, defaulting to the drone anytime they were confronted with something more complicated than moving to assigned workstations or transmuting quadrium.

A wraith grabbed the edge of a loose sled. It pushed an omnium cube back into place, then froze. The wraith transmitted data from its visual cortex to the drone. Between the cubes were several blocks labeled DENETHRITE. EXPLOSIVE CHARGE, 1 EACH.

The drone activated the wraith's aggression programming a split second before the charges erupted with a thunderclap of noise and light. A wave of overpressure slapped the drone into the ceiling, breaking off several stalks.

Wraiths picked themselves off the ground, their armor saving all but the closest to the blast from injury. The remains of much of the drone's work crew were red stains against the walls or scattered across the floor.

Marines rushed into the cavern. Plasma shots hit the drone before it could attack, breaking it into a dozen pieces that disintegrated before they hit the ground.

****

Hale shot two bolts of plasma into a charging

wraith. Its armor cracked like glass struck by a rock and it stumbled to the ground. Hale pressed his muzzle against the temple of a one-armed wraith struggling to get to its feet and blew a hole through its head.

"Gunners, lay down covering fire!" Hale shouted to Orozco and Crimson's gunner, a short Marine named Lin, as they ran into the cavern.

"Incoming!"

A dozen wraiths materialized through the smoke and dust. One leveled its spike at Hale. A red beam cut through the haze and struck Hale's arm. Pain lanced through Hale's shoulder and sent his rifle flying as his hand went into spasms.

He backpedaled, his mind struggling to focus against the inferno raging against his arm and the muted shouts from his Marines. A plasma bolt snapped over his shoulder. He looked up and caught a wraith's bull rush against his chest. Hale hit the ground hard and the wraith landed on top of him with enough force to push the air from his lungs.

The wraith's face pressed against his visor, a mask of atavistic rage screaming at him. Hale snapped his Ka-Bar out of the sheath and slashed across the wraith's neck. Blood gushed out, splashing over Hale's helmet. He shoved the slack body off and slapped at his face, trying and failing to clear his vision.

Hands grabbed him beneath the arms and dragged him away. Hale ran a thumb across his visor and swiped a clear patch. Dead wraiths littered the ground, tripping up their reinforcements. The heavy gunners' cannons knocked wraiths off their feet and blew limbs away with each hit.

Hale struggled to draw his gauss pistol with his off hand. A red beam cut through the dust and gouged out a burning trench that missed Hale by inches. He aimed for the source of the beam and snapped off shots until the pistol clicked empty. He tried to drop the magazine with one hand but succeeded in dropping his weapon.

The drag stopped behind a wrecked sled. A Marine with a corpsman's stencil on his armor set Hale's back to the sled then grabbed Hale's head with both hands.

"Are you OK?"

Hale managed a groan. His right arm felt like someone had stabbed it with a burning-hot fork and was trying to stir it around.

"Pain is good." The corpsman—Niles, according to the name on his armor—ran a line from his gauntlet to a port on Hale's chest. "OK, good news is we're in atmo. I need to remove the damaged armor before it...let's just remove the armor." He touched his gauntlet.

The armor sleeve covering Hale's right arm went slack. Niles tugged at the deltoid plate and an electric charge of pain went up Hale's arm.

"Sorry! Sorry, sir," the corpsman said.

"What're you doing to my patient?" Yarrow slid to a stop next to Hale and knelt down.

"He's my patient and I've got this," Niles said, reaching out and trying to push Yarrow away. Yarrow slapped the hand away.

"His pseudo-muscle layer melted." Yarrow shook his head. "The heat's burning through the pressure lining but hasn't melted all the way through. We need to get it off before it hits his bloodstream and shuts down his heart."

"How do we do that without further—"

"Hold his arm." Yarrow braced his forearm against Hale's chest and looked into the captain's eyes. "Sorry, sir."

Yarrow grabbed the melted armor plate and ripped it off Hale's arm. Hale fought against a scream as searing pain erupted across his arm. Yarrow pinned Hale to the sled as his commander struggled to get loose.

"Nu-skin spray. Now," Yarrow said to Niles. Hale heard a hiss and the pain in his arm subsided to mere agony. "I know this isn't much of a consolation, sir, but it was just a flesh wound."

Hale breathed hard. Control over his hand came back slowly. He cocked his head up, waiting for the sound of plasma rifles or screaming wraiths but there was nothing but background noise through his IR.

"Jacobs, Cortaro, status report," Hale said.

"All hostiles down," Jacobs said. *"We're securing the cavern."*

Hale tried to get up and but the corpsman pushed him back down.

"Skin hasn't cured yet, sir," Niles said. "Stay still for a few more minutes."

"You lost everything covering your bicep." Yarrow held up a small armor plate, still dripping with blood. "The environment layer that protects you from vacuum is quite toxic if it melts. We don't treat that often in void combat as casualties tend to expire from other injuries before toxic shock."

"If you want a thank you for ripping my skin off, you're fishing in the wrong pond," Hale said.

"Just be glad Steuben isn't here," Yarrow said.

"Sir, try not to get shot again," Niles said. "I'd rather not have any more stories about treating you while under fire."

"Don't waste your breath. The good captain's

always looking for trouble," Yarrow said. "Sir, can you flex your arm for me?"

Hale pulled his fist to his shoulder, stopping halfway when pain that felt like a live wire came to life in his arm. He swore and let his arm flop down.

"Bet you've got some tendon damage." Yarrow pressed Hale's injured arm against his torso. Mag locks pinned Hale's arm in place. Niles took out a roll of tape and fastened it over Hale's arm.

"How am I supposed to shoot like this?" Hale asked.

"Sir," Cortaro said, handing Hale his gauss pistol, "you worry about controlling the battle. Let us grunts do the trigger pulling." Cortaro held out a hand and helped Hale to his feet.

Dead wraiths littered the cavern floor. The heavy smell of copper—spilled blood—filled the air.

"Any other casualties?" Hale asked.

"Egan got a little singed. One of Crimson took a punch to the helmet that cracked her visor. Both say they're fine. Armors are still void capable," Cortaro said.

"We made a hell of a noise. Won't be long before the Xaros come looking for us," Hale said.

"Every minute they're running around is a minute they're not working on that gate, right?"

"We're not here to distract them." Hale pointed to two tunnels he could make out through the floating dust. A low thrum came through the tunnel on the left. "That sound like drones to you?"

"No, sir. Pitch is higher. Cycle's faster than what we've heard before. Makes you wish Steuben was here, don't it? Swear he can tell us apart by our heartbeats."

"If there's something unusual down that tunnel, then that's where we're heading." Hale stepped over dead wraiths and kicked one over. He picked up his plasma rifle and shook off dirt and blood.

Hale pointed his barrel toward a tunnel.

"Follow me."

****

Standish felt vibrations pulse through his feet. The tunnel ended a few dozen yards ahead. He saw what looked like a rapid-flowing river past the exit. He continued on, glancing at a Marine on the opposite side of the tunnel and a few steps behind.

"Why am I on point?" he muttered. "Crimson. They're all the new guys. They should be on point. I bet putting me up here was Orozco's idea. Most dangerous spot in any formation is the point man. He doesn't want me to get my spot back in that damn movie and get a chunk of his royalties. I want my movie cash too, damn it."

"Who're you talking to?" hissed Weiss from a few yards behind. "You see something, put it out on the IR."

"When I want shit from you, I'll squeeze your head," Standish snapped. He hurried to the end of the tunnel and pressed against the side. A rocky pathway cut across the end of the tunnel, ending a few yards away with a steep cliff.

A pulsating vibration went through Standish's body through the tunnel wall. Beyond the cliff was a wide stream of dirt and rocks flowing in midair. The material lurched faster with each thrum of vibration.

"That…is not something I've seen before," Standish said. He snapped pics with his rifle optics and sent them to Cortaro and Hale. With one eye, he slowly peered around the corner, then pulled back.

"Oh boy," Standish said, opening a squad channel. "Cap, Top, you're going to want to see this for yourself."

"Moving," Hale said.

Standish held the optics on top of his rifle just around the corner and snapped more pictures.

"Jesus," Weiss said as the pics hit his visor. "What the hell is that?"

"Did I ever tell you about the time I fought a Jinn wyrm? Or when I defeated the face-eating Kroar of Nibiru? Neither of those were as big as this baby," Standish said.

"What the hell's a Kroar?" Weiss asked.

Hale and Cortaro ran up to Standish. Hale moved awkwardly; no Marine trained to move with one arm fixed to his side. Standish looked over the new environment layer fused over Hale's injury and the blackened and warped armor plating on the captain's right arm. He wasn't sure how the captain managed to keep going, but Standish had never known Hale to quit anything.

"That's spoil, sir," Cortaro said, pointing to the river of material. "You're mining anything and there's going to be plenty of rock you don't need. Got to send it somewhere. Explains all those rocks we saw on the surface."

"The size of that funnel…this must be the shaft leading out of Norgay Montes," Hale said.

"Movement." Standish went to a knee and raised his weapon. On the opposite side of the river, a sled loaded with cubes of omnium and two wraiths raced along a road running parallel to the spoil stream. The sled zipped out of view.

"Who wants to wait right here until a different

sled goes right in front of us? Not me," Standish said. "I don't have a vote but if we're considering personal pref—"

Cortaro put a heavy hand on Standish's head.

Hale tapped his gauntlet screen and the images Standish captured popped up on his visor.

At the origin of the spoil stream were massive rings, the widest hundreds of yards across and studded with blunt teeth, grinding through Pluto's crust. The next ring was flush with the outermost, crushing stone into dust. Five rings formed into a mining drill, a glowing crystal in the very center.

Tiny black figures stood along the roadways. Beams from wrist spikes pulled quadrium from the passing spoil, transmuting it to omnium where it was loaded onto waiting sleds. Several drones cut into the rock just behind the drill's progress, building the roads deeper into the surface.

"They're laying track as they go," Cortaro said. "Clever."

"We need to destroy it," Hale said. He looked up at the top of the spoil funnel. "How much denethrite do we have left?"

"Enough to do about as much good as a spitball against armor," Cortaro said.

"Sir," Jacobs said as she approached, "I have an

idea."

"Another officer with an idea. God help us," Standish said under his breath.

"We don't have to destroy the drill, just stop the omnium from getting to the surface, right?" she asked. "The Xaros are using the wraiths and drones to transport the omnium. We take them out and the enemy can't finish their jump gate, right?"

"There are ten of us, hundreds of wraiths and drones," Cortaro said. "We're good, but we're not going to win a head-on assault."

"Wait." Hale flicked his fingers across his gauntlet screen. "There's another tunnel entrance closer to the drill. Can we get there from here?" Hale asked Cortaro.

The first sergeant shrugged and consulted the data sent from Earth.

"Xaros are aggressive, brutal," Hale said. "I've never seen them let up from an attack before, or hold anything back. We can use that."

"How do you mean, sir?"

"Bailey?" Hale waved the sniper up the line. "You ever heard of a 'come on' ambush, Lieutenant?"

"No, sir."

"You're kidding. What're they teaching at the Basic Course these days?"

"Fighting Xaros and fighting Xaros," she said.

"Sir," Cortaro said, tapping his gauntlet, "you're right. We can get to that other tunnel. We've got to double back quite a ways."

"That works," Hale said. He pointed across the stream of dust and rocks when Bailey arrived and asked, "Can you hit a target on the other side with your rail rifle? Cortaro, how much denethrite do we have?"

****

Bailey snapped her gum and touched the power line running from the stock of her rifle to the battery attached to her lower back. The rail rifle had taken a few knocks since landing on Pluto. Her status screen had been known to lie to her before. Confident that the line was secure, she put her finger back on the trigger.

With the optics in her visor linked to the weapon, she could punch a hole through a turret on the other side of the moon. Shooting across a river of rock and dust was going to be tricky.

"Got one coming," Standish said from the corner. He and Egan pulled back from their observation post and stopped a few feet behind Bailey. They pressed their hands against their helm audio ports.

"Yeah, that's a good idea." Bailey swallowed her gum and braced herself against the weapon. Firing a rail rifle in atmo was never a pleasant experience, especially when she was firing on full power.

A sled appeared on the opposite side of the spoil. Bailey locked on with her optics and shifted the rifle to keep her bead on the target. Boulders the size of cars tumbled through the spoil stream, blocking her shot.

"Here we go." Bailey waited for a boulder to tumble away and pulled the trigger. The rail rifle accelerated a slug the length of Bailey's hand to supersonic speed, breaking the sound barrier with a thunderclap. The bullet tore through the spoil stream. Dust ignited with the round's passing, leaving a line of fire tracing from Bailey's position to the sled.

The bullet hit the sled, blasting it into splinters and shattering the omnium cubes. The cubes broke into jagged hunks, evaporating to nothing within seconds.

"You're up!" Bailey grabbed her rifle and disassembled it. By the time she had the barrel and bolt assembly mag-locked to her back, Egan and Standish were nearly at the tunnel exit.

"Face-first into battle!" Standish skidded around the corner and leveled his plasma rifle. He fired from the hip, sending off a spray of shots toward the wraiths and drones working near the drill. Egan bothered to aim, putting fewer shots down range.

Red energy beams slashed past the tunnel opening, striking the wall and sending out puffs of vaporized rocks.

The two Marines dove into the tunnel. Disintegration beams tore through the ground they were standing on just moments ago.

"It worked," Standish said as he scrambled to his feet. "Definitely pissed them off. Lots of very angry horrible things coming right for us."

"Damn my short legs." Bailey ran through the tunnel, the sounded of screaming wraiths closing fast. The sound of the Dotok twisted into banshees still haunted her dreams. She had a bad feeling the barbaric roars of the wraiths would prove a cruel complement to future nightmares.

Orozco and Lin stepped out of the side tunnel, their cannons slung at their waists. Plasma bolts streaked past Bailey, hot enough that Bailey felt their passing through her armor. She heard the crack of falling rocks behind her as the heavy gunners blew hunks out of the roof, dropping caltrops of broken stone.

"Hurry!" Orozco yelled.

A ruby beam snapped over Bailey's shoulder. She

flinched aside and went tumbling head over feet. Two more beams seared over her head.

There was a grunt of pain and the clatter of falling armor.

"Lin's hit." Orozco looked at the twin smoking holes in the fallen Marine's chest, then grabbed Bailey and hauled her to her feet. He pushed her through the side tunnel. Standish and Egan disappeared down the jagged passageway.

Standish ducked his head back and yelled, "Move your asses!"

"Lin?" Bailey glanced back and saw the denethrite charge over the side tunnel exit, the timer on the fuse promising a detonation in one hundred twelve seconds. She ran on, scraping against jutting rocks but making forward progress all the same.

"Dead," Orozco said.

The scream of wraiths echoed through the tunnel.

Bailey had never scored top marks on the strike Marine PT runs. But now, even in her armor, she ran like the wind. Orozco dogged at her heels, unable to run around her.

She ran into the cavern where they'd ambushed the wraith work party. Jacobs waved to the fleeing Marines from the entrance to their escape tunnel. The lieutenant hit a button on her gauntlet and timers connected to denethrite charges across the cavern started their countdown. Jacobs fell in behind Bailey and Orozco as they ran down the tunnel.

"Fuck." Bailey struggled to breathe as her lungs started to burn. "Fucking. Hate. Running."

The exit to another cavern appeared as the tunnel veered to a side. Bailey felt a surge of energy as the finish line neared. The cries of nearing wraiths urged her forward even faster.

Explosions sounded far behind the fleeing Marines as the denethrite charges blew. A blast of overpressure slapped Bailey across the back and pushed her against the tunnel wall. The rumble of an earthquake filled Bailey's helmet. Flakes of rock broke from the ceiling as the rumbling intensified and bounced off her armor.

A small boulder struck her back and sent her sprawling. She lay in the dirt, struggling to get up, when she felt hands grab her. Orozco tossed her through the exit with the grace and gentleness of a dock worker at the end of a long shift. She rolled over several times before she bumped into Standish's legs.

The ground slapped against Bailey and a shower of dust washed over her. She got up on her knees and looked around. The tunnel Orozco threw her out of had

190

collapsed. A gray armored hand stuck out from between cracks in the rock.

"Oro!" Bailey ran to the broken pile and threw a boulder aside. "Hold on!"

More Marines joined Bailey as she scooped up debris and tossed it aside. She got Orozco's arm uncovered.

Standish wedged himself between a boulder larger than him and pressed his feet against it. The artificial muscles beneath his armor strained as they tipped the boulder over, revealing Orozco's cracked helmet and his shoulders.

"Get his arms," Cortaro said as he grabbed Orozco underneath an armpit and pulled. Yarrow got the other and the two yanked Orozco hard. He slid a few inches out from the collapsed rocks, one arm still buried. Bailey grabbed the heavy gunner by his chest armor.

"Ready. Heave!" Orozco's upper body emerged from the rock slide. The arm pinned to his side came into view with the next pull, revealing another armored hand gripping Orozco's forearm.

"That's Jacobs," Weiss said as he grabbed his lieutenant's hand.

Orozco came free a moment later. The rest of the Marines went to aid Jacobs as Yarrow and Bailey knelt beside Orozco, his armor dented and caked in dirt.

"His vitals are still strong," Yarrow said. "Maybe another concussion. This guy needs to stop getting hit on the head." The corpsman touched a button on Orozco's helmet and the visor popped free. Yarrow took a small capsule from his belt, crushed it between his fingertips and wafted it under Orozco's nose.

The big Spaniard jerked up. He looked at Bailey, then to Yarrow, then swung his head from side to side.

"Where's my weapon?" he asked.

"On your back, you big oaf," Bailey said. She gave him a pat on the shoulder, then hugged him.

"What? What I do?" Orozco asked.

Jacobs brushed dirt off her armor and did her best to limp away from the cave-in with some sense of dignity. She stopped next to Hale and leaned on him.

"Guess it worked, sir," she said. "Every last wraith and drone that followed us into the caves won't be a problem."

"Can you keep moving?" Hale asked. "We need to get to the other entrance and put a stop to that drill. No rest for the weary."

"Or the wicked." She looked at the cave-in. "Lin…"

"Endure, Lieutenant," Hale said. "We can mourn

later. We have to fight now."

****

His arm ached. A dull presence of pain radiated out from his abused muscles and up his shoulder. Hale tried to focus on something else as his Marines marched through a tunnel wide enough to fit four walking side by side.

Years ago, he'd suffered a stress fracture during a road march at the Basic School. A bone in his foot snapped in half at mile ten of a twenty-mile hike. He finished the march without a word of complaint and endured some halfhearted criticism from the instructors when he finally turned himself over to the corpsmen the next morning. Pain was part of an infantryman's life.

Hale looked up at a floating glowing orb. The objects ran from one end of the tunnel to the other, a few dozen yards between them.

"Cortaro," Hale said, pointing his free hand at an orb, "why do you think those are here? Why would the Xaros bother with lights?"

"The wraiths, I guess. Make the environment safe for them," Cortaro said.

"For a species that moves planets from solar

system to solar system, it should be easy to put their workers in an environment suit." Hale tapped a finger against the side of his pistol. He turned around and aimed it at a globe behind the Marines and fired.

The globe shattered, the fragments disintegrating before they hit the ground.

Marines swung around, weapons up and ready for battle.

"As you were," Cortaro said. "Keep moving."

The globes on either side of the new gap in the line burned brighter. Hale picked up a rock and tossed it.

The rock arced away, then floated slowly at an angle when it crossed through the gap. The stone neared another globe and fell to the ground.

"The globes generate the gravity," Hale said. "Bet there's a force field that keeps the air in as well."

"Great, sir, we know something new," Cortaro said. "We aren't entirely sure if this tunnel will get us to the drill, or back to the surface, but we've figured this puzzle out."

"This might prove useful," Hale said.

"Sir, got an opening coming up on the right," Jacobs said through the IR.

"Check it out." Hale glanced at his gauntlet screen. "Should be the side tunnel we need to get to the drill."

"Moving."

"You doing all right, sir?" Cortaro asked. "I see your face twitching. If it hurts that bad, then Yarrow can give you something."

"And then I won't be thinking straight," Hale said.

"Have you been thinking about how we're going to get the hell out of here? If the *Breit* didn't make it…"

"If she's gone, then Earth will send another fleet through the Crucible. We'll hitch a ride back with them. We, high command, can't let the Grinder come online," Hale said.

"Sir! There's—" Jacob's warning cut off into static.

Hale ran for the entrance, but Cortaro stopped him with a hand to his chest.

"No weapons fire," Cortaro said. "No noise. Could be interference that cut her off."

"Could be the enemy." Hale ran forward, his pistol held ready next to his helmet. He made his way into a small cavern where he found Crimson squad standing in the middle of the room, dead wraiths all around them. The trail of dead led to a doorway piled high with bodies.

"What is—" An arm wrapped around Hale's neck and jerked him backwards. The razor-sharp edge of a silver blade pressed against his visor just beneath his eye.

"You have blundered into an ambush. Disappointing," a low voice growled.

Hale pushed the arm away and spun around.

"Steuben!" Hale lowered his pistol. "What happened here? Where have you been?"

"Landing was a bit rough," Lieutenant Mathias said from a terrace above Hale's head. Four more Marines stood around him. The lieutenant held up a thin chain with several dog tags on it. "Took casualties before we ever got into the tunnels. Lost Bronx and half my team to those banshee-things a few rooms back. Bunch more just charged in here after that explosion. I assume that was you, sir?"

Hale brought the lieutenant and Steuben up to speed on what he and the other Marines had been through. The rest of Hale's squad joined them in the cavern.

"Sounds like you've been through worse," Hale said.

"You are hurt. Again," Steuben said.

"Flesh wound." Hale waved Cortaro, Jacobs and Mathias over to him. "Take a knee, everyone."

Hale holstered his pistol and drew a circle in the sand. "OK, the drill is…" He stopped, feeling the thrum of distant machinery through the ground. "Close. Here's the plan. Pipe up if you have a better idea."

****

Standish stepped over a wraith corpse and inched closer to the end of the tunnel. The thrum of the drill jarred pebbles and dust loose with each pulse.

"You think this is going to work?" Weiss, a few feet behind, asked over the closed IR.

"I've fought giant Xaros constructs with Hale before," Standish said, swallowing hard. "On Earth, we had the Iron Hearts to pull our asses out of the fire. Takeni: Iron Hearts and orbital fire support. Classified space vault I'm not telling you about: Iron Hearts and a space god…thing. This time, we have a couple more Marines," he glanced down at his plasma rifle, "and peashooters. Fuck."

"So…no?"

"We'll be *fine*," Standish said. "Probably. Probably fine. The captain and the lieutenants had a good idea pow-wow." The Marine detached the optics from the top of his rifle and reached them just around the corner.

Video feed of the road running perpendicular to the tunnel and the river of spoil flashed across Standish's visor and went to every Marine behind him. A little more than a dozen wraiths pulled quadrium from the flowing rocks while many more worked on the opposite side of the river.

"Got some hostiles," Standish said, "less than before. Nice when a plan comes together. No sign of a sled. Wait…there's one." Standish zoomed in on an empty hover sled driven by a single wraith slowing on the opposite side of the gigantic mineshaft. "Wrong side, though. Go or hold, sir?"

"Hold," Hale said. *"Give it a few minutes. See if another comes our way."*

"Roger." Standish swept the optic back and forth over the target area.

"So, you were really on Takeni?" Weiss asked. "You ran through that burning forest?"

"Yes. That sucked, by the way."

"You were the one that pulled Torni out of that river when she jumped in to save that little Dotty girl?"

"What? No, never happened. You can ask Torni about that yourself," Standish said.

"Sergeant Torni's dead. How am I going to do that?" Weiss asked.

Standish tapped the side of his helmet. "Damn IR's funny in these tunnels." The optic froze. "Here we go. Captain Hale, got one empty sled arriving."

"Collapse the stack, ready on my mark," Hale said.

Standish crouched slightly and Weiss stepped closer and stuck his rifle over Standish's shoulder.

"Hey, Weiss." Standish craned his head up to look at the other Marine, his face pale and moist with sweat. *"Gott mit uns."*

"Gott mit uns." Weiss nodded emphatically.

"Attack!" Hale shouted.

Standish rushed forward in a crouch. He cleared the exit and twisted to the left.

The sled idled a few feet over the road. A neat line of wraiths holding omnium cubes waited to hand over their cargo to a lone wraith standing on the flat bed.

"Don't shoot the sled!" Standish drilled a plasma bolt into the forehead of a wraith holding a cube. He sidestepped and leaped onto the bed where the lone wraith on the sled with him hurled an omnium cube right at Standish's face.

Standish ducked and rolled forward. Following his momentum, he got to his feet, swung his rifle over his shoulder and drove the butt of the weapon toward the Wraith's face.

The wraith caught the rifle butt with one hand, freezing Standish's strike in place. The wraith's dead eyes clicked from the rifle to Standish.

"Well, shit." Standish let go of his weapon and

ducked forward, ramming an elbow into the wraith's stomach. There was a grunt and the wraith's hips shot backwards. Standish swung an uppercut into its chin. Blood and teeth sprayed out of the wraith's ruined mouth. Standish grabbed it by the shoulders and hip-tossed it through the air and into the spoil stream.

Boulders smashed into the wraith, crushing it into armor fragments and bloody paste as the stream carried the body to the distant exit.

A ruby beam snapped passed his elbow. Standish fell flat and rolled over the side of the sled. He fell next to Hale, who had his plasma rifle over the driver's controls, firing on wraiths on the other side of the stream. A dying drone disintegrated at the end of the road. Dead wraiths who'd been shot down before they could be directed away from their mining tasks lay like discarded puppets in the dirt.

The Marines fired on the wraiths on the other side of the river, but few of their plasma bolts and few attacks from the wraiths made it across the spoil.

"Get this thing moving, Standish!" Hale ordered.

"Right, let me just—" He stood up and barely missed another beam of energy sent over the top of his head. "Jiminy Christmas! I don't think they want us to leave, sir."

"Bailey! Take your shot," Hale said.

The sniper raised her rail rifle and fired. The supersonic round sent a clap of thunder against Standish's helmet, hard enough that his ears popped. The bullet hit the opposite side of the tunnel, just below the road's edge. Dirt, rock and wraiths went flying, all sucked into the spoil and crushed into tiny bits.

Standish jumped back onto the sled and found the controls: several round dials with lit rings. The last sled they found was push operated, but this...

"Ugh, Egan?" Standish asked for the team's pilot.

"Busy! Very busy!" The snap of plasma bolts and clipped commands from Cortaro stepped on Egan's reply.

Standish looked over his shoulder and saw a drone rise up from the edge of the road, stalks lit and ready to attack. Orozco's heavy cannon beat it into the spoil. The rush of material propelled the drone forward. A stalk shot out and nearly took Standish's head off before boulders clapped against the drone and spat the crystalline pyrite inside the shell out into the stream.

"OK." Standish looked at the controls. "I've hotwired everything from a 1997 Pontiac to the new hotness Teslas. I can figure this out." He touched a fingertip to one of the dials and ran it clockwise around the lit ring.

The sled lurched to the side, straight toward the spoil. Small rocks pelted the side of Standish's helmet as he spun his finger the other way. The craft banked the opposite direction, heading straight for Hale.

Hale dove to the ground as the sled almost scalped him. The sled smashed into the tunnel wall hard enough to pitch Standish off his feet and into the rock.

"Standish!" Hale shouted.

"Yes! Sorry, sir. She's a bit sensitive." Standish gingerly touched another dial, and the entire sled fell to the ground. He moved his fingertip the opposite direction and it rose higher. "Think I've got it now." He touched another ring and the sled lurched forward.

"Yup! All aboard the Standish Express!"

Hale waved an arm over his head. "Shift fire!"

Half the Marines swung their rifles at the drill and aimed for the outermost ring. Their plasma bolts smeared across the metal with no effect.

"Bailey, plan B!" Hale called out.

Bailey dropped a spent battery from her belt and attached the power cable running from her rifle to a new battery. She took a tungsten dart from an ammo pouch and slipped it into the acceleration cradle at the base of the rail gun vanes. She aimed at the drill, then raised the weapon to the rocky ceiling just above the spoil stream.

Marines covered their audio receptors and ducked away.

Bailey shot the roof, knocking loose fragments of Pluto's crust the size of houses. The giant rocks floated in the spoil stream, then moved slowly downstream.

"Load up!" Hale shouted.

The Marines broke away from the firefight with the wraiths on the other side of the spoil, the firing lines for both sides blocked by the new debris. He loaded up the sled, rifles oriented to the front and to the spoil.

Hale was the last one on, needing help from Steuben to climb aboard.

"Go, take us slow," Hale said.

Standish touched a dial and the sled jerked forward. Bailey slung her plasma carbine off her back and laid flat on the bed. Each time the moving sled passed beneath a floating orb, she destroyed it with a well-timed shot.

Wraiths ran up the opposite road, shooting red beams of death after the Marines.

"Not that slow," Hale said.

Standish increased the speed, and Bailey missed a shot.

"Hey! This is hard enough without you driving like a sloppy drunk!" she protested.

"I'm getting mixed messages here," Standish said.

Cortaro stood up and hit the globe Bailey missed. With each globe they destroyed, the spoil stream shifted to the opposite side, toward the functioning globes still generating a gravity field. The once-smooth highway of the spoil stream degraded into a traffic jam of boulders and rocks compacting against each other.

The spoil stream ground to a halt and spilled over the opposite side, crushing the wraiths to bits. The entire cavern filled with rock as the drill kept eating away and filling the space with more rubble. A wall of spoil advanced a few more yards, then stopped.

Standish risked a couple quick glances over his shoulder.

"Well, I'll be damned. That was a great idea, sir!" Standish said. "You got the drill to bury itself."

"Think it'll stop?" Hale asked Cortaro. "Or will it cut through the entire planet and spawn more drones?"

"I don't think the Xaros can handle the pressure at the core of a planet, sir," Cortaro said.

"Let's hope not."

****

Hale's good arm grabbed the edge of the pit and

he hauled himself onto Pluto's surface. Gravity lessened instantly as he moved beyond the effects of the last glowing orb. A brown haze of dust filled the sky directly over the pit, giving way to blue as the distant sun scattered through tholin particles in the upper atmosphere.

He searched the sky and found no sign of the Grinder...or the *Breitenfeld*.

"Egan, get comms going. Find our ship," Hale said.

"I don't think I can get anything through all the particulates in the atmosphere," Egan said. "We could go radio," he said, pointing to Abaddon cresting over the horizon, "but that'll bring every Xaros drone still out there right on our heads."

"Try," Hale said.

"Sir," Jacobs came over to Hale, "where did the task force go? The Grinder would have burned up if it was destroyed. It's gone...shouldn't the ships be out here trying to find us, at least send something down the tunnels to look?"

"Valdar wouldn't leave us behind." Hale felt a chill spread from his gut to the rest of his body. Where was the *Breitenfeld*?

Hale looked at his air and battery gauges; both were amber and dangerously close to low.

"Steuben, where is your drop pod?" Hale asked.

"Clear over those mountains." The Karigole pointed to distant icy peaks. "It took significant damage when we landed."

Hale scratched that course of action off a shrinking mental list of ways his Marines could survive.

"Sir," Cortaro got close to Hale, "Drebin in Slate has life support for the next fifty minutes. His O2 scrubber got banged up and is malfunctioning. Rest of us have between one and four hours."

Fifty minutes before his Marines started to die.

"What do we do, sir?" Mathias asked.

"Get Drebin back in the pit where there's still atmo. Have him breathe that instead of his suit reserves until we're ready to move," Hale said. "Worse comes to worse, we'll send a radio beam to Earth, see if they can—"

"Sir, got something." Egan waved to Hale from a satellite dish stuck in the dirt. "Distress beacon on the search-and-rescue freq."

"SAR freqs are radio spectrum. Are you sure?" Hale asked.

Egan's face fell. "Yes, sir, I'm sure. Coming from an escape pod, telemetry says it's off the *Scipio*."

"Got it." Niles held his rifle steady and pointed to the sky. "Sending."

A pic of a corvette came on Hale's visor. A tear in the hull ran across the rail gun; one vane was bent and misshapen. The ship lolled on its side, trailing debris.

"That looks like the *Scipio*," Hale said. "I wonder why we're getting a life pod hit off it and not the ship's distress signal."

"Hold on." Egan touched the side of his helmet. "Getting another transmission off the beacon…dot dot dot, dash dash dash, dot—SOS. There's someone up there, sir."

"Doubt they can come pick us up," Cortaro said.

"You ever serve on a corvette?" Hale asked Cortaro. "How bad does the *Scipio* look?"

"Did a few Luna jumps off one. Didn't get a real good look around, but you look at her on the infrared spectrum and her battery stacks are still hot. Ship could still have power," Cortaro said.

"And atmo in her tanks," Hale said. He looked at Abaddon. "If there were Xaros inside that thing, they would have come out to finish off whoever's sending out the distress call. Egan."

"Sir?" Egan looked up from his gauntlet.

"Xaros drones can break out of gravity wells much stronger than Pluto's. You think that sled can get us up to the *Scipio*?"

"Only one way to find out," Egan said.

CHAPTER 15

Of all the things Stacey regretted about her life before the Xaros invasion, not learning to be a better public speaker was at the top of the list. She wished her grandfather, Marc Ibarra, the world's richest man and the one who'd engineered Stacey's birth to serve as humanity's ambassador to the races united against the Xaros, had encouraged her to practice giving speeches—or done anything to teach her to deal with the crippling onset of anxiety that came before every one of these meetings.

The bastard knew I would end up here. Why didn't he send me to Model United Nations or Toastmasters instead of astronomy camp? she thought.

She paced back and forth on the small pod used by Bastion's ambassadors for their full meetings. It took five steps to get from one side of the dome-shaped craft to the other and Stacey pinged from side to side so fast the turns were making her slightly dizzy.

Pa'lon shared the pod with her, the Dotok ambassador's eyes watching her go from side to side. He kept his hands clasped behind his back, rocking back and forth on his heels slightly.

"Do all humans act this way before public events?" he asked.

"You want to go back to your own pod? You can." Stacey shook her hands from side to side then patted her cheeks.

"You've been an ambassador for many years now. Perhaps the topic of discussion is causing this…behavior," Pa'lon said.

"Ambassador Ibarra engages in this routine before every Congress, even during sessions where she is not scheduled to speak," said Chuck, Stacey's AI assistant, from a speaker on the control panel. "Variations include self-talk, snapping fingers, unexpected flatulence—"

"Thank you!" Stacey shouted. "Thank you for all that unnecessary information, Chuck. That happens one time—"

"Eight."

"—one time and it gets filed in some gigantic behavioral database." Her face flushed red and she looked away from Pa'lon.

"I can make the request to Congress," Pa'lon said. "My species is in as much danger as yours."

"No, this is my job. I will get Bastion to send their fleets to help defend Earth. I failed miserably when the Toth came knocking. I'm not going to screw this up again." Stacey took a deep breath and let it out slowly. "My bargaining position is significantly better this time around."

"I wouldn't go there, Stacey. There are already too many ambassadors afraid of what humanity could do with what Bastion's provided: the procedural generation technology for new soldiers, the omnium reactor, the Crucible. We will win more support by being magnanimous, thankful."

"Earth has lost billions of lives to Bastion's plans. Don't think we're going to let the Xaros steamroll us just because it's convenient for some race that's never seen the business end of a disintegration beam." Stacey set her face and threw back her shoulders. "Chuck? We ready?"

"The final ambassador is in place," Chuck said. "The Vishrakath ambassador, Wexil, has petitioned to address the council before the vote."

"Of course he has," Stacey said.

Wexil had swayed Bastion away from supporting

Earth when the Toth attacked, offering the reptilian aliens the proccie technology and the lion's share of humanity. Wexil's plan would have had Earth repopulated with more "compliant" humans from replacement proccie tubes to serve the Alliance. Relations between Stacey and Wexil had reached a nadir soon after she learned of this plan, and they had not improved.

The dark covering on the pod's dome rolled aside. A gigantic stone pillar with a flat top large enough for a football field was in the center of the grand Congress. Hundreds of ambassador pods surrounded the pillar, all floating on an even plane.

A giant disembodied head appeared over the pillar: one of the Qa'Resh appeared as a middle-aged woman with a long braid of hair. "She" was really one of the giant crystalline entities that made up the Qa'Resh; that Stacey had seen their true form put her in a very exclusive club on Bastion. The Alliance's hosts and nominal leaders were notoriously shy and paranoid, especially after the Toth killed one of their number in a kidnapping attempt many years before Stacey arrived in the station.

"Members of the Alliance," the Qa'Resh said, "the Xaros are at the gates of a member world. Earth, which holds our only Crucible jump gate, is under threat. Ambassador Ibarra and Pa'lon have petitioned for military aid. It is time to decide."

A pod rose from the other side of the pillar. Stacey felt anger swell in her chest as Wexil came level to the Qa'Resh's pillar. Few things helped Stacey focus during public forums, but one was her hatred for that man.

"To our hosts." Wexil bowed to the Qa'Resh. He looked like a patrician man in his late forties with slick black hair. Stacey did not know what the Vishrakath really looked like; Wexil hid behind the human projection Bastion kept around him at all times. Every ambassador looked human to Stacey, just as she resembled the races of each ambassador when they saw her—all in the name of cohesion and communication, according to Chuck.

"Ambassadors." Wexil's pod spun around and he held his hand to the side. "Earth and the Dotok are right to ask for our aid. They are under threat and have done much to aid our efforts against the Xaros." He looked at Stacey and gave her a slight nod. "But expending resources to save that planet is no longer in our best interests."

Stacey's hand snapped out to activate her pod's speakers. Pa'lon caught her by the wrist and shook his head.

"Let him finish. We're in control. Let's act like it," he said.

Stacey jerked her hand away.

"We now have the means, thanks to our arrangement with the being known as Malal, to create our own Crucible jump gates. Once Malal finishes constructing his codex, we can access the entire Xaros network and strike at the heart of their leadership, this Apex of theirs.

"We have the path to victory beneath our feet, but defending Earth would be a mistake." Murmurs spread through the ambassadors. Wexil raised a hand and a hologram of Abaddon appeared over the plateau. "This is what the Xaros sent to destroy Earth. A drone mass on par with the largest maniple ever to attack a world. The Xaros struck out from their gate around a nearby star and reached the Earth in a few years. A few years. If we commit lives and ships to stopping this attack, the Xaros will return again and in even greater numbers.

"I will mention that the Xaros' arrival is earlier than the estimates we made when the decision to save humanity was made. A human ship, the *Breitenfeld*, against this council's decision, went to the planet Takeni and there the Xaros saw that ship and then they knew—they knew— that something had gone awry on Earth. Our finely laid plans were ruined because of an impulsive human captain that could not see beyond the impact of his actions."

Pa'lon smashed his palm against the broadcast button. Their pod shot into the air and came level with

Wexil's.

"That decision saved the last of the Dotok species, you vile bit of—" Stacey slapped Pa'lon's hand away from the button before he could say more.

"Way to be magnanimous, Pa'lon, good job," Stacey said.

"The Crucible near Earth is compromised," Wexil said. "We have learned much from it, achieved great technological strides from its use, but now it is time to abandon it and Earth. With Malal, we can build another Crucible deep within Bastion space, far removed from the threat of the Xaros. We can take our time to carefully design a fleet to defeat the Xaros leadership and shore up defenses around that device.

"We cannot throw resources at defending Earth, not when the planet's doom is assured when the third wave of the Xaros arrive. I will remind you all what happened to Jelben's Star and the great defeat we suffered there," Wexil said.

"What's he talking about?" Stacey asked.

"Ancient history, one of the first attempts to fight the Xaros when they first arrived. A group of five species in a close star cluster combined their fleets at Jelben. Beat a small force of Xaros that arrived, then the Alliance sent every ship they could build and crew to beat the second

215

wave. They kept up the same pattern for the next two hundred years, kept the crews in suspended animation and bled the planets white to fight the third wave. Third wave was…trillions of drones. Swept the fleet aside like it was nothing and wiped out the species that were in that alliance. Rest of the galaxy took a dim view of going toe to toe with the Xaros after that."

"I propose an amendment to the motion before us," Wexil said. "The humans and Dotok evacuate what they can to a member world and aid in the construction of a new jump gate. They scuttle their Crucible and let us trade space for time and confront the Xaros in a more deliberate fashion.

"How much do you want to bet that new jump gate will be well within Vishrakath space?" Stacey asked.

"I wouldn't put it past him," Pa'lon said.

Text for Wexil's motion came up on the dome wall.

Stacey cleared her throat and hit the broadcast button.

"To my fellow ambassadors." Stacey felt butterflies in her stomach as she flicked a button and brought her pod higher than Wexil's. "Earth is under siege. We did not join this Alliance to be shunted aside when it proved convenient for other members. We joined to fight, to beat the Xaros with *your* aid and fight beside you and save *your* worlds when the time came. Xaros maniples are a few years away from the Ruhaald and Naroosha Collective. Will this body decide to let them slip beneath the Xaros tide too? Will Wexil argue that your race should be left to their own devices for the greater good as well? When will we stop retreating and finally take a stand against the enemy?

"Defend Earth. You've all seen the projections from the data gathered from Malal's vault. The Crucible on Earth can be completed within months. Then we can strike the Apex while it is still beyond our galaxy. If we wait too long, the whole of the Xaros leadership will arrive and we will be forced to deal with who knows how many Masters instead of the General that's been encountered. The time to turn this war around is now.

"I know I'm the newest ambassador here. I haven't been around for centuries to watch the slow erosion of free space back to this little corner of the galaxy. I saw what the Xaros did to my world firsthand and I am not willing to let that happen to another planet if I can help it."

Stacey paused. She looked over the ambassadors and saw many scrutinizing Wexil's proposal.

I'm not going to fail again. I won't let them throw us under the bus like they did with the Toth, she thought.

"Let me make something clear," she said. "If the Alliance does not send ships to defend Earth, we will not part with Malal." There was a pause before the implication of what she said registered with the ambassadors. "You will not make your own Crucibles or access the Xaros network without Malal. If you do not help us now…Earth will withdraw from the Alliance and you will be back where you started before that probe ever contacted my grandfather."

Stacey stepped back and the pod sank slowly to become level with the rest of the Congress. Hundreds of vid screens popped up on the inside of the dome. Ambassadors attempted to speak directly to Stacey, stepping over themselves with anger, support and bewilderment.

A dark covering swept over the dome, isolating Stacey and Pa'lon.

"That could have gone better," Pa'lon said.

"It's time to play hardball, Pa'lon," she said.

The long-haired Qa'Resh woman appeared against the dome.

"There is disquiet." The Qa'Resh looked at the two ambassadors, her face emotionless.

"You don't say," Stacey said, shrugging slightly.

218

"The decision comes from Earth. We're not going to stuff our ships full of civilians and scurry off to another planet. Eventually, we will run out of places to hide. Humanity was born on Earth. We will die there."

The Qa'Resh glanced at Pa'lon and then focused on Stacey and said, "We gave your species Terra Nova. A sanctuary world safe from the Xaros. Your species will survive there."

"What's she saying?" Pa'lon asked. "Her lips are moving but there's no sound."

"You didn't hear that?" Stacey frowned.

"Now you're not making any sound," Pa'lon said.

"You did not share Terra Nova with the Dotok," the Qa'Resh said. "Your species has few friends in the Alliance. We do not wish to see you lose another."

"You gave us Terra Nova to survive the Toth, out of guilt for letting us fight those monsters on our own. We would have left the Alliance without that show of good faith from you, the Qa'Resh. We trust you, the Dotok, and the Karigole. Don't expect us to bleed for anyone else unless they prove they're in the fight with us."

The Qa'Resh cocked her head slightly.

"They are ready for the vote," she said and vanished.

"What's going on? What was that all about?"

Pa'lon asked.

"The system's overloading with people screaming at me," Stacey said. "She had to cut your audio to get through to me. The Qa'Resh wanted confirmation that I really would leave the Alliance. I told them as much. And it's time to vote."

"That's suspiciously fast," Pa'lon said. "Normally there would be hours between an amendment like Wexil's and a vote."

"Well, I doubt anyone's ever threatened to take their ball and go home before. Look at me, Grandpa. I'm a trailblazer," Stacey said.

"The Dotok council instructed me to stay in the Alliance even if you leave. I trust we'll still be welcome on Earth."

"Your people are on Hawaii, some of the best real estate on the planet. If we leave, you'll have to move someplace worse—like Antarctica or Siberia."

"What? The place with that vile substance...snow, is it?"

"I'm just kidding," Stacey said. The dark shell over the dome opened. The Congress was at peace, the ambassadors touching their screens to vote. Two choices popped up on the screen before Stacey, one for her proposal to send forces to Earth, the other for Wexil's.

Stacey touched her bill, and Pa'lon did the same from the other side of the pod. The choices vanished from the screen.

"Where's the tally?" Stacey asked. "Every other vote has had the count live as votes come in."

"The circumstances are unusual. Voting against you is essentially a vote to have humanity out of the Alliance," he said.

The two proposals reappeared on the screen, hers in blue, Wexil's in red. Bar graphs formed beneath the two, and the blue column was decidedly larger.

"We did it?" Stacey asked. "We did it!"

She went to give Pa'lon a hug and was rebuffed by a force field.

"Contact not authorized," Chuck said.

"Where's Wexil? I want to rub his nose in this," she said.

"Magnanimous, Stacey. Be the bigger person. The war is far from over and we'll need the Vishrakath in the future," Pa'lon said.

Stacey caught sight of Wexil as his pod lifted over the rest and sped toward an exit. The alien inside gave Stacey a hard look, but betrayed no other emotion.

Two vid screens popped up on the inside of the dome: Darcy, the Ruhaald ambassador, and a man with sandy blond hair and freckles, the Naroosha representative.

"Darcy, good to see you, and…" She'd never dealt with the Naroosha before. As best she knew, no one on Bastion had much contact with the reclusive species.

"My approved designation is Tamir," the Naroosha said.

"The word is given," Darcy said. "Our fleet will begin shuttling to Earth as soon as I return to Ruhaald Prime. We've only one functioning jump engine, but it can get a sizeable force through the Crucible in one go. Just remember to come lend us a hand when the Xaros hit our system in twenty years."

"If there's a blood debt between Earth and Ruhaald Prime, it will be honored," Stacey said. "The same for the Naroosha, though your people will be in danger sooner than the Ruhaald, I believe."

"5,299 Earth rotations until expected encounter with the Xaros," Tamir said. Stacey couldn't help but notice that his mouth didn't move when he spoke. Some of the species represented on Bastion were a good deal more exotic than their forced human appearance. Stacey knew the Ruhaald's true form. Anyone on Earth expecting aid from a race similar to the Dotok or Karigole were in for a shock.

"I will return to Earth right away with the gate codes for your arrival," Stacey said. "Come as fast as you can."

Their screens snapped away.

Stacey crossed her arms over her chest and tugged at the bottom of her lip.

"Pa'lon…what do you think?"

"When obstacles suddenly vanish from my path, I believe a trap lies ahead," the Dotok said.

"The Ruhaald I trust because of their ambassador. She's always been for us. The Naroosha…but what are we supposed to do? We're beggars right now, can't afford to be choosey with who comes to save the day," she said.

Worry nagged at the back of her mind and would dog her thoughts until she went back to Earth.

CHAPTER 16

Torni's stalks plied over a thin sheet of clear crystal, then froze suddenly. Her stalks quivered and smashed together, breaking the crystal into shards that flew across the workshop. Her body shifted to her human form and she fell onto her hands and knees.

Torni's mouth opened to scream, but there was no sound. She pounded against the deck, denting the metal plates. Steam rose off her back and shoulders as embers burned across her surface.

"Torni, what's wrong?" Lafayette asked. He edged toward the door, his eyes locked on her.

Discordant noise came out of Torni's mouth then she inhaled deeply.

"It was him." The words were tinny, disjointed. The embers faded away, leaving Torni's body looking like a fire-ravaged tree trunk. "The General, he…he's here. Angry. Felt him through the gestalt."

Torni slapped a palm against the omnium cube and her body restored itself.

Lafayette's arm beeped. He twisted his hand over and Ibarra's hologram appeared.

"What happened?" Ibarra asked.

"The General. His presence is…affecting me," Torni said. "I can finish the device—don't worry. Just give me a minute."

"If he is here, we can kill him," Lafayette said.

"Do you know how to kill a photonic being, Mr. Karigole? According to Torni, that thing's been around since the Xaros first hit the galaxy thousands of years ago and survived the passage from their home galaxy," Ibarra said.

Torni tapped the base of her palm against the side of her head.

"If only we knew someone who was an expert in immortality," she deadpanned.

Ibarra and Lafayette glanced at each other. Ibarra pointed to an empty bench and waved his hand. A hologram of Malal appeared. The ancient being sat with his head lolled to the side, like he'd been turned off.

"Malal," Ibarra said, "when you spoke with Stacey,

you mentioned you rejected the photonic form used by the General. Why?"

Malal's head cranked upright and locked in place.

"Irrelevant to my purpose here," Malal said.

"If the Xaros manage to overrun Earth, you'll be the General's problem, not ours," Ibarra said, "so you tell us how to kill it and maybe we'll survive long enough to get to your bigger picture."

One side of Malal's mouth pulled aside, distending and revealing sharp teeth of an impossibly wide jawline.

"The conversion to photonic existence is simple," Malal said. "A consciousness can be maintained for eons with minimal degradation, so long as the containment vessel is stable. I rejected that path. The possibility of death means the certainty of death. My peers were jealous of my work and accomplishments. They would have found a way to destroy me. I opted for godhood, not immortality."

"That's not helping us," Torni said.

"You can disrupt his photonic matrix, dissolve his consciousness," Malal said. "It won't be so simple as broadcasting an interference pattern. You'll have to break through his armor and broadcast a discordant—"

"How!" Ibarra shouted.

"With this." Malal's chest morphed into a diagram

of a blade with inlaid circuitry. Torni looked over the schematics. She could fabricate the weapon from omnium easily enough.

"Or…you can release me," Malal said. "I'm weak now, but with enough strength I—"

Ibarra drew a hand across his throat and Malal's hologram vanished.

"Not no, but hell no," Ibarra said.

"And why not?" Lafayette asked. "When the Karigole plan operations, all viable options must be discussed and decided on. Not rejected out of hand. I am aware of the impact Malal had against the Xaros when Stacey released him during the operation to his vault. He has the potential to turn the tide of this battle."

"Let me tell you a children's story," Ibarra said. "Once upon a time there was a scorpion sitting on a riverbank that wanted to cross the river. He went to a frog and asked to stand on the frog's back while it swam to the other end.

"The frog said, 'No, scorpions sting frogs. I can't trust you.'

"'But Mr. Frog,' the scorpion said, 'if I sting you, then I'll drown. I'd never do that.'

"So the frog agrees and takes the scorpion onto his back. Halfway across the river, the scorpion stung the

227

frog.

"'Why?' asked the frog. 'I am poisoned and you will surely drown. We're both dead.'

"'Because I am a scorpion. Scorpions sting frogs. It is our nature.'

"Right now," Ibarra's tone changed as the story ended, "Malal is weak, still running off the fumes from the Shanishol he consumed I don't even know how long ago. He needs to be stronger to fight the General and the entire armada of drones. He thrives on sentient life. Where do you think he's going to get that strength?"

"Earth," Torni said, "all the people we've got down there."

"And what do you think he'll do once he's back to his godlike strength after draining the life out of hundreds of millions of people? Even if he does beat the Xaros for us, he won't stop there," Ibarra said. "He'll keep the proccie tubes on full production until he's ready to go after the 'peers' that left him behind. Malal is a tiger, and we've got him by the tail. We cannot let go."

"What is a tiger?" Lafayette asked. "I assume a frog is some manner of—"

"We are not going to let him loose," Ibarra said. "We didn't take the Toth's offer of handing over our people in exchange for some of us surviving. I sure as hell am not going to trust Malal more than the Toth. I sacrificed billions for a chance at survival once before. The Xaros were inevitable, already on the way to Earth. What I did was the only path forward. Now…we can still win this fight without having to put our trust in some alien savior."

Lafayette frowned.

"Not you, Lafayette," Ibarra said. "I mean, yes, you're an alien that we're trusting. But the whole kit and caboodle doesn't depend on you alone. We trust Malal and we might as well leave the fox in charge of the hen house."

"I agree with you," Lafayette said. "I was on the vessel that brought the Shanishol to Anthalas. I did not see the carnage on the surface, but I saw the results of Malal's plans."

"Then why did you even suggest letting him loose?" Torni asked.

"Discussing a plan does not mean I endorse it. Allow me some Karigole foibles. I can't help who I am," Lafayette said.

"The weapons? How long until you can make them?" Ibarra asked.

Torni scooped omnium up from the cube with both hands and spread her arms wide. The omnium stretched from her fingertips and spun slowly, forming the shape of a blade.

"A few minutes," she said, "but it will be long, and heavy. I don't know who can wield this with any amount of skill or effectiveness."

"Make me one and get back to fabricating the second device. I'll replicate more blades through the omnium reactor. As for who's going to kill the General, I have the right people in mind," Ibarra said

CHAPTER 17

Elias stabbed his fingers into a crack on a drone's surface and ripped it in half. He sprayed fire from his rotary cannon at a dozen drones attempting to combine into a walker. The drones burst apart as black smoke from their decaying mass joined the red wind sweeping through the battle.

"Elias, this is Carius. What's your status?" came over the radio.

"Busy." Elias smashed a heel against a drone attempting to fly past him and crushed it against a boulder.

"I'm sending an extraction for you and your armor. It'll get to the Breitenfeld, *and she'll take you back to Earth,"* Carius said.

"Plenty of fight here. Don't think Valdar wants me on his ship." Elias fired at moving shadows through the sand storm.

"Not a request, son. Now clear an LZ. Got a big horse coming for you in one minute."

Elias backed up until he made contact with Bodel. Caas and Ar'ri found their way over and the four formed a circle, weapons facing outward. The Xaros they'd been fighting were nothing but burning fragments.

"What's going on?" Caas asked.

"Extraction incoming," Elias said. *"Breit*'s taking us to Earth. Didn't get anything more than that."

Running lights on a Destrier transport filled the sky overhead, diffusing through the fine sand blowing around them into a wide glow.

"Any word from White platoon?" Bodel asked.

"Nothing." Elias looked up and saw the Destrier's rear ramp lowering.

****

Valdar squeezed his eyes shut as the blinding light of wormhole transit assaulted his senses. His head felt like a vice was tightening against his temples and the scars of old war wounds burned like hot wires.

He hated his ship's jump engines. Hated them with the passion of a burning sun but he could never share this with his crew. He'd earned his sea legs in the blue water navy; he'd never had the desire to become a spacer until the navy forced him into it.

The pain faded away as the blinding light lessened.

Valdar shook his head to regain focus and looked out the front screens on his bridge. The *Breitenfeld* was in orbit over Mars, and tiny flashes of distant explosions sparkled through the atmosphere. Gossamer-thin clouds stretched out around the ship.

"We're in the upper edge of the atmosphere," Ensign Geller said. "Not as bad as Takeni but I'll get us clear."

Columns of black smoke rose from mountain ranges like they were smoldering volcanoes.

"Comms," Valdar said, pulling up a data slate from his armrest, "get me contact with Admiral—"

The bridge trembled as a shadow swept over them. A carrier larger than the *Breitenfeld* flew past the prow, smoke and fire burning from dozens of tears in the hull. The dying ship rolled to its side and corkscrewed into a final descent.

"Valdar!" Admiral Garret's face appeared on the data slate. The man looked ten years older than the last time they'd seen each other face-to-face. Sweat ran down his face and blood stained the left side of his head. Garret wore an emergency void helmet, not the armored combat helmet he should have donned before a battle.

"*Breitenfeld* here as ordered. Where do you want my guns?"

"Earth. You're to rendezvous with our remaining *Manticore* frigates over Mount Olympus, take on whatever armor can reach you and jump back to Earth as soon as your engines have the charge."

Valdar glanced at Levin, his chief engineer.

"Twenty-two minutes to open a wormhole to the Crucible. Longer if we've got to take more ships with us," Levin said.

"I monitored." Garret's face jerked from side to side, the reflection of a chaotic holo screen against his faceplate. "Looks like you'll have fifteen—fourteen now—frigates with you. We'll hold the Xaros off until you're away. I'm taking the rest of your task force away from you to hold the line here."

Valdar felt his ship shift as Geller set the *Breitenfeld* toward Olympus.

"Aye aye, sir, but if the *Breitenfeld* can make a difference to this fight why are—"

"Earth is on the brink, Isaac," Garret said. "Luna has fallen. Xaros are pressing on the Crucible and if we lose that station, they'll bring in reinforcements and it'll all be over but the screaming."

A flash of yellow light hit the right side of Garret's face.

"Believe it or not, we're holding our own up here," the admiral said. "Get your ass to Earth and win that fight. I'm counting on you for another miracle, Valdar. You haven't disappointed me yet. Garret out."

"The rest of our flotilla is moving to join with Mars fleet," Ericcson said. "The *Chimera* and *Argus* are waiting for us at the rendezvous point the admiral sent us…rest of the frigates are no more than fifteen minutes away. Also tracking several transports coming up from Mars."

"Tell the flight deck to prep for pass-through traffic." Valdar swiped across his data slate and looked over the battle. More than half the Mars fleet was lost, locked in a knife fight with Xaros constructs. Valdar had a hard time believing the admiral's assessment of the battle.

Valdar swiped to the next data feed from Earth. The information wasn't real-time, and whatever battle he planned to fight wouldn't be there when he arrived.

Valdar looked over the Xaros forces assaulting the Crucible…and picked up a stylus.

CHAPTER 18

The Destrier flew through the *Breitenfeld*'s aft hangar entrance and set down once it had enough real estate to land on. The rest of the flight deck was full of armor soldiers. Eagles packed the sides of the flight line. Nearly a hundred suits filled the deck, grouped in packs of three to twelve. Most bore scars across their armor; others were missing arms, legs, and even a few lacked their helms.

The Destrier opened its forward ramp and Elias took a step down then froze in place. He hadn't seen so many armor since the Second Battle of Brisbane where the combined armor of the entire Atlantic Union destroyed the Chinese People's Army III Corps and saved the city from falling to the invaders.

Every last suit of armor was looking right at Elias.

Elias thumped his fist against his chest in salute.

The armor returned the salute with a ripple of metal-on-metal bangs.

"Elias, 'bout time you got here." Carius walked up the ramp in his deep gray armor with black bands around the shoulder plates. He lifted a thick chain bound to the General's damaged faceplate and placed it over Elias' helm. A cam bot flew up the ramp and panned over Elias.

"You've got an admirer, my boy. Not the kind that sends fan letters. This…General is on Mars and he's been head-hunting armor," Carius said. "Took out an entire squadron at Gradivus cannon." The colonel's helm shook from side to side. "We're pretty sure he's looking for you."

"Then why am I not on Mars looking for him?" Elias asked.

"We've learned a little about the Xaros leadership from that Torni friend of yours. Seems the alien bigwigs aren't above pride and vengeance. We're going to use that to our advantage—get the General to come chase you to Earth, take some of the pressure off Mars," Carius said.

"Send us back. I ripped his face off once. I can do it again," Elias said.

"You'll get your chance. Right now we need to set the trap and you're the bait. Hope you don't mind," Carius said. "Now smile to the camera. We're about to broadcast

237

this across the solar system."

Elias looked straight into the cam bot. He held up the General's mask and leaned toward the camera.

"I want the rest of you."

****

Ibarra paced back and forth across the Crucible's command center. He'd returned to this old habit once the Xaros entered the outer solar system. His holographic feet couldn't wear a rut in the deck, and they never grew sore or tired. There were a few advantages to having his consciousness live on inside the Alliance probe, but he had no fist to smash against anything when the desire arose.

"Jimmy, what's our status?" he asked the probe in the center of the domed room.

The probe's answer was a flat holo screen showing the Crucible, surrounded by nearly a hundred ships of the line. Point defense cannons sparred with swarms of drones trying to slip through the defenders.

A few drones had made it through, only to be destroyed by the doughboy and Marine defenders manning small bunkers atop the many control nodes and inside the long hallways running through the conjoined thorns making up the Crucible.

The probe didn't answer with words. All but a sliver of its computing power worked to stymie the Xaros trying to regain control of their nearly complete jump gate. The hacking attempts started once the leading Xaros forces reached a few light-minutes from Earth. The Xaros managed to throw off the Crucible from sending more graviton bombs, but the probe could control the quantum field within the great crown of thorns to keep the door open for the *Breitenfeld*…or reinforcements from the Alliance.

Where are they, Stacey?

Ibarra zoomed out from the Crucible. An enormous mass of Xaros drones lay between Ceres and Earth. Constructs the size of strike cruisers and great murmurations of drones stood guard between the fleet protecting the Crucible and humanity's home. Another, smaller force of Xaros waited in the void beyond Ceres' orbit…waiting for the defenders to make a mistake.

If the fleet guarding the Crucible made for Earth, it would be mauled by the cruiser-sized constructs and the waiting Xaros would swoop in and take the Crucible. If the Xaros assaulted the Crucible, the defenses in the void around the jump gate and built into Earth's second moon would defeat the attackers.

The standoff had held for hours, and Ibarra

wasn't sure how much longer the human defenders could maintain their patience.

"Crucible, this is Captain Gor'al on the *Vorpal*." The Dotok's face came up on the holoscreen. "Earth command reports that we just lost the orbital over Guam. Ground stations across the Pacific Rim are sending me...I don't know what this is."

A camera feed from Okinawa came up. A great dark swell of drones poured through the atmosphere, skirting the fire from the remaining orbital batteries in low orbit.

"Not again..." Ibarra shook his head.

"What 'not again,' Ibarra?" Gor'al asked.

"They're forming an extinction arch," Ibarra said. "The Alliance has seen it on many worlds, and I saw it up close and personal when Earth fell. Watch."

The drones pressed together, melding into a slight curve that grew to over a hundred miles in length within minutes. The arch in the storm clouds rolled over Okinawa. Sharp points grew out of the bottom like a predator's teeth. Red energy grew from each tip. The camera feed cut out in a wave of light and static.

"The Xaros will move the arch over populated areas. They'll carve mountains apart to get at us," Ibarra said. He switched to feeds from the surviving platforms and watched as the arch drifted north. "It moves slowly, but we'll lose all of Japan in hours."

Drones broke away from the Xaros blocking fleet and flew toward the extinction arch.

"The orbitals might put a dent in that thing," Gor'al said as his eyes widened with a realization. "Earth's mobile defense is gone…if we don't break station from the Crucible, it'll hit the Himalayas, the Ural line, the Alps. Everything. Everyone on Earth will die if we don't stop it."

"Hold your station, Captain. We get taunted off the Crucible and *everyone* will die when the Xaros come pouring through from a wormhole that's got billions more drones just waiting to join the fight," Ibarra said. He ran through a least-time projection on the annihilation arch's path across Earth's fortresses…eighty-two hours. Much less if the Xaros made another massive breach in the orbital defenses and created another such construct.

"Your people are dying, Ibarra! We're sitting on our nests watching it happen." Gor'al's face pressed closer to his camera. "There are hundreds of thousands of drones loose on Earth's surface in addition to this arch of theirs. You didn't go through all the trouble to rebuild humanity and rescue the Dotok to bring them here and just let it get washed away now."

Ibarra resisted the urge to lash out. Earth was teetering under the current assault, and the next wave of drones—a wave nearly twice the size of the force laying siege to Earth—was due to reach the planet in mere hours. He could handle that problem, but only if Lafayette and his team completed their project…and if Gor'al didn't throw away the strategic situation Ibarra needed to make his plan work.

I made everything work when I could lie and obfuscate. Telling the truth is an enormous pain in the ass, he thought.

"Help is on the way, Captain. Either the Alliance will send reinforcements or—" The Crucible shifted around as the probe readied a wormhole.

"There, see? Just had to be patient." Ibarra closed the channel and swiped his hand over the screen to see a white field blossoming within the Crucible.

"What've we got, Jimmy?" he asked the probe. "Alliance to turn this fight around or the *Breitenfeld* to spit in the wind?"

The strike carrier ripped through the wormhole and streaked away like a bat out of hell. Ibarra instinctually ducked behind a workstation and watched as Captain Valdar's ship raced toward the fleet blocking her path to Earth.

"What in the hell is he doing?" Ibarra turned his

face away as the Xaros battleships struck at the *Breitenfeld*, carving fissures across her hull as she bore down on the aliens. The *Breitenfeld's* rail cannon batteries flashed as she zipped past, striking Xaros ships on either side with quadrium munitions.

Lightning chained from one ship to the others, burning hundreds of drones out of existence.

The *Breitenfeld* continued toward Earth, engines flaring to guide her into high orbit.

Frigates leapt out of the wormhole, each with the same insane velocity as the *Breitenfeld*. The Toth energy cannons fired and pummeled the disabled Xaros battleships. The *Manticore frigates* pounded the Xaros, cracking their hulls and blasting them to pieces. A battleship cracked in half, burning from within. The rest of the Xaros fleet was nothing but expanding ash within minutes.

"Valdar?" Ibarra blinked hard, unsure what he'd just seen.

"Ibarra, what the hell is that over Japan?" the *Breitenfeld's* captain asked.

"Your next problem. There are two million fighting beneath those mountains. They've got less than an hour before the extinction arch that wiped out Okinawa reaches them," Ibarra said.

"Are you aware of the next wave of Xaros coming toward Luna?" Valdar asked.

"I'll worry about that. You worry about Japan." Ibarra glanced at the ceiling. "Wait, do you have Elias with you?"

CHAPTER 19

The sled rose through a reddish-brown haze. Dust and flakes of rock spewed out of the Xaros tunnel and hit Hale's visor with a *tink*. He shifted his feet against the soles of his boots, testing that the mag lock to the sled still held.

His Marines knelt against the bed, each maintaining several points of mag-locked contact with the sled.

The *Scipio* lay ahead, the automated distress call from one of its drop pods pulsing through his comms. The Morse SOS signal came and went every few minutes, never broadcasting too long.

Hale zoomed in on the corvette. She bore scorch marks over her hull and two of her maneuver engines were mangled. The ship's shuttle bay door was open, but Hale couldn't make out anything inside.

"Cutting the anti-grav," Egan said. "We'll coast the rest of the way."

"Not to be needy, but I've got eighteen minutes before I suffocate," Drebin said.

"We'll be there in five. If I try to rush, we'll overshoot, then this canoe is way up shit creek and I don't see any paddles," Egan said.

"Sir," Jacobs spoke to Hale, Steuben and Mathias on a private channel, "do you…do any of your Marines know how to work a corvette?"

"We all have basic damage control training. You?" Hale asked.

"Nothing," Jacobs said.

"Same," Mathias said.

"Adapt and overcome, Marines. Adapt and overcome," Hale said. He looked at Steuben, waiting for an answer.

"I am a warrior, not an engineer," the Karigole said. "If Lafayette were here, I would have no concerns with your plan."

"Wait, you have concerns?" Hale asked.

"The ship is unpowered and in a degrading orbit. It will crash within a few hours."

"Why didn't you mention this observation before

246

we loaded up and broke atmo?" Hale asked.

"You still would have taken this chance. My observation would have made no difference."

"Steuben. My XO. The next time you see the chance for catastrophic failure, speak up," Hale said.

"As you wish," Steuben shrugged.

"Almost there." Egan touched the controls and the sled jerked beneath Hale. "What do you think, sir? Shuttle bay or the Xaros-made entrance across the rail gun battery?"

"Shuttle bay. Can you get us inside or do we need to float in?"

"I can land it." Egan maneuvered the sled to outside the shuttle bay.

Inside, a wrecked Mule lay crumpled against the inner bulkhead. The shuttle bay was tiny, with barely enough room for a single Mule, compared to the stem-to-stern flight deck of the *Breitenfeld*. Blackened streaks scarred the inner walls.

"Looks like there was one hell of a fight," Orozco said.

"Shh!" Egan edged the sled over to line up with the shuttle bay deck and inched the sled inside. Once the rear of the sled had cleared the threshold, Egan set it down with a thump heavy enough to jar Hale's teeth.

"And the Canadian judge takes off a point for the landing," Standish said.

"You can walk away from it, can't you?" Egan stepped away from the controls.

A pair of Marines jumped off and went to the sealed double doors leading to the rest of the ship. When the control panel failed to function, they unsnapped the manual locks in the door frame and twisted the circular handles, the dogs, and slowly opened the doors.

"Mathias," Hale said, pointing at the lieutenant, "see if the atmo chamber in the Mule is still functional. Stuff Drebin in there until we've got the rest of the ship up and running, then get the blast doors secure. Jacobs, find the source of that distress call. I'm going to the bridge."

Hale got off the sled and locked his boots to the deck. He felt the ship creak beneath him. Pluto twisted slowly outside the shuttle bay as the ship rolled over.

I've got thirteen Marines counting on me, Hale thought. *This had better work.*

****

Jacobs grabbed a broken crossbar and shoved it out of her way. The deck was a mess of wrecked framework and broken bulkheads. Sparking electrical wires and fractured pipes floated in the weightless passageway. Lumps of ice bounced off her armor as she stepped over a rent in the flooring caused by a Xaros beam.

"We're going to have to seal off this whole section if we want to walk around in the ship's atmo," Weiss said.

"You volunteering for that detail?" Niles asked.

"Heck yeah, you think I want to stay buttoned up in my armor for the next three weeks until the fleet can get something out here? I'm getting a rash just thinking about it," Weiss said.

Jacobs pushed aside a large piece of broken hull and found an oval-shaped hatch to an escape pod. A metal spar was impaled against the door frame. She leaned over and knocked on the door's glass porthole. She looked inside and saw another human face staring at her.

The woman inside opened her mouth and raised her arms, cheering. Jacobs saw high fives exchanged with other occupants in the escape pod.

"Ship must have taken a direct hit when they were getting ready to punch out." Weiss pushed away a floating hull plate and stuck his head into a compartment open to the void. "Pod got jammed in the shoot."

Niles flicked his finger against the spar embedded in the frame.

"Well, there's your problem." The Marine took a

cutting torch off his belt and activated a white-hot plasma cutter.

****

The *Scipio*'s bridge was silent. Restraint buckles floated in vacuum, tugging against acceleration seats. Stars rolled over through the forward view ports that wrapped across three-quarters of the bridge.

The hatch at the rear of the bridge swung open. Standish and Egan stepped inside, weapons up and ready.

"Clear," Standish said. He tapped on the control panel of a circular holo table. "No power up here either."

Hale followed them in and went to the helmsman's station. He grabbed the control sticks and whipped them back and forth. The corvette continued its slow, dying ballet around Pluto.

"Damn it," Hale said.

"Captain Hale?" Jacobs said through the IR. *"We found the source of the distress call. Escape pod never made it off the ship. We got the crewmen out, at least."*

"Does the senior sailor have comms?" Hale asked.

"Petty Officer Tagawa here, sir," a woman said. *"Myself and two other sailors really appreciate you getting us out of that death locker."*

"Tagawa, what's your job on this ship?"

"Supply, sir."

Hale slapped the palm of his hand against his visor.

"Can any of you get the *Scipio* back online?" Hale asked.

"Engineers Mate Allen and Yeoman Morris will need a look at the battery stacks. We'll do all we can, sir. One more thing…are you the Hale? From the movie?"

"Yes. Now get to work, Tagawa."

"That's never going to happen to me," Standish said. "It'll always be, 'Oh, how'd you end up with Hale? Can you get his autograph for me?' not 'My son has your action figure. Lunch is on me.'"

"Dude, let it go," Egan said.

"I was erased from the historical record, fly boy. I don't have to be happy about it. A man has his pride," Standish said.

Cortaro reached through the hatch and grabbed Standish by the arm.

"A man better get his flapping gums to engineering and help get this ship back online before I take his air tanks away for the good of the team." Cortaro pulled Standish through the door.

****

Hale stood next to the captain's chair, thrumming his fingers against the armrest as Tagawa spoke. The petty officer held a slate with a wire diagram of the *Scipio*, red marks across much of the hull.

"Deck three is sealed off," she said. "I've got the atmo tanks patched to the living quarters and we can move the air scrubbers as soon as we clear a path through gauss cannon B."

"Air and power," Hale said.

"Right…" She tapped her gauntlet. "Allen, what's your status."

"Main conduit yoke got barbequed. Chief Franks could have got it back up in a heartbeat, but his body's down here with me. I got the auxiliary installed. Everything should work once I flip the breakers," Allen said. *"Give me a minute to clear the room. I double-checked everything, but Skippy took a hell of a beating. If there's more damage I haven't found, then I'd rather not be in here at go time."*

"Allen, this is Hale. We've got maybe another hour until our orbit decays past the point of no return. We don't have time to make things perfect. Flip the switch."

"Aye-aye, sir. Stand by and cross your fingers," Allen said.

Hale opened a wide IR channel. "All units, we're about to jump-start the ship. Make ready."

Lights and workstations came to life. Screens filled with static.

"Hey, there we go," Mathias said.

The power snapped off.

"Son of a bitch." Mathias banged a fist against the bulkhead.

The bridge came to life again. Power held steady for several seconds. Hale held a finger up to Mathias before he could speak again.

"Allen, how we looking?" Hale asked.

"Minor fire. Very minor. Got it taken care of. Should have power back to the engines in a few more minutes. We can re-pressurize parts of the ship, if you want."

"Drebin is still in the Mule's atmo-box," Mathias said.

"Engines are the priority," Hale said to Cortaro and Tagawa. "Life support after."

"We're on it," Cortaro said.

"Egan, can you get us a link with Earth?" Hale asked.

Egan leaned over the comm station and examined the displays. "Antennae showing green across the board. Give me a few minutes."

"Great, after we've got positive comms, I need you to fly this thing." Hale pointed to the helmsman's station.

"This is a bit bigger than a Mule, sir," Egan said.

"Orozco is our other trained pilot," Hale deadpanned.

"Can be done! Absolutely can do, sir." Egan ran a wire from the comm array to his gauntlet. "Lot of traffic coming through the Mars repeater…Jesus, the Xaros are already there."

"What about Earth?" Hale asked.

Egan tapped on a keyboard. "Civil defense net is lit up like a Christmas tree. Hard to tell. Hold on, we're getting a data packet…that's taking over my work station."

"*Scipio*, this is the Crucible. Stand by for instructions," Ibarra's voice came through every IR channel on the ship. Screens across the bridge switch to show the same image; Abaddon.

"To the senior ranking officer of whoever's mucking around the *Scipio*. You are hereby ordered to destroy Abaddon immediately,"

"Is he crazy?" Tagawa asked. "She's barely holding together with duct tape and hope and he wants us to *destroy* a moon?"

The screens zoomed toward Abaddon and passed

254

through the outer shell. A dome appeared. Several red arrows popped up on the screen, all pointing to the dome within Abaddon.

"There is a Xaros conduit, a connection to the rest of their network, somewhere inside that thing," Ibarra said. "Shoot it. Blow it up. Slice it into ribbons. I don't care how you do it. Take it off line permanently it will trap the Xaros general in our solar system. Do that, and we've got a chance to kill him once and for all."

Hale suddenly wished Elias had come on this mission.

"Don't wait twelve hours for your questions to be answered," Ibarra said, "get moving right now."

The screens went black.

"Message repeats after that," Egan said. "They must have been broadcasting on a loop."

"Sir? What're we going to do?" Mathias asked.

"No rest for the weary. Sitting around waiting to be rescued isn't what strike Marines were made for, especially not when we can do something useful. We're going in," Hale said.

****

Hale removed his helmet and took a deep breath

of ozone-tinted air. He set the helmet on a hook on the side of the captain's chair and flipped up a control screen. He looked over the dazzling array of data points coming through to him and frowned.

"How do the squids keep all this straight?" he asked.

"Sir?" Tagawa asked from a forward workstation.

"Nothing. What are you looking at over there?"

"System status," she said. "We're leaking air from several compartments…sending locations to Cortaro now. Two point defense turrets are manned and online. Main gun is down, obviously. Both forward torpedo bays are offline, same with the starboard tube. Port tube was destroyed."

The lights overhead flickered.

"What is working?" Hale asked.

"Atmo scrubbers and tanks are functional, barely. Main drive is still online. Same with maneuver thrusters. And the automated galley is still up and running. Later tonight we can all have tacos," Tagawa said.

"Egan, get us moving," Hale said.

"I would, sir." Egan tapped on a blank screen. "But—"

"Inertial navigation is down," Tagawa said.

"Point us at the giant alien space station and hit

the gas," Hale said.

"Roger, sir."

The ship shuddered. The view out the front view ports stabilized. Egan steered the ship to Abaddon and held her course steady.

There was a groan of metal and a snap that shook Hale's chair.

"What was that?" he asked.

"Number four engine came loose," Tagawa said. "It wasn't functioning to begin with. We're still good."

"What am I looking for once we get to Abaddon?" Egan asked.

"Open portal on the surface," Hale said. "According to Torni, the conduit should be in the very center. Tagawa, are there any explosives on this ship?"

"There were eight breach charges in the storage locker on deck four," she said. "We fired off all our torpedoes during the assault on the Grinder…wait. The torpedo in tube three failed to launch."

"Can we still fire it?" Hale asked.

"No, the exit port is slag."

"Then can we cut through the ship and dig out the warhead?" Jacobs asked.

"That's…possible," Tagawa said. "Allen knows that part of the ship. I'll get him on it. Egan, we'll need you to fly steady."

"No bouncing around while you do a cesarean section on our torpedo baby. Got it," Egan said.

Abaddon loomed larger through the windows.

CHAPTER 20

Elias held onto a heavy ring bolted to the side of the Destrier as it entered Earth's upper atmosphere. Bodel stood next to him, Caas and Ar'ri behind. They rocked slightly through turbulence, the only passengers inside the heavy transport.

"I don't understand why the colonel is spreading the armor across the planet," Ar'ri said. "If that General is really after Elias, then why don't we make him fight all of us at the same time?"

"He knows exactly where I am and he'll come in full force," Elias said. "The maniple that broke off from Mars is too strong for any one fortification. The armor will be fighting in every city. He either spreads out trying to find me or waits in the void, taking a beating from the orbitals."

"We won't bombard our own positions," Bodel said. "The safest place for his drones is right on top of the city."

"So we want to get into a close fight around the cities? Wouldn't that put the civilians at risk?" Caas asked. "Every Dotok is inside a bunker cut into Mauna Loa right now. I'd rather beat the Xaros in orbit."

"There are too many to beat in a fleet engagement," Elias said. "We make them spread out over Earth. Divide and conquer. The cities are ready for a siege. They can hold until reinforcements come through the Crucible. Then we defeat them in detail."

"One of the first things Colonel Carius taught us was to never depend on the enemy doing what you want him to do," Caas said. "He referenced the human deity named Murphy, who confounds all plans."

"He taught us to have a plan. Fight your plan. Adapt as soon as the plan doesn't fit the situation," Bodel said. "He never mentioned that to you?"

"This seems contradictory," Ar'ri said. "Have a plan…but you don't have to follow the plan."

The Destrier rocked slightly.

Elias turned around and pointed a finger at Ar'ri. "There's something you've got to learn, bean head. War is—"

260

A crimson beam burst through the floor and out the top of the transport ship. The beam swiped to the side, cutting through the hull. The Destrier ripped in two with a screech of metal and a howl of wind as freezing cold air blasted through the cargo bay. The forward section corkscrewed away, lost from view as the rear half of the ship with the armor tipped over and went into free fall.

Elias saw nothing but clouds through the half-severed opening behind him. His altimeter was dropping fast.

"This is the god Murphy at work," Caas said.

"Jump. Use your packs to slow once you're close to the ground." Elias released his mag locks on the broken section of the transport and pulled against the handle to launch himself into the open air.

"We never trained for this!" Ar'ri said as he came out of the tail section.

"You have the rest of your life to figure it out." Bodel keyed his jet pack and put some distance between him and Elias.

Elias looked down. Desert stretched beneath his feet, and he made out the highways surrounding Phoenix. Elias swung his head down and fell toward Earth even faster.

"You'll reach terminal velocity in seconds," Elias

said. "Lock and load. The drone that killed the transport is still around."

"Contact!" Caas shouted. "Drones to the…the—" She said something in Dotok and fired her forearm cannons. Elias followed the rounds' path and saw ten dark points against the sky.

"Take 'em out." Elias swung upright and put a hand over the top of his cannons, pressing down as he fired. The recoil bucked him backwards and sent his feet tumbling past his head. He activated his jet pack and stabilized his fall.

The battery levels on his jet pack decreased far more than was comfortable. He needed most of the charge to keep him from splattering across the Arizona landscape. He could use the jet pack for maybe a few more seconds and still survive the landing.

Short bursts from the other armor streaked toward the approaching Xaros.

A Xaros beam snapped past Elias. He twisted to the side and felt the next beam singe his chest. He let off a burst and saw one of the drones explode into a cloud of fragments.

The drones sped up, stalks splayed out like the business end of a trident, heading right for the falling armor.

"Move!" Elias fired his jet pack and zoomed out of the way, nailing two drones as they tore through the air he'd just occupied.

There was a bright yellow light as Ar'ri burned his jet pack at full strength. His rotary cannon opened up and made quick work of the remaining drones.

"Got 'em!" Ar'ri said.

Elias twisted his body and tried to glide beneath the Dotok armor who was now many yards overhead, but Elias' armor had the aerodynamic properties of a brick and barely moved.

"Ar'ri, how much charge do you have left?" Elias asked.

"Four…percent," Ar'ri said. Elias could almost see the young man's face as he realized that he had just saved his fellow armor but doomed himself to a landing he couldn't survive. Ar'ri's arms and legs flailed about as panic set in.

"Ar'ri, listen to me." Elias glanced around and saw Caas close by, Bodel too far to matter. "Calm down and go flat. Your sister and I will be right there." Elias pointed to Caas, saw her nod, then pointed to Ar'ri. Elias pointed his feet at the ground and fired his jet pack. He slowed his fall and got to Ar'ri. He grabbed Ar'ri by the waist and mag-locked his hands to the Dotok.

"Clamp on. Caas?" The other Dotok came toward them too quickly. Elias twisted himself and Ar'ri around, missing her as she sped past.

"Sorry!" Caas shouted.

"The ground is coming very fast," Ar'ri said.

Elias didn't bother to check the altimeter. His maneuver would save, or kill, them all.

He reached up and grabbed Caas' hand. He pulled her in and she wrapped her arms over her brother's shoulder.

"Caas, fire your pack—don't let up—on my mark." Elias glanced down and made out bushes and large rocks against the slope of a mountain directly beneath them.

Here goes nothing.

"Mark!" Elias activated his pack and felt his true body thump against his womb as the fall of three armor soldiers slowed considerably. They came down over a saddle extending away from the mountain and the combined force of Elias' and Caas' jet packs brought them to a complete stop…thirty feet over the ground.

Caas' jet pack ran dry and Elias cut his to stop them from spinning out.

Caas and Ar'ri screamed in fright as they went into free fall. Elias put a hand against Caas and shoved her away.

Elias tried to twist around to take the fall on his feet and hit on his back. He felt his jet pack crumple beneath the impact and went down the slope of the hill. He and Ar'ri rolled like an out-of-control barrel until a boulder brought them to a jarring halt.

Damage icons flashed against Elias' vision, but none too severe.

He tried to get up, but Ar'ri had his helm buried against Elias' chest and arms wrapped around him.

"Ar'ri. Let go." Elias thumped a fist against Ar'ri's back.

Ar'ri's helm shot up. He crawled away and got to his feet.

"You saved me," Ar'ri said.

"So did your sister." Elias looked back and found Caas sliding down the side of the hill.

"All three of us could have died…because I was an idiot. Burned through my thrusters."

"If this is the worst thing that happens to us today we're damned lucky." Elias turned and saw Phoenix in the distance. "You can feel bad later."

He detached his jet pack and let it fall to the ground without ceremony.

Bodel landed nearby, his feet hitting the ground so

smoothly it was almost as if he was coming down a flight of stairs.

"I watched your landing," Bodel said, "smooth."

"We Dotok have a saying." Caas came to a stop on a cloud of dirt and loose rocks. "'Any landing you can talk about, you can brag about.'"

"So that's Phoenix?" Ar'ri asked. "I thought it would be bigger."

"One day I will ask Ibarra why he chose this sweltering hell hole as his headquarters," Bodel said, "and not some beautiful place like Berlin or Munich."

Elias unlimbered his treads and drove off, the rest following close behind.

CHAPTER 21

The *Scipio* flew to an open portal the size of a battlecruiser and slowed to a stop. Nothing but darkness greeted the human ship.

On the bridge, Hale tried and failed to navigate the data filter options on his command screen.

"Egan, Tagawa, what's in there?" he asked.

"Nothing on sensors," Tagawa said. "Want me to risk a radar pulse?"

"Not yet," Hale said.

"Setting screens to IR," Jacobs said. The image through the windows changed to a heat scale. Just beyond the opening, a rocky column more than twice the width of the *Scipio* extended from the inner surface and into the center of the sphere.

"Looks like we've got a path," Egan said.

"Go. Keep us close to it," Hale said. He opened up a ship-wide channel. "Point defense teams, you are cleared to engage any Xaros you encounter. Stay alert."

As the ship crossed into Abaddon, a slight shudder went through it. Egan put the pillar to the starboard side and increased the ship's speed.

"'And I beheld a straight and narrow path, which came along by the rod of iron,'" Jacobs said.

"What?" Hale asked.

"Sorry, sir. Something from scripture," she said.

"I can see maybe ten seconds ahead with the infrared," Egan said. "After that, there's just nothing."

"Makarov had some idea about this," Jacobs said. "From the notes recovered off the *Midway*, she thought the Xaros had carved up a dwarf planet or Kuiper belt object from the outer orbit of Barnard's Star. The enemy would convert the mass to drones on the way over. Looks like they did just that."

"I saw the estimates on the force moving to Mars," Hale said. "If they converted this whole thing to drones...where are the rest?"

"Eighth Fleet wrecked Abaddon's propulsion rings. The drones had to burn themselves out to get this thing to our solar system. The graviton mines her fleet set up made them work that much harder," Jacobs said.

"Makarov gave Earth a fighting chance. I'm glad I got to meet her," Hale said.

"Slowing down," Egan said. "We should be at the center soon, and I don't know if this ship can take a sudden stop."

"You really think the Xaros would leave this place unguarded, sir?" Jacobs asked.

"The Xaros attack in mass," Steuben said. "Overwhelming force always has a lower casualty rate and chance of success for an attacker. Leaving a force to protect a spent asset does not fit their behavior."

"Then why is there something worth blowing up in here?" she asked.

"The only other invasion where that General has shown up was Takeni, right?" Hale looked at Steuben, who nodded. "He must think we don't know about the conduit. He must not know about Torni."

"Torni's alive?" Jacobs and Tagawa asked at the same time.

"Captain Hale," Steuben said, shaking his head, "I am glad you are commissioned in the infantry. You would have made a poor military intelligence officer."

"Got something," Standish said from a point defense turret. *"Big and long something—heh heh—at our ten o'clock, mark two."*

An image of a section of another rocky column popped up on Hale's visor, angled downward. Hale mentally traced its course.

"It'll intersect with the pillar we're following," Hale said. "We must be close."

"Slowing," Egan said.

A minute later, the column ran into a basalt-colored orb the size of a stadium. Thick columns of rock spoked off the surface in many directions.

"This is the place." Hale unbuckled from the command chair and got to his feet. "I don't see an entrance, but it looks like the same material the Crucible is made out of. We can cut through that."

"I will lead the assault team," Steuben said. "We will bring the warhead inside the structure and set it for remote detonation. The explosive should suffice."

"No, I will—"

"You are the commander of this vessel, Hale. I am XO. I am to do all duties you do not wish to do or have time to do and you do not have time to heal your arm." Steuben gave Hale a curt nod and walked off the bridge.

"Sir," Jacobs said as she unsnapped her restraints, "permission to—"

"Go." Hale sat back in the command chair, looked at his injured arm, and hated himself for sending others into danger he wasn't able to share.

****

Cortaro landed on the basalt surface. His boots scraped against the rock, gouging out bits of rock as he slowed to a stop. He tested his footing. The command center felt spongy, almost soft beneath his feet.

"That's different," he said.

"Coming in." Jacobs touched down a yard away, her feet slipping and shooting out from under her. Cortaro snapped his hand out and caught the lieutenant before she could go flying into the abyss.

"Careful, ma'am," he said.

The sky was lightless. Rock pillars extended from the command center and vanished in the inky dark. A sense of absolute stillness fell over Cortaro. He heard only the sound of his breathing, and felt a growing sense of dread.

"I'll admit it," Jacobs said. "I'm not a fan of this place."

"Let's blow it and get the hell out of here."

Orozco, Yarrow and two Marines from Crimson team landed near them. Yarrow took a breach charge off his belt and strung it across the surface.

"Warhead team," Cortaro said, "get ready. This stuff self-repairs pretty quick. Start moving soon as you see the charge go off."

There was a double click on the IR as the other team acknowledged the order.

Orozco swept his plasma cannon across the sky.

"There's nothing out here," he said. "It's like we're in Satan's belly."

"Fire in the hole." Yarrow unsnapped a detonator switch from the line, stepped away from the charge and clicked the switch three times. Light flared from the breaching charge and a ring of burning gas shot away from the command center as the line burned through the outer layer.

Cortaro felt a slight tremor as the charge cut through the inner hull. The ring of gas died away.

"Partial, damn," Yarrow said from the edge of the burnt hull. "Didn't cut enough to knock our new door free. I need a pick to haul out the section we cut loose."

"No time. I'm doing a body breach." Cortaro jumped up and pulled his knees to his chest to somersault away from the command center. He straightened his body, pointed the soles of his boots at the center of the glowing circle and overcharged the gravity plates. His boots pulled him to the command center far faster than he would have ever fallen on Earth. Cortaro hit the breach, the momentum pushing the severed section into the orb like a champagne cork going the wrong way.

Cortaro released his grip just as he entered the command center. He fell twenty feet and managed to land with his feet and knees together, rolling with his momentum. He swung his plasma rifle off his back and across his new surroundings.

The hull section bounced against a black floor so polished Cortaro could have used it as a mirror. Rows of chest-high workstations like he'd seen on the Crucible radiated away from a plinth in the center of the room. There, in a sparkling column of light, was a set of red armor plates that would have fit a giant.

Something heavy landed behind Cortaro. He swung his rifle around and found Steuben behind him.

"What you did to gain our entry was unusual," the Karigole said. "Teach me."

"Later. Later." Cortaro pointed his rifle to the General's armor. "What about that?"

"That would appear to be the entity the Iron Hearts and Lafayette encountered," Steuben said. "I do not believe the entity is here, as we are not fighting for our lives."

"...*some activity...hurry...*" came over the IR.

"Figures." Cortaro looked up at the hole and waved to the Marines looking through. "Get that bomb in here!"

Weiss pulled a torpedo warhead nearly half his size through the hole. The two floated down on an anti-grav harness wrapped around the device. Weiss landed gracefully and kept control of the warhead like it was a child's balloon.

"First Sergeant! Steuben!" Yarrow yelled from the opening, which was shrinking slowly. Flashes of plasma shot over his head. "We got drones! Get the hell out of there!"

Cortaro grabbed the warhead and pulled it toward the ground. He ripped the harness off and it fell with a metal clang.

"Set the timer. Five minutes," he said to Weiss.

"Is that going to be—" Cortaro slapped Weiss on the side of the head before he could finish. "Yes, First Sergeant!" He opened a panel on the side of the warhead and pecked at keys.

Steuben drew his sword and set his feet in a wide fighting stance.

The light at the center of the room grew slowly. The armor plates shifted against each other.

"Go. I will hold him off," Steuben said.

"You're tough, but you're no Elias." Cortaro aimed his rifle at the base of the dais and let off three shots. The dais fractured, sending hunks of stone bouncing off the workstations. The armor plates clattered to the ground.

Steuben looked at Cortaro and grumbled.

"Weiss?" Cortaro asked.

"Timer set. Can we leave now?" Weiss asked.

"Look." Steuben pointed to the dais, which was slowly reforming. The armor plates leapt off the floor and found their place in the light. Steuben and Cortaro pounded the dais with their rifles, blasting it down to a heap of rubble and scattered armor.

"Let's go." Cortaro backed away, watching as the armor slowly returned to the dais. The first sergeant touched the control panel on the warhead and took a minute off the timer.

Weiss jumped into the air and pushed himself to the shrinking exit with a burst from his anti-grav linings.

Cortaro crouched and keyed his boots to do the same. An error message popped up across his visor telling him his anti-grav linings had just shorted out.

"Ah, damn it." Cortaro looked at the diminishing timer on the warhead.

"Don't worry," Steuben said, grabbing Cortaro by

his belt and shoulder, "we've done this before."

"No! No, Steuben wa—" Steuben yanked Cortaro off his feet and tossed him to the exit like he was a piece of luggage. Cortaro bounced off the side of the hole and went flying into the abyss. A hand grabbed his ankle and slammed him back to the surface.

Cortaro mag-locked a hand to the sphere as plasma bolts flashed overhead.

"What were you doing in there?" Orozco aimed his cannon at a lump rearing up from the surface and hit it twice. Pyrite broke out of the lump and scattered through the void.

A stalk shot up next to Cortaro's face. He pressed his rifle against the base and severed the stalk with a single shot.

"They're coming out of the floor," Cortaro said.

"Welcome to two minutes ago." Orozco ripped shots across another mound that formed like a wave.

Steuben came through the hole and landed. He swung his sword and cut through another stalk growing from the surface.

"We should leave," Steuben said. The Karigole grabbed Cortaro by the waist and jumped toward the *Scipio*. The point defense turrets blasted away at the surface, leaving a narrow corridor for the Marines to return to the ship.

"Captain, bomb is set," Cortaro said. "Had to rush the time table. We've got maybe two minutes before this neighborhood gets even worse."

"Get on board. We're not leaving you out there," Hale said.

Cortaro looked to the command sphere, then to the open shuttle bay on the *Scipio*.

"I don't think we're going to make it," he said.

****

Hale locked the command chair restraints across his chest and slammed his helmet on.

"Egan, get us the hell out of here soon as we've got everyone back on board," Hale said.

"This is turret three," Standish said over the IR. *"I'm down to fifty rounds and I swear every inch of that sphere is about to become a drone."*

Hale looked over the crowded command screen and slammed a fist against the armrest. "Tagawa, how much longer until—"

A flash of white light seared through the windows. The *Scipio* bucked like it had been kicked. A fragment of the sphere the size of an armor suit hit the bridge at an angle, shattering the starboard window and denting the ceiling.

Air rushed out of the bridge, leaving a sheen of frozen water vapor across Hale's armor. Hale slammed from one side of his restraints to the other. A rocky column twisted over and over through the front window.

"Egan! We're hit!" Hale shouted.

"I'm trying!" Egan's hand struggled to reach a control panel over his head as the ship's roll tugged his hand back and forth. He finally got his fingertips against the panel and tapped a button with his thumb several times. The spin abated as maneuver thrusters across the starboard hull flared to life. The ship came to a halt and Egan cut the thrusters. He fell back against his chair, his arms loose at his sides.

"That should do it," Egan said.

"Cortaro? Steuben?" Hale asked.

The IR was silent.

"Here. We're all here, sir," Cortaro said. *"Had a pretty shitty ride in the shuttle bay."*

"Bridge lost atmo. Get me a casualty report and start patching holes," Hale said. "Damage report."

"Still have pressure in several cabins," Tagawa said. "For what it's worth, there wasn't much left to break. Except for that." she nodded to the cracked window.

Why the hell didn't I put the ship in combat conditions and drain the air? he thought. *Maybe this is why officers don't command ships and ground troops at the same time.*

Hale looked at the column just beyond the ship's prow.

"Egan…is that the same one we followed to get to the center?" Hale asked.

"I got disoriented. I'm not sure, sir."

"Turn to starboard and follow it. That will take us back to the command center, I think. We need to make sure the job's done," Hale said.

"Moving." Egan sent the ship to the right and flew over the column. It ended in a broken spike a minute later. More broken ends of the many columns that led to the command center pointed to Abaddon's now empty core. Burning motes flit through the empty space like summer fireflies.

"Mission accomplished," Tagawa said.

"It is…but which way is out?" Hale asked, looking at each cracked column. Any of them could lead to the open portal they used to enter the hollow world and their escape…or to a dead end.

****

279

Hale crossed his arms over his chest. He looked over the team of Marines welding a metal plate over the shattered window then out the front of his damaged bridge. The broken columns felt like accusing fingers, all denouncing Hale for his failures in planning and leadership.

"We could take each one," Jacobs shrugged. "Process of elimination until we figure out which is the way out."

"Not to intrude, ma'am," Egan said from the helmsman's station. He tapped on a screen with blinking red icons. "The reactor's on her last legs. I push it any more than one or two trips out to the surface and we're dead in space."

"Radar pulse?" Mathias asked. "Maybe we can map out the interior and find the exit."

"Radar is meant for short range," Tagawa said. "Hundred miles at most. With the distances to the shell, we'll have beams bouncing all over the place. Like trying to listen to static."

"The IR antenna utilizes a tight beam," Steuben said.

"I aim it down the spikes and see where the signal *doesn't* reflect back," Egan said. "IR's going through the shell. That's our exit and Bob's our uncle."

"Get to it," Hale said.

Egan switched workstations, his hands moving with a great deal more certainty on the communication section than at the controls of the ship.

"Do you think we killed that Xaros leader? The General?" Jacobs asked.

"We did not see him in the command center when we retreated," Steuben said. "It is unwise to believe an enemy dead unless he lies at your feet."

"You blew up the conduit before he could leave," Hale said. "He's stuck in our solar system. Don't ask me if that's a positive. Something tells me beating the drone's programming is a lot easier than beating someone who reacts, who makes intuitive decisions."

Cortaro cleared his throat.

"Sir, ma'am, not to rain on the parade, but how are we going to get back to Earth? Or someplace we can wait out an extraction? Don't tell me this thing can make the long haul to Uranus? Or Neptune? I don't even know where the hell we are compared to the rest of the solar system," Cortaro said.

"We'll get out of here and contact Earth. We'll sit tight until they've got an answer for us on an extraction," Hale said.

Mathias and Jacobs glanced at each other.

"We spoke with Allen before we came up here," Jacobs said. "We've got maybe three days before the ship goes dark."

"Then we've got three days to figure something out—plenty of time," Hale said. "For now we need to wait for Egan to—"

"Ha! Got it." Egan pointed to a column off the port bow. "That was our way in, and it'll be our way out. Don't everyone thank me at once."

"I blame Standish for his attitude," Cortaro muttered. "Get your ass to the other seat and get us moving, Marine."

CHAPTER 22

The Iron Hearts and their Dotok companions rolled to a halt at the stories-high doors leading into Camelback Mountain. Turrets on either side had their gauss cannons pointed high, scanning for any Xaros on approach.

Elias shifted back into his walker form and went to a camera panel beside the doors.

"Open up," Elias said.

"Yes, hello," came through a speaker. "We're on force protection condition alpha plus. I challenge: ellipse. Please provide the countersign."

Elias looked back at Bodel, who shrugged.

"Ellipse. I need the correct response before I open the gate."

"I am Elias of the Armored Corps. You either

open up or I will reach through this wall and crush your skull," Elias said.

One of the doors swung loose ever so slightly. Elias stomped over and waited as hydraulics slowly moved the door.

Inside, an army major in full battle armor waited with his hands clasped behind his back. The hangar behind him was full of techs in lifter armor moving large-caliber munitions crates and ammo dollies loading up. Elias saw a container that held spare ammo and parts for his and the rest of the team's armor.

"Major Dane, Camelback command, welcome to our little slice of heaven…" Dane stepped aside and held his hand out to a large case at the back of the hangar. "This is for you. Showed up in a white flash of light. Marc Ibarra, *the* Marc Ibarra, cut through my comms and told me not to touch it until armor showed up. I was told to expect more than…four."

"We're all you've got." Elias went to the case, which popped open on his approach.

Swords as long as Elias' forearm gleamed within. Elias grabbed one by a stubby handle and lifted it into the air. Light went through the clear blade that looked like it was made of glass; tiny gold lines of inlaid circuits ran through the length.

"Is Ibarra kidding?" Elias asked.

"No, I'm not." Ibarra's hologram appeared from a projector in the case. "Elias, I know your work. Nice to meet you at last."

Elias knocked the flat of the blade against the side of the case and tossed it inside.

"Explain," Elias said.

"The General is a photonic being. The armor is just a containment vessel. For total decoherence we need to disrupt the quantum matrix…you want the whole thing or brass tacks?"

"Get to the point."

"You shoot the General, rip his heart out, won't matter. He'll just retreat and reform, but we've got him stuck in this solar system until he builds another conduit. You need to stab the bastard and keep the blade in his guts until he's good and dead," Ibarra said.

Elias picked up a blade and sliced it through Ibarra's neck, tugging at the hologram as it passed.

"I won't take that personally," Ibarra said. "It'll fit in your pike housing. Now, I have to go and explain the weapons to a dozen other teams before they break them. I swear, you tanks are just as bad as doughboys."

"We're not tanks!" Caas shouted.

Ibarra rolled his eyes and his hologram began to

fade.

"Wait," Elias snapped. "You said the General can retreat. How?"

"He's photonic. We've seen him pop around the battlefield pretty damn fast. Then he has some manner of quantum displacement field that lets him move through solid matter, albeit a bit slow," Ibarra said. "I suggest hitting him hard and fast. Don't wave the swords at him."

Elias unfolded his aegis shield.

"Can he get through this?" Elias asked. He looked up and pointed to the aegis plating surrounding the hangar. "Can he get through that?"

Ibarra's holo came back completely. He looked off to the side and nodded.

"Probably not," Ibarra said. His face contorted in anger. "And just how the hell did you come up with that idea? When I, in all my wisdom and with the help of some of the deepest repositories of knowledge ever even heard of, didn't?"

"I fought him before with a shield made out of banshee armor. He couldn't get through that," Elias said. "Don't confuse knowledge with experience."

"I will pass this on," Ibarra said as he faded away, "but I'm taking all the credit!"

Elias tossed a blade to Bodel, who balanced the

flat of the blade on a finger, testing its balance point.

"Hilt heavy," Bodel said, "you think we should trust Ibarra's science project?"

"We have a choice?" Elias removed his pike and fixed the blade to the socket. He retracted the blade, then snapped it out with a *ching*.

"I'm carrying weapons that can kill a starship in orbit," Caas said, picking up a blade and examined it in the light, "and Ibarra wants me to *stab* something to death?"

"I'm oddly comfortable with the idea." Ar'ri picked up a blade.

"Major," Elias turned to Dane. "Explain this city's defenses to us right now. Every detail."

The Iron Heart took the chain with the General's facemask off his belt and put it over his helm.

CHAPTER 23

Torni finished another crystal and placed it into the device.

"That should do it," she said. Her stalks twitched in the air.

Lafayette ran a data line from his arm to a control switch. His pupils jittered from side to side as he communed with the machine.

"Everything is in order," Lafayette said.

"You want to tell me what this thing is now?" Torni asked as she shifted to her human form.

Ibarra appeared over the diminished omnium cube.

"I've got some good news and I've got some bad news," he said. "The home fleet is decisively engaged with a maniple that broke away from Mars early on." His hologram diffused and reformed to a map of the solar system. Red Xs marked where human and Xaros fleets were engaged through much of space surrounding Earth and most of Mars. A large force of drones moved from beyond Mars' orbit toward the Earth.

"This is real time," Ibarra said. "The force on the way to Earth will take some hits from the macro cannons on Mars, but the swarm that's coming for us will break through the orbitals and hit the cities. The Mars fleet can't make a run for us without getting slaughtered."

"We need two ships for our plan to work," Lafayette said.

"Every ship of the line is duking it out against the Xaros as we speak," Ibarra said. "I can't...wait. There is one ship. Get one of your science projects to the shuttle bay. You're going to Pluto, Lafayette."

"One ship does not solve our problem," Lafayette said.

Ibarra looked at Torni and tapped his foot.

"I'm telling her," Ibarra said.

"That is unwise," Lafayette said. "We do not know if the Xaros can—"

"I tell her and *maybe* it doesn't work. She doesn't help us and the whole plan falls to pieces," Ibarra said.

"If I feel the General trying to control me, I will

release my hold on the kill command," Torni said. "Destroy myself and any knowledge he would want in the process."

"That's my girl," Ibarra said. "At your feet is a hack job of two very different devices. The first is a Tikari shield array; the other is a bastardized jump engine. I say bastardized because it can make short-distance jumps but it's designed *not* to function like the engine on the *Breitenfeld*. The tear in the fabric of space-time will stay open for a longer period and allow more through before it destabilizes. We bashed a jump drive and a Crucible together to make a very ugly baby, one that has a few percentage points of probability to create an unstable rip in space that will annihilate the galaxy."

"Like what happened to the Xaros' home." Torni took a step away from the device.

"Yes…yes, that's a gamble," Ibarra said. "One we're going to risk. If this works, we actually have a decent chance of winning this thing."

"I still don't understand how two faulty jump engines are going to make a difference," Torni said.

"I'll explain it on the way to the shuttle bay," Ibarra said. "Lafayette, you still know how to use that pod you and the rest of your buddies came in, right?"

****

The *Scipio,* trailing wisps of air and sparks from her wrecked engines, limped out of Abaddon.

Hale breathed a sigh of relief. He ran a hand over his face and wondered just how long it had been since he and any of his Marines had any sleep. He touched his helmet on the side of the command chair and cast a suspicious glance at the patch over the starboard window. The repair work managed to keep air and pressure steady, thus far. He went over the symptoms of hypoxia in his head.

Without a canary on the bridge, the crew would have to watch out for each other if the patch sprung a leak.

"Bring us to a halt, Egan," Hale said. "Then get us in contact with Earth."

"Roger, sir."

The smoggy layer over Pluto had nearly faded away. Much of the matter the drill spewed into the atmosphere had fallen to the surface. The massive mineshaft lay dormant. Hale felt more confident that he and his Marines really had shut down the Xaros operation.

Hale's gauntlet buzzed with an incoming call.

"Looks like Earth found us," Egan said.

Lafayette came up on Hale's gauntlet, a padded

acceleration seat and alien machinery surrounded him.

"I assume your mission was a success," the cyborg said. "Good. I was beginning to worry."

"Yes," Hale frowned, "wait, are you speaking to me in real time?"

"Very astute of you. I see Steuben's praise is well deserved. My pod is four kilometers from your ship. Please collect me at your earliest convenience as I have an ersatz jump engine that will bring us back to Earth," Lafayette said.

"I've got him," Tagawa said. "Weird looking ivory colored escape pod. Should barely fit in the cargo bay."

"We're on the way," Hale said.

****

Frost clung to the Karigole pod as Marines strapped it to the deck.

Standish leaned close and rapped his fingers against the side. He waited a moment and tapped again.

An oval-shaped section of the pod sprang loose with a hiss. Standish jumped back like he'd just seen a snake. Lafayette pushed his way through the pod and stepped onto the deck. His metal feet clicked against the corrugated plates.

"Standish, no screaming this time. Quite the improvement," Lafayette said.

"Piss off." Standish tilted his nose in the air and stomped away.

"Lafayette, we're glad to see you," Hale said as he and Steuben approached the pod. "Can't say I'm exactly sure why Ibarra sent you, but still good to have you."

"This vessel is in worse shape than I anticipated," Lafayette said, looking over the damaged shuttle bay.

"Anticipated...for?" Hale asked.

Lafayette's arm snapped back and pointed into the open pod.

"My Karigole brothers and I brought humanity's first jump drive with us. I have another such device we need to install as soon as possible," Lafayette said.

"You're bringing us back to the fight," Hale said. His tone left little doubt that his words were a command, not an inquiry.

"But of course," Lafayette said.

"Niles, Standish," Cortaro said, pointing to the Marines, "get in there and help Lafayette."

The cyborg raised a hand. "This is a precision piece of engineering. I will carry it. Just show me the way to your fusion reactor."

****

Lafayette attached a clamp to a power line with one hand and rewired a junction switch with the other. For as long as he'd known Lafayette, Steuben had yet to get used to watching the cyborg's limbs function independently from each other.

Steuben sniffed the air over the jump engine.

"I scent Stacey Ibarra…and omnium," Steuben said.

"The omnium is Torni. She's proven most useful these past days," Lafayette said.

"This isn't like the same jump engine design we brought the humans. Not the same design of jump engines we've been around since we lost our home world," Steuben said.

"We've made some improvements." Lafayette reached beneath the fusion reactor. There was a groan of metal and the jump engine hummed to life.

"Why improvements now? The Qa'Resh were never ones to stifle technology. The jump engines are theirs." Steuben narrowed his eyes, sensing something that Lafayette wasn't telling him.

"Progress can come in fits and stops, or it can be iterative," Lafayette said. "Malal. Torni." He tapped the jump engine. "Now we have a tad bit of progress."

"That," Steuben said, pointing a claw to a sphere on one end of the jump engine, its surface covered in thin lines running from the poles, "is a Tikari shield generator. Which has no place in a jump engine. Explain."

"I always suspected you had more technical knowhow than you let on. All this time together and you still surprise me," Lafayette said.

"All these years together and you've never lied to me."

The faux skin over Lafayette's face twitched. He reached up and touched his knuckles to Steuben's temple.

"You have your part in this battle, old friend," Lafayette said. "I have mine. If you reach our brothers first, in the afterlife, speak well of me." He removed his hand and touched his forearm screen. "Hale. Cycle the reactor to full power and send your crew to the shuttle bay. I will reach the bridge shortly and handle the jump."

"Baar'sun, what are you planning?" Steuben asked, addressing Lafayette by his true Karigole name.

"Come on. We do not want to be in here when the gate forms." Lafayette walked away.

****

Niles stood to attention as his team leader sidestepped in front of him. Jacobs did a cursory inspection over the ribbon-chute fixed to his armor, testing that every tie-down and clamp was secure. Jacobs slapped him on the shoulder and stepped aside.

Hale took Jacob's place in front of Niles.

"What's the plan, Marine?" Hale asked.

"High-orbit, low-opening drop to Phoenix, sir." Niles' eyes widened slightly. "Join up with the city's defenders. Kill Xaros."

"You ready? This drop's a bit longer than standard qual jumps," Hale said.

"Been doing a lot of things I hadn't trained or planned on lately," Niles chuckled.

"Welcome to war." Hale slapped him on the shoulder and stepped out of the line of Marines.

Hale flexed his injured arm. The pain was only enough to make him wince. Whatever Yarrow had injected into his bicep was doing wonders for his mobility. The corpsman had mentioned something about long-term damage, but that worry would wait until after the battle.

Cortaro came out of the Karigole pod carrying a ribbon-chute pack. He brought it to Tagawa and began attaching it to her void suit. The other two sailors had their ribbon-chutes affixed, both looking as awkward as little kids trying to wear their father's suit. Cortaro mimed how to open the ribbon-chutes for the sailors, repeating himself several times until the three nodded in unison to his instructions.

"Four minutes," Lafayette said to Hale over a closed IR channel.

Hale clicked his mic twice.

Hale finished inspecting what remained of Crimson team and made his way to the front of the formation. He stopped at the edge of the open shuttle bay.

"Marines," Hale boomed, "you have done a great thing this day. The Xaros thought they had an ace up their sleeve. Thought they could keep us away while they opened up a back door to flood our home with their machines. You think they're ever going to underestimate us again?"

Profanity-laced shouts answered Hale.

"You accomplished the impossible. Races across the galaxy will remember this day, but this day is not over. The fleet is slugging it out with the Xaros over Mars. The Xaros made it to Earth and they are trying to burn us out of our homes. I remember Phoenix the day the Saturn fleet came back to retake our planet. Cold. Empty. Never again, do you all understand me? We live. Phoenix lives.

"There was nothing but a spark left, a tiny ember

that grew to a fire that beat the Toth. That saved the Karigole. That saved the Dotok. Now, it is time to save our own world." A white light rose behind Hale.

"Prep for drop and follow me," Hale said.

The light blinded Hale, then faded away in a heartbeat.

Outside the shuttle bay doors was Earth. White bands of clouds crossed over a tan desert. Hale made out Baja California and the Pacific Coast. They were right where they were supposed to be.

Hale took a running leap out of the shuttle bay, fired the thrusters attached to his boots and rocketed forward. A red dot appeared on his visor, his beacon to the landing zone just south of Phoenix. Wide red rings joined the red dot, marking his flight path.

Just stay in the rings, he thought.

He looked back at the *Scipio* and counted Marines as they followed him through the upper atmosphere.

"All clear," Cortaro sent. *"Had to throw Allen."*

"He'll get over it," Hale said.

"Hale, this is Lafayette. I'm taking the Scipio *to the Crucible.* Gott mit uns *to you."*

"Wait, you're not coming with us? Why are you taking that wreck?" Hale asked. He wiped condensation from his visor and twisted to the side to re-center his flight path.

"Tell Steuben that I am *shol mar cul* when the time is right. He will understand," Lafayette said.

"Laf, what does that mean? Lafayette?"

The channel shut off.

A gust of wind buffeted Hale to the side, rolling him over and over. He snapped his hands and arms to the side, steadying himself in the thickening atmosphere. A yellow strip flashed on the right side of his visor. He looked over and saw the rings of his intended flight path hundreds of yards away.

"Um, sir? Is our flight path changing?" Jacobs asked.

"No. Got bad air. Keep to the beacon while I correct," Hale said. A wave of embarrassment welled up in his chest. Telling Marines to follow him only worked if he went the right damn direction.

He tapped the thrusters on his left hand and heel, edging him closer and closer to his flight path. The path went right over his head, and he was losing altitude too fast to ever close the gap.

Hale entered a cloud. Rain patted against his visor and ran down the sides.

"Crimson, Slate, this is 6. I'm off path and will hit south of the landing zone," Hale said. There was no answer. He looked around and saw nothing but the cloud that was absorbing his transmission.

He shot through the cloud ceiling. Phoenix spread out ahead of him, far larger than he ever remembered with highways spoking away from Euskal Tower. Red flashed from Xaros beams, striking buildings south of Camelback Mountain east of the tower.

There was sparse desert below, miles from the edge of the city. Hale realized he was in for quite a hike once he hit the ground.

"There he is!" Bailey shouted.

"Told you he went through that big miles-wide cloud," Orozco said.

Hale twisted around. His Marines were right behind him, sticking out like sore thumbs against the backdrop of the gray cloud.

"Before you get mad," Standish said, "we figured you didn't want to be all by your lonesome out here, especially not with all the drones. Also, First Sergeant told us to follow you."

"Cortaro?" Hale looked to the ground and swung his feet down.

"Last thing I heard you say was 'follow me,' sir. Everything after that was broken and unreadable," Cortaro said. "Rest of the teams are still on course. Steuben's got them."

Hale mumbled under his breath. Cortaro's story didn't pass the smell test, but he was glad to have his team with him.

The captain got a solid grip on his ripcord and watched his altimeter blink from amber to red. He pulled the pin, releasing a clear foot-wide ribbon of composite polymers from his backpack. The ribbon-chute twisted into a corkscrew, spinning rapidly as it stole Hale's speed. He activated his boot linings and slowed to a complete halt inches over the ground.

Hale thumped to the ground and hauled the chute out of the air. He found a capsule full of liquid at the base of the ribbon and crushed it with his fingers. The clear chute melted as the released chemicals ate through the material. Hale ripped the harness off his back and tossed it beneath a spiky ocotillo tree. Steam rose off the disintegrating chute.

"Sound off," Cortaro said. All the Marines checked in.

Hale took his plasma rifle off his back and zoomed in on Phoenix's distant spires. Xaros drones flit through the towers, hounded by plasma bolts and gauss rounds from the ground.

"Doesn't look so bad," Hale said.

"Not down here, but look east," Egan said.

Explosions blossomed over the horizon. Energy blasts stitched across the sky in a dogfight that must have stretched for miles.

"Can we hurry?" Yarrow asked. "We need to get to Phoenix. My—the civilians need us."

"Traveling over watch, let's move." Hale took off running.

Hale set a punishing pace for anyone not wearing powered armor. His suit could keep moving for hours at a pace of five minutes per mile, taking much of the burden off the wearer.

"I think I remember this place," Standish said. "Didn't we land around here when we pulled Ibarra out from under his tower? The *Midway* was over on the left, crashed in the mountains."

"It was a little south," Cortaro said.

"And we had Stacey Ibarra with us and she would *not* stop breaking noise discipline. Then we had to take her to the Crucible where—"

"Standish," Hale said.

"Yes sir, shutting up."

CHAPTER 24

The maniple of drones between Earth and Mars contracted, fusing deep within its center to form a pointed oval shape the size of a small capitol ship. Inside the new construct a conduit to the rest of the Xaros network formed. Lumps of the surrounding chamber pulled away and formed into the General's armor over the plinth.

The General's being arrived soon after. He reached back to the gate that was under construction over Pluto…and felt nothing. Abaddon…nothing. Data from his drones showed a small human strike force destroying both.

No matter. His drone force over Mars would keep the main human fleet tied to the planet and unable to aid Earth once his armada arrived. The battle was as good as won.

The chamber darkened as an inky mass spread from the top and worked down the walls. Bright-colored nebulae arose through the darkness and contracted into stars, the work of billions of cut into mere seconds. Constellations known to the Xaros home world surrounded the General.

+Keeper.+ The General failed to hide his disdain.

+I thought this issue would have been decided by now,+ came from all around the General. +The vessel you used to travel from the nearest gate...where are the rest of your drones? There should be more drones.+

+There was a complication on the way. The humans will be extinct soon and why are you distracting me from my purpose? I do not visit the Apex and fret over the geode's energy balance.+

The stars swirled around the General, settling into a new pattern of constellations once visible from a destroyed paradise world of islands and shallow seas.

+You asked me to awaken the others because of this anomaly with a vagrant species. I came to see it resolved...but it is not,+ Keeper said.

+It will be soon.+

A macro cannon shell from Mars clipped the outer net of drones traveling to Earth. The loss of several hundred drones fed into the chamber.

+Your service to the Apex has been flawless…until now,+ Keeper said.

+This solar system will be purged.+ The General rose off the plinth, his body burning white hot with anger. +When this galaxy is ours and it comes time to choose our domains—all worlds that *I* secured—this will be where I rule. This insignificant species will be the last that dares stand against us. I will broadcast their final agonizing moments to whatever species still cower in worlds untouched by my drones and show the futility of standing against *my* armies.+

The General formed a hand into a long blade and touched the point against the conduit.

+Now you can either leave before I destroy this conduit and spare myself from your prattling or stay for the rest of this campaign and watch me work,+ the General said. +Choose quickly.+

The star field along the walls drew into a point over the conduit and vanished.

The General hacked at the conduit, breaking away chunks and severing his connection to the rest of the Xaros network. If there were to be any more embarrassing episodes, he wouldn't let Keeper see them.

CHAPTER 25

In a low crouch, Hale ran past a burning car. He stopped against a wall and took a quick look around the corner. A walker construct the size of a two-story building swept ruby beams across the sky.

The walker clipped a squat-high rise, slicing a corner away. The corner crashed to the ground and exploded in a cloud of pulverized quick-crete.

"Are we too late?" Yarrow asked as he hit the wall behind Hale. "I don't see anyone. No civilians anywhere."

"Look at the walls, any of the buildings," Hale said. "No beam holes. Xaros picked through civilians and killed them the first time they attacked. Civvies must have evacced to bunkers."

The roar of an Eagle fighter filled the air. Hale ducked away from the edge as the fighter's gauss cannon ripped through the street next to him and traced a line through the construct.

"That pilot's either a master who knew where we were," Standish said, "or an asshole that just didn't care about hitting us."

"Maybe both," Bailey said as she fit her rail rifle together. "Want me to take care of that thing, sir?"

"Nice big boom from your rifle would tell every Xaros in the city we're out here," Yarrow said. "Can we get past it? Let the big guns take care of that thing?"

"Yarrow, with me. Grenades," Hale said, taking one from his belt and twisting the cylinder to activate the shaped-charge setting, "set for lance. Rest, take it out once we hit it." He broke open a window with his shoulder and climbed through.

The building had rows and rows of robot fabricators. Spindly arms with many fingers bent over workbenches full of rifle components. Power cables lay on the ground, disconnected from each bench.

The two Marines shuffled along the outer wall, the electric crash of the walker's beam sounding through the wall. The walker thundered past a window, the shifting metal of its tree-trunk legs shaking the ground with each step.

Yarrow touched a hand to the window, ready to

break it with the slightest tap of his augmented knuckles.

"No," Hale whispered, "need a few yards for the grenades to arm."

The construct stopped and raised its twin cannon arms to the sky. Red light flashed through the factory as Xaros fired on a target high above.

"Now!" Hale smashed a fist through a window and swiped broken glass out of the way. He hurled his grenade and ducked beneath the sill. Twin thunderclaps from the Marines' attacks shattered the rest of the windows.

Hale looked over the daggers of glass. The construct stumbled forward, two smoking holes against its back. The Xaros swung an arm toward Hale.

"Move!" Hale dove aside as a disintegration beam the width of a telephone pole ripped through the wall and destroyed the idle robots. Hale got his plasma rifle off his back. He stood halfway up when another beam cut through the wall just over his head and across the entire factory's façade.

There was a groan of metal as the building tilted over, straining against a section of undamaged framework behind Hale.

"Back! Back!" Hale vaulted over a workbench and made for the growing tear across the outer wall. The building toppled over like a felled tree, raining shattered glass as the failing structure collapsed. A wave of dust and smoke washed over Hale. His world was nothing but a growing rumble and a purgatory haze.

He wiped at his face and air filters and spun around.

"Yarrow? Anybody?"

A ruby beam as thick as his arm stabbed through the fog, missing his head by a few feet. Hale dove to the ground and crawled away, looking for any kind of cover.

The ground shook—heavy footsteps on approach. A giant humanoid shadow loomed through the dust. Hale rolled to his side and fumbled with his rifle...and the shadow ran right past him.

The flash of a gauss cannon snapped through the haze. The sound of ripping metal filled the air. What looked like a bent log flew up and arced through the air, landing a few feet from Hale—one of the construct's cannon arms, disintegrating rapidly in the dust.

Hale ran to the sound of metal pounding on metal and scrambled over a pile of broken masonry.

An armor soldier stood over the defeated construct. The armor's shoulders shifted up and down, like it was breathing hard. Scorch trails and heat blotches marred the armor's plate; antennae on half its helm were bent and broken.

As the dust settled, the armor turned to Hale. A red, bent faceplate with two slits for eyes hung over the armor's chest.

"Hale."

"Elias."

"Steuben said you'd come through this way." Elias raised a foot and slammed it against the construct's chest, kicking up burning embers. "Where are the rest?"

"Captain!" carried through the fog. Hale heard the bricks knocking against each other.

"Over here!" Hale called back.

"I've got a spider hole for you a few blocks away," Elias said, "that'll get you to the mountain. Need to hurry, next wave will be here soon."

"There he is!" Yarrow struggled through the wreckage as the rest of their team followed behind. "Sir, thought we'd be out here for hours digging for you."

"Look at that," Standish said, pointing to the smoldering construct. "Captain took out the walker all by himself. Oh…hi, Elias."

Three more armor soldiers rolled over on their treads.

"Sector twelve and twenty-three are clear," Bodel said. "Air support says we've got clear skies for at least ten more minutes."

"Climb on." Armor panels on his legs lifted up and folded against themselves, exposing his treads. Elias shifted down to his travel form and motioned for Hale to come over.

Hale and Standish jumped onto either side of the armor.

"The worst ride is better than the best walk," Standish said. "Hey…where's Kallen?"

Elias' treads bit into the rubble and drove them down a side street.

"Elias, did you hear me? Where's Kallen?" Standish slapped his palm against the armor's shoulder. There was no answer as Elias pulled to a stop in front of a Chinese restaurant, its tall double doors hanging by bent hinges.

"I'm talking to you, god damn it." Standish reached up and struck Elias' helm with the back of his knuckles.

Elias kicked the tread beneath Standish into the air and sent the Marine sprawling onto the road. The armor reared up to his full height and raised an open hand into the air. He slammed his hand toward Standish, pinning him beneath the armor's fingers.

Standish stared defiantly at Elias, both ignoring

the shouts around them.

Elias' hand closed around Standish…and he lifted him gently onto his feet. Elias knelt in front of the Marine, bringing their heads level.

"She fell, Standish."

Standish nodded slowly, then did his best to give Elias a hug.

"Did she tell you? How much she cared?" Standish asked.

"She did. Her and Bodel tell me what a help you were back when I was locked in my tank. I haven't thanked you, have I? Thanked you for getting me out of that hospital?"

"You just keep on saving our ass, big boy," Standish said, pulling away and slapping a palm against the helm's enormous cheek, "and we'll call it even."

Elias stood up and pointed to the open doors.

"There's a hatch on the kitchen floor. Passage beneath will take you straight to the mountain. Close it behind you or they'll blow the whole tunnel after ninety seconds," Elias said.

"What about all of you?" Hale asked.

"We're staying out here," Elias said. "Need to pick a fight."

****

A pair of double-barreled gauss cannons built into a turret greeted Hale and his Marines as they neared the end of the tunnel. Each flanked a vault door with no handle.

"What could go wrong here?" Standish asked.

"The cannons have to be manned," Egan said, "won't risk a program that the Xaros can hack. Soon as whoever's supposed to be manning them sees we're not drones, they'll open up."

"Go knock on the door," Cortaro told Egan. The commo Marine did a double take at Cortaro, then walked to the vault door, his arms wide, rifle held by the barrel in one hand. Egan reached up to the door.

The cannons whirred to life, panning across the hallway quickly. Egan jumped back from the door, still holding his rifle at arm's length.

"Friendlies!" Egan shouted.

The vault door cracked open, then swung slowly into the hallway. There was a thin layer of quadrium metal between the reinforced armor plates making up the vault door.

A Ranger in jet-black armor stood in the doorway, a pistol in his hand. There were two more soldiers behind

313

him, rifles low but pressed to their shoulders.

"Captain Hale, I presume," the Ranger said.

"That's right." Hale stepped forward. "Mind if we come in…"

"Major Dane, 25th Regiment, or what's left of it." Dane stepped aside.

Hale looked up and down the hallway. There was no one manning the cannons, or anyone else in the poorly lit area but the Rangers who greeted them.

"I thought those were active when we first saw them." Hale pointed a thumb to the triggers and vision slits behind each cannon.

"I need manpower on the redoubts, in the air. Xaros haven't figured out the tunnels…yet. Guess the quadrium linings do work as advertised, confuses the drone's scanners," Dane said. "Come with me. I need you on the walls."

"We've been out of the loop for a while. What's the situation?" Hale asked as he walked side by side with Dane.

"Mars is slugging it out. Fleet's down to half-strength but the macro cannons are still beating the piss out of the Xaros. Garret's got his hand on the Xaros' belt. They can't withdraw from Mars without taking severe losses…course, Garret can't leave Mars to come help us

314

either.

"Graviton mines broke their advance up. So we're dealing with a few million drones at a time instead of everything they got past Mars all at once. We lost Korea and most of Japan to the first orbital they got up. Himalayas held on only because the *Breitenfeld* popped into high orbit and blew that thing to hell."

"She's here? The *Breitenfeld* made it back?" Hale asked.

"She did. Brought all the armor off Mars with her. Strangest thing, giant force of drones pulled back from Mars soon as the armor made landfall here and set course for Earth. That wave will be here in about twelve hours…which is going to be a significant emotional event for everybody."

"Why's that? How many drones are coming?"

"We did all right when a million plus drones hit. We held on by our fingernails and lost the Luna macro cannon when ten million came at us. This next wave is twenty, twenty-five million," Dane said quietly.

"We getting any help from Bastion?" Hale asked.

"Hell if I know. Phoenix is my piece of the fight. I don't have time to worry about things beyond my control." Dane looked back to the Marines behind them. "Now I've got the heroes of Takeni with us. Should help morale a bit."

Dane gave Standish and Egan a quizzical glance. Standish rolled his eyes and tossed a hand up in mock surrender.

"Your XO's got the rest of your Marines on the wall. He's got my assignments for everyone but you." Dane put a hand on Hale's shoulder. "You…General Robbins needs you to come be a hero for a bit."

They turned a corner and came to a hallway as wide as a football field and nearly three stories tall. One side of the hallways was broken rock carved out of the mountain; the other was a fortress wall, dotted with turrets up and down its length. Soldiers, Marines and doughboys came in and out of honeycomb tunnels against the rocks to open sally ports big enough for armor in the fortress walls.

"We can get to most anywhere in Phoenix and the connected defenses from here. General Robbins is cycling out positions, changing out the fighters who've been in the shit for the last twelve hours."

"Lot of doughboys," Hale said. The massive soldiers towered over their human leaders as shuffled through the hallway.

"Couldn't do this without them, but…can't do much more than point them at the drones and let them fight," Dane said.

Dane pointed to an open but unused sally port. Steuben came around the corner and waved his hand in the air.

"He's got your team, but you're coming with me, Hale."

"Excuse me, sir," Yarrow said. "Captain Hale's been under my medical care. I need to get him to a level two facility for treatment. So I need to come with him. Medical necessity."

Hale's eyebrows furrowed. He flexed his damaged bicep and felt only a bit of pain.

"I think I'll be—"

"Infection, sir. Need to have it looked at," Yarrow nodded vigorously.

"Fine, come on," Hale shrugged.

****

Yarrow ran the back of his fingers against the stubble on his face. He desperately wanted a quick trip to a shower pod to clean up, but General Robbins wanted both him and Hale as they were, fresh from the battle.

A metal blast door rose in front of Hale, Yarrow and Dane. The clink of chains and thunk-thunk-thunk of metal on metal drowned out whatever Dane was saying until it ground to a halt.

"—fourteen more civilian pods like this one beneath Camelback and Mazatzal mountains. More scattered under Phoenix. Ibarra's proccies have all been military-aged men and women. All the families and children are from the original Saturn colony.. We had enough warning to get everyone off the streets, at least," Dane said as pushed his way through a lighter set of double doors.

Bright lights embedded in the ceiling cast a uniform glow across a cavernous room full of cots. Restroom pods the size of cargo containers and thousands of people lined up along a makeshift pathway delineated by nothing but a strand of rope the width of Yarrow's finger.

A cheer went up as Hale walked into the room. The Marine took a step back, his hands jerking toward his rifle before he caught himself. Thousands of civilians waved and called to Hale and Yarrow. Parents held children up on their shoulders. Yarrow had never seen so many people so happy, so full of hope.

"What am I supposed to do?" Hale asked.

"We're broadcasting this to the other pods. Just get to the end. Show your face and tell them we'll win," Dane said to Hale before he turned to Yarrow. "Same to

318

you. They know you from the movie."

Yarrow swallowed hard. He'd caught only a few minutes of *The Last Stand on Takeni*. Whatever actor they had under the holo skin might have looked like him, but he hadn't sounded like Yarrow at all. In Yarrow's opinion.

Hale went to one side of the line, shaking hands and smiling at everyone.

Yarrow went to the other side, nodding and pretending to care about whatever the civilians said. He moved quickly, searching for a beautiful woman with lavender hair and a little girl. He made it through half the room with no sign of them.

The corpsman caught sight of an elderly couple sitting on a cot and recognized them both.

"Enzuna, Belit!" Yarrow waved to them. The old man glanced up. A wide smile came across his face and he tottered to the line. "Move aside. Let him through." Yarrow tried to push the packed crowd aside gently, then shoved them away with a push from his power armor.

"Forgive Belit, young one," Enzuna said. "She's still angry we never got to see Lord Mentiq. I keep telling her, 'They were going to kill us,' but she doesn't believe me."

"Where is Lilith? Is she here?" Yarrow asked.

"Oh no…they're in the Scottsdale pod. Eight or

nine *beru* away from here," Enzuna said.

Yarrow's heart sank at the news. He nodded slowly.

"Ah, look, Belit wants you." He pointed to the old woman. She raised a hand to Yarrow and gave him the finger.

"We saw that in your movie," Enzuna said.

Yarrow gave him a pat on the shoulder and moved on. He answered a few questions on what Bailey was really like and if Orozco was single, trying to put on a good front for the civilians.

The children got to him. All the scared faces, toddlers clutching at their parents, some had little plastic action figures of Marines and armor soldiers. He'd spent more time with Dotok children than human. This was the first time he'd been around humanity's future, and seeing it up close and personal made him proud of what he'd done as a Marine. The larger purpose of all his pain and suffering came into focus when he looked into the face of a newborn baby.

If only his child was here.

They got to the end of the line and went through another set of double doors.

Dane held up an Ubi hand slate, and a bright camera light shown over both Hale and Yarrow.

"Anything to say to Earth, Captain Hale?" Dane asked.

Hale's mouth worked for a second before he said, "We're in this together and we'll win this day."

Dane angled the Ubi at Yarrow.

"Lilith, Mary, D-D-Daddy loves you and I'll find you when this is all over," Yarrow blurted out.

The major tapped the screen and went to open the blast door.

"You…what?" Hale asked Yarrow.

"Sir, Lilith and I…during shore leave—"

"I can figure that part out. When did you know about…Mary?"

Yarrow went bright red and tugged at his collar. "There was—I mean Egan found a way to open comms with Earth and email came through so…I know there was a commo blackout but my bank account—"

"Stop." Hale squeezed his temples with one hand. "I've been a company commander less than a week and there are already baby issues. I will get you to them once this fight is over. I promise."

"Thank you, sir," Yarrow said.

"We're done with the grip and grin," Dane said. "I'll get you back to your company."

"Don't we need to stop somewhere, Yarrow?"

Hale asked.

"Sir?"

Hale looked at his injured arm.

"Yes! A field station. Doctors. Antibiotics. Absolutely the reason I came with you, sir." Yarrow pointed down a hallway without any idea of where it led to.

"This way." Dane went the opposite direction of Yarrow's finger.

****

Landing Zone Baker 7 was a hollowed-out section of the Superstition Mountains. The flight deck was a dome sixty yards wide and almost as tall. The armored doors, big enough to get a Destrier transport in with a reasonable amount of skilled flying, were sealed shut.

Eagle fighters and Condor bombers, all being worked over by crew that looked like they hadn't slept for days, faced the outer edge of the circle.

Standish walked up to a craft much larger than a Condor, turret balls on the upper and lower sections of its stubby wings, rotary gauss cannons slung under the cockpit and dual rail cannon vanes in the fuselage. A crewman stood on the outside of the cockpit, a welding torch in her hand and sparks flying from where it touched the hull. More crew worked on the upper hull, all welding plates over cuts from Xaros beams.

"What the hell is this?" Standish asked. Bailey, Orozco and Egan looked over the giant machine, all as unsure as Standish.

"Tail number 29," Bailey said. "This is our assignment."

The crewman jumped off the bridge and ripped off a welding helmet. She had short blond hair, a soot-stained face and pilot's wings on her coveralls.

"You're the replacements?" she asked. "Which of you is Egan?"

"That's me." Egan raised a hand slightly.

"You're Mule rated?"

"I've got my wings for that and small craft, not for...what is that?"

"Osprey. Where the hell have you guys been? Even the doughboys know what these are." She wiped a sleeve over her face and managed to make it even dirtier. "Don't matter. You can fly a Mule you can co-pilot my Osprey. Control setup's the same. What's your call sign?"

"Gooey," Standish snapped. "His call sign is Gooey."

"Woah. Hold on..." Egan raised a finger in

objection.

"I'm Firecracker," the pilot said. "I suggest the rest of you get something to eat and hit the head in the next ten minutes because we sortie in thirty. Pick a turret and get comfortable. Come on, Gooey. Let me explain our girl's quirks."

****

Standish attached air and data lines to the base of his helmet and wiggled against the turret chair. Aegis plates bolted to the side of the turret took away a bit of his view but none of his firing arc as he maneuvered the twin gauss cannons through their full range of motion. Counters popped up on his visor, showing each cannon with a little more than nine hundred rounds available.

"Ball two up and ready," Standish said.

"Three, good," Orozco said.

"One, hoping this goes better than Takeni," Bailey said.

"What're you complaining about?" Standish asked. "So your turret had to eject and you landed in the middle of a bunch of banshees who wanted to eat your face. How could this go worse?"

"Wait," Firecracker said, "you're *that* Bailey? And

324

that Orozco? I thought it was some sort of coincidence."

"And *that* Standish!" He slammed a fist against the turret wall winced in pain.

"Orozco…would you sign a little something for me later?" Firecracker asked.

"*Sí, mamacita,*" Orozco said in his Castilian Spanish.

Standish heard a giggle and rolled his eyes.

A whine went through the ship as its batteries cycled to full power. Standish felt his limbs grow heavy and his stomach do its routine flip-flops before combat.

"My body is ready," Standish said to himself.

"Getting updates in from the tower," Egan said. "Drone swarm broke atmo off the California coast. They're coming in low from the west. Orbital support's trying to thin their numbers but we should expect 'serious' contact."

"Here I was hoping for noncommittal contact, maybe just a passing contact," Standish said.

"He always talk this much?" Firecracker asked.

"Never shuts up," Bailey said. "Just yak-yak-yak since the minute we met."

The aegis doors opened and a crack of sunlight filled the hangar. An Eagle rose off the landing pad and shot through the doors, banking aside to squeeze by before they finished opening. The entire floor rotated clockwise, bringing the next fighter to the exit.

"That's new," Orozco said.

"Faster deployment time," Firecracker said. "Whole mountain range is full of pockets just like ours."

Standish watched as fighters and bombers tore out of the hangar until his and one other Osprey were left. Their craft rose off the deck and accelerated into a sky full of red and orange as the sun set to the west, shining through the tops of clouds pregnant with rain.

Eagles and Condors flew high overhead, forming into squadrons stacked on top of each other. The Osprey banked to the side and flew over a canyon, maneuvering better than any Mule Standish had ever rode in.

"Aren't we going to join the party?" Standish asked.

"Not our job," Firecracker said. "We cover the city, take a swing at any big boys that show up."

"Jesus, Mary, Joseph and the sheep," Bailey said, "would you look at that."

Standish swung his turret around. Over the Superstition Mountains, bright streaks descended through the atmosphere, too fast and too narrow to be a dying spaceship. Standish couldn't prove it, but he swore he felt the Earth shake each time the burning lines passed over the horizon.

"Kinetic strikes," Orozco said. "Never thought I'd see that on Earth. There hasn't been an orbital bombardment since the Chinese wiped Hong Kong off the map."

"There's nothing human west of the mountains," Firecracker said. "Free-fire zone."

A shockwave buffeted the Osprey enough that Standish slapped his hands against the turret ball to steady himself.

"What was that?" he asked.

"Air bursts," Orozco sounded almost giddy. "I see the fireballs rising over the mountains. Big guns upstairs set the k-strikes to go off way above ground level, slap the drones right out of the air. If only I could be up there."

"That means they're close, doesn't it?" Standish shifted his turret around to face the mountains. Streaks of rail cannon shots burned through the sky from the Eagles and Condors overhead, all leveled at the distant peaks.

"Here we go," Bailey said.

"Hold your fire until they're too close to ignore or I say otherwise. Garrison command wants us as a knockout punch, not throwing jabs," Firecracker said.

A dark shadow crested over the Estrella Mountains and flowed down the leeward slopes. Standish zoomed in and saw Xaros drones flying so close to each other their stalks nearly touched. He glanced at the round count on his guns and felt a wave of dread pass over him.

The first rail cannon shots reached the Xaros wave. Quadrium munitions exploded into chain lightning, burning hundreds of drones from existence instantly and sending many times that into freefall against the jagged rocks below.

The barren land between the mountains and Phoenix's outer limits came alive with tracer rounds as hundreds of bunkers rose up out of the desert and gauss rotary cannons fired so fast Standish thought they were sweeping laser beams through the Xaros.

"Doughboys," Firecracker said. "Every bunker down there's full of doughboys. Damn things are too dumb to be anything but brave."

A rail cannon shot seared past the Osprey. Standish's head snapped to the side to follow it and watched as the round blossomed into flechettes and tore a burning chunk out of the Xaros advance. He traced the round's path back to a gun emplacement embedded in the side of Camelback Mountain that looked like it belonged on a battleship.

"Construct!" Firecracker called out. "Got a cruiser analog coming over the Estrellas. Time to shine boys and girls."

The Osprey swooped up and pulled into a half loop before Firecracker rolled the craft over. Eagle fighters shot past the Osprey, gauss cannons blazing as they fired into a wall of drones massing between Phoenix and the Estrella Mountains.

A Xaros ship floated on the other side of the ridge, banks of energy cannons arrayed against its flanks and a glowing red depression in its leading edge.

A beam hit an Eagle just behind Standish and turned it into a fireball.

"I'm going to start shooting now," Standish said. He swung his turret to the left, found a drone on the tail of a Condor, gave the enemy just enough lead and fired two shots. One round connected, fracturing the drone's shell and sending it tumbling away in a shower of sparks. He slammed the guns to the right and sent out a peal of shots that nailed two drones.

He slewed the guns straight up and destroyed another drone that was coming straight down on the Osprey, stalks already glowing in anticipation of the kill.

"Anytime the rest of you want to—"

A blinding flash of red light erupted from the cruiser and a beam the width of a house tore through the doughboys' bunkers. The cruiser moved the beam from side to side, systematically carving a smoldering canyon that zigzagged through the defenses.

Standish tore his gaze away and pounded at a group of drones breaking through their scrum with a squadron of Eagles. He stopped firing, but his turret was still shaking.

"What the—"

A pair of Condor bombers swept over the Osprey. The two craft fired six rail cannon shots in quick succession then pulled into a loop and flew off.

"Big birds thank whoever's keeping the drones off 'em," Firecracker said. "Looks like they broke the shell. Stand by for rail cannon."

Standish's hydraulics lost power. He cursed and grabbed a small handle on the turret ring and spun it madly to twist the turret toward the front of the Osprey at an agonizingly slow speed.

A glowing crack ran along the Xaros cruiser's flank, and the main cannon flickered.

The Osprey's twin rail cannons thundered, rattling Standish against his restraints. One round hit the mountainside, throwing up a shower of dirt and shattered rock. The other hit the construct on the prow, breaking the forward third clean away. The construct angled down and crashed into the mountains, gouging up an avalanche as it slid down.

A drone veered out of its dogfight with an Eagle and angled for the Osprey. Standish spun the handle the other way.

"Got a bandit coming in on our two o'clock," he said, "would appreciate some hydraulic power."

The Osprey twisted onto its side and swung away from the scrum. Standish lost sight of the attacking drone.

"Bailey! You see it down there? Should be your—" The Osprey leveled out and Standish saw the drone pursuing them from behind. He spun the wheels faster. "Six. Six o'clock!"

Power returned and Standish swung the guns around. The drone fired before he could line up his shot and a scarlet beam struck the top of the Osprey, cutting a rudder away and tracing a laser straight to Standish's turret.

The Osprey banked to the side as the lost rudder threw off the plane's aerodynamics. The beam meant for Standish zigged around his turret and wrecked the antennae array.

Standish fired wildly, joined by Orozco's turret. The drone went down in the crossfire.

A Xaros beam struck the aegis plating next to Standish. Black smoke stained the side of the turret. A small fire burned through a hole in the armor and the turret dome. Standish slapped at the flames.

More drones were coming for them.

The Osprey shot forward, wobbling as the afterburners cast blunt torches of fire behind them.

"We're pulling back to the defense lines along the Salt River," Egan said. "Another wave's coming in."

Standish turned his guns on the swarm. The Xaros pulled back, oblivious to the losses inflicted by him and the rest of the defenders' air fleet, and coalesced into a sphere a hundred yards wide. The sphere blasted apart, revealing a jagged sphere of light at its center.

Standish zoomed in and saw the General, surrounded by interlocking rings of circling drones. The General raised a hand, then pointed to Phoenix. The drones instantly swarmed past the General, obscuring him from sight.

"OK, looks like the Xaros brought their big bad to play. Anyone have a silver bullet, wooden stake…bucket of water? Also, we've got incoming." Standish fired his cannons, determined to shoot off every bullet before the drones reached them.

A drone reared up over the tail and spat past Standish's turret before he could swing it around to engage. The drone ripped a disintegration beam across the cockpit and the Osprey flew into a barrel roll.

The world around Standish went end over end, the centripetal force too strong for Standish to reach the ejection handle beneath his seat.

"Gooey! Firecracker? The ground is coming…doesn't…look…friendly," Standish managed to say.

The Osprey fell into a flat spin, whipping Standish back and forth against his restraints until it nosed down. Standish got a good look at a doughboy bunker just before the Osprey pulled out of the dive…and flew straight toward a mountainside.

Standish brought his hands over his face. There was a rip of metal and the ship's tail swung around. The Osprey belly flopped against a slope and careened down the mountainside. Standish jostled against his restraints as the slide got rougher over every rock. He spotted a boulder the size of a car directly ahead of him.

"Ah…crap…" The Osprey hit the boulder and went tail over nose. The ground came straight at Standish as his turret ball slammed to Earth.

There was a bang…then silence.

Standish opened his eyes and found crushed weeds and pulverized rocks against his turret ball. The impact had bent the barrels of his gauss cannons into scrap metal. His turret had sunk into the recession beneath the seat, crushing the hydraulics. Blood rushed to Standish's head—he was upside down.

"I owe the designer a drink," Standish said. The lights in his turret ball faded away, leaving him with a sliver of sunlight from a crack in the fuselage.

"Hey," Standish said, knocking against his turret, "anyone hear me?"

"Standish?" Bailey asked. "I'm trapped in my turret."

"Me too. Better stuck here waiting than going home in a bucket, I guess."

"I love engineers. Bless their nearsighted, basement virgin, problem-solving little hearts," she said.

There was a squeal of metal, the clang of something hitting the outside of the ship.

"Ah, think we're good and fucked now," Bailey said.

Standish reached for the holster strapped to his chest and drew his gauss pistol. He gave it a derisive look. It wouldn't make much difference against a drone.

"Bailey?" No answer. Standish swallowed hard and felt his heart race as the sound of tortured metal got closer.

"This is not how I wanted to die," he said quietly.

His turret shook slightly, then pulled deeper into

the Osprey. The ball went rolling across the desert, oscillating Standish's view between blinding sunlight and dirt until he came to a sudden stop. Tall figures with wide shoulders and hefty rifles surrounded him.

A Cro-Magnon face with mottled skin stared at Standish through the glass. A hand the size of an oven mitt knocked on the turret.

"OK?" a gravelly voice asked.

"Where the hell did we land?" Standish kept a tight grip on his pistol.

"Move." Orozco, a crowbar in hand, stepped around the giant soldier. He jammed one end against the seam on the turret ball, popped a panel free and helped Standish out.

"Oro…" Standish cast a sideways glance at the soldier watching the two Marines. "You make new friends, or something?"

"These are doughboys. Where have you been?" Orozco pointed the bent end of the crow bar at the wrecked Osprey. "They got us out."

Egan sat against the twisted metal, sharing puffs from a vape stick with Bailey.

Standish took off his helmet and turned his face to the sky.

"Ah, sunlight, dry heat." He waved a hand over

his face. "Bugs. Good to be home."

The Osprey's two flight techs crawled out of a rip in the back of the ship. One tossed away his helmet and vomited.

"Firecracker?" Standish asked Egan.

Egan shook his head and held up an arm. A burnt line ran down his forearm. "Drone got her. Made flying a lot harder."

Standish looked to the mountain they'd rode down. The flash of gauss cannons and Xaros beams traced lines of conflict over Phoenix.

"Everybody," Standish said, clapping his hands, "up. We need to get back in the fight." He turned around and found himself face-to-chest with a doughboy. He craned his neck up.

"You. Big man. English?"

The doughboy grunted.

"We need a tunnel back to the city. Any help?"

The doughboy cocked its head to a round bunker jutting out of the desert floor.

"That'll do." Standish turned back to the survivors. Egan was on his feet, limping badly to the bunker. Standish went to him and put Egan's arm over his shoulder. "Thought it was just your arm."

"Everything hurts," Egan spat.

336

"Maybe next time we let Orozco fly. What do you think?"

"Hell no."

"If he had some more—"

"No."

The sound of explosions from the heart of Phoenix echoed through the mountains.

CHAPTER 26

Torni lifted the last open hatch on the Karigole pod off the ground and slowly brought it upwards.

Lafayette, crammed into the pod with a jump drive and several dozen ribbon-chutes, nodded to her as it closed.

"Reminds me of my first encounter with humans," Lafayette said.

"Just without Standish screaming," Torni chuckled.

The hatch shut with a hiss as the pod sealed itself off from the outside world.

"Torni, I need you to get a lifter team and move the pod to the airlock doors," Ibarra said through an IR bud tucked behind Torni's ear.

Torni reached under the pod, widened her stance and lifted it up with little effort from her omnium body.

She carried it toward the end of the air lock as the doors peeled opened.

"Or that. That works too," Ibarra said.

Orbital stations around Ceres and the Crucible fired bursts of anti-air fire every few seconds. Torni saw explosions in the atmosphere against Earth's horizon, long trails of dying ships streaking through the clouds as they succumbed to gravity.

Fires burned against small pockets of the lunar surface. Distant stars wavered around Earth, not from the shifting air currents like she'd see from Earth's surface, but from the passage of drones. Great spikes from the Crucible's structure formed a giant crown of thorns, each shifting against each other.

"I need you to give the pod a good push to the center of the Crucible. Lafayette, you'll get your wormhole in a jiffy. Bring back the Scipio *as soon as you can,"* Ibarra said. *"We have a couple hours to make this work. Don't dawdle."*

"I am an engineer. I do not 'dawdle,'" Lafayette said.

Torni carried the pod over the threshold and let it float just beyond the doorway. She morphed a hand to grip the deck and stretched her other arm out like a tentacle to grasp the pod. She pushed the pod into the Crucible's empty center and pulled herself back into the air lock.

There was a flash of white as the Crucible sent the pod to rendezvous with the *Scipio*.

"Now, the next part." Ibarra cleared his throat. *"I need you to take the other jump engine to the Tsiolkovskiy crater on the dark side of the moon."*

"I'm sorry, take the what where?"

"Transform into a drone, pick up the other jump engine and fly it to the moon," Ibarra said slowly.

"You do know that every gun in this solar system is itching to blow drones to pieces, which would include me," Torni said.

"You'll be safe from the local defense platforms, Scout's honor. Luna is lost. There's no one, drone or human, to shoot at you. Things will happen in a hurry once Lafayette returns and it'll take you at least twenty minutes to get the device into place. Chop chop."

"Don't you 'chop chop' me." Torni picked the jump drive up off the deck and morphed into her drone form, holding the device between her stalks. "I don't even know where the soil cove—thing—place is."

"I'll guide you. Aim for the upper half of the dark side and don't spare the gas."

****

Torni flew over the mountains ringing the

Tsiolkovskiy crater, her stalks gripped to the jump engine behind her like a squid's tentacles against a caught fish. She zipped toward the center of the miles-wide plain, kicking up a storm of loose dust in her wake.

+I'm here.+ She slowed to a stop, scanning for any movement across the crater.

"Wonderful, my dear, well done. Excelsior. Now the hard part," Ibarra said. *"I need you to stay and aim."*

+Aim?+

"When Lafayette is in position, he'll open a wormhole that links to the Crucible, which will then funnel to your device."

+And what position is that?+

"The sun's corona. Lafayette will open his portal in the path of a solar flare and send that raw power through your device. You will direct the flare against the Xaros swarm coming for Earth. You should see them by now. Look for the occluded stars."

Torni shifted to her human form, stepping into the pristine lunar soil. She looked around and found a massive dark patch against the starry sky that shifted and roiled like a living thing.

+Wait. Wait…now hold on just a second.+

"You will be protected by the Tikari shielding for a few seconds. That should be enough to wipe out the maniple. It has to be there and it has to be now. The moon will take the brunt of the heat and radiation. An up-close and personal look at a solar flare would

destroy the Earth. Now, are you ready?"

+What about Lafayette?+

"He won't survive. This was his plan. He volunteered to take the Scipio in. He's the only one that can keep the wormhole open so close to the sun. If we had more time, we could have come up with something else, but here we are."

Torni clutched the jump engine tight and looked to the millions and millions of drones on their way to Earth.

"The shielding should keep you safe from—"

+Don't worry about me. I don't care what the Xaros did to me. I am still a Marine and if I have to die here, now, to give Earth a chance, I will. You should never have kept the details from me, Ibarra. They wouldn't have mattered.+

"Sometimes I forget that not everyone is a dishonorable cheat like me. Put the end with the crystal against your chest and lead the Xaros maniple by about two fingers' width. Sweep the blast across the swarm if you can. The activation will be sudden and unpleasant."

+You're a real son of a bitch, you know that, Ibarra?+

"I do, my dear, I do. The shield will function automatically. Brace yourself when you see it charge up."

Lafayette buckled himself into the command chair on the *Scipio*'s bridge and ran a data line from the back of his head into a port on the chair. The ship's systems came online and fed directly into his mind. He shifted through the damaged systems and found that the Marines and a few sailors had done a passable job at repairing her.

He activated the jump engine connected to the ship's fusion core and routed the Tikari shielding along the *Scipio*'s hull. The Tikari shields were a marvel of engineering from the now extinct species. The technology had spread through the Alliance and was viewed by many as a panacea against the Xaros invaders. Central to the shield's function was a small oscillation buried within the finer details of string theory, which the Tikari had studied extensively for many hundreds of years. It seemed that the Xaros had a more thorough understanding of the underlying physics to the shields and once the Xaros encountered the Tikari fleet equipped with the technology, the drones had ripped through them with ease and put an end to the Tikari.

The Alliance abandoned further research in the technology. Only the Toth kept the shields in use on their larger ships. Lafayette felt disgust rise in what remained of his throat as he remembered salvaging the *Naga* to recover their shield emitters. The Toth shields had been the genesis for this plan, after he'd made a number of significant improvements to their design.

"Lafayette, the Marines are clear. You ready?" Ibarra asked.

The Karigole checked the jump engine's power levels and gripped the handrests tightly.

"Everything is in order. I trust you will send this ship to the right place."

"I have monitored the sun's energy output since I first entered the solar system," the probe said. *"It kept my subroutines active and engaged."*

"It stopped him from being bored. I tried to turn him onto soap operas. He wouldn't have it," Ibarra said.

"See that my personal effects make it to Steuben. He'll need them," Lafayette said. "Be sure he knows I volunteered for this, or he will suspect otherwise of you."

"Thank you, Lafayette. The human race will not forget this," Ibarra said.

"I do this for my village, my people, for the allies that saved us from the abyss. Let's get on with it."

"Stand by."

Lafayette activated the Tikari shielding. A ripple of energy washed across the bridge's view ports, like the leading edge of a wave slowing against a beach. Lafayette looked to Earth and picked out the African continent where a battle raged over Mount Kilimanjaro. The last of his people were safe behind the walls, for now. As much as he wanted to stand atop the battlements and strike at the foe, what he was about to do could turn the tide.

The ship groaned as something deep in the hull buckled. An electrical panel on the navigator's seat fritzed out and sent sparks into the air.

"How did they ever learn to master fire?"

A wormhole formed before the *Scipio* and engulfed the corvette.

Lafayette's heart pounded against his metal chest as the ship's sensors went wild. The white abyss faded away and Lafayette looked out across the sun's photosphere. The surface stretched for far longer than any gas giant he'd ever visited. Giant pillars of fire several times the size of Earth rose off the surface, arced down and formed great archways larger than any structure ever built by mortals. Dark spots tens of thousands of miles across seethed on the sun's surface.

Lafayette had never felt so small before.

"Shields are working, as I haven't been burnt to a crisp." He checked the power levels…and found they were decreasing faster than anticipated.

A flare rose up beneath the *Scipio*, heading right for the ship.

"At least the probe's calculations were correct." Lafayette activated the jump drive and watched as the wormhole struggled to form between the incoming flare and the *Scipio*, solar winds buffeting the portal like a sail in a storm.

Heat warnings popped up across the ship. Temperatures rose to levels that would have killed a human being within seconds. Lafayette felt the armrests go slack as the metal softened. The shields lost half their remaining charge in less than a minute.

The wormhole stabilized.

An avalanche of superheated plasma hit the wormhole...and did not rip through it. The rest of the flare engulfed space around the *Scipio* and the tiny wormhole. The ship survived in a small shadow of safety behind the wormhole. The might of Earth's sun ripped into the portal and out the other end on the dark side of the moon. The plan was working.

"Thirty-four seconds." Lafayette felt his feet melting against the deck. His shields' strength flashed red as they began to fail. A timer popped up and a choice lay before him.

He had enough power to jump away from the sun

in the next several seconds and give Torni only a fraction of the sun's power she needed to destroy the swarm coming for Earth, or he could redirect his jump energy reserves to the shields.

Lafayette didn't hesitate. He tapped the fusion core to power the shields and sealed his fate.

The portal would remain open just long enough to accomplish the mission.

Lafayette tore his restraints away and got a step away from the command chair, ripping his leg away from the melting foot. His broken leg touched he deck and slid out from under him as it went slick with molten metal.

Lafayette's hands hit the ground to arrest his fall. His fingers fused together almost instantly.

He looked up at the wormhole, the rage of the star around the edges. He thought of the Karigole village on Nibiru, where he'd seen children playing, his mother caring for newborns.

"I will not be the last," he said.

The wormhole collapsed and the flare annihilated the *Scipio*.

****

Torni's IR bud started beeping, the sound growing

faster and louder as she felt the jump engine in her arms
start to hum. She flipped a switch on a control panel and a
sphere of Tikari shielding popped up around her, throwing
up a ring of dust as the shield pressed against the lunar
surface.

A wormhole formed a few meters above her, so
wide she could barely see the void between the portal and
the moon's surface. She shifted the jump engine from side
to side and found the white portal followed the
movements.

+Here we go.+ She braced herself against the
ground.

Blinding light burst around the edges of the portal.
The raw heat from the sun instantly scorched the surface
beyond her shielding to black, molten glass. She tried to
shift the portal to the side, but it was as stubborn as a
stuck door. She put all her strength into the push and
managed to move it a few inches.

In the space beyond the Earth and her satellites,
the solar flare streaked out and closed the distance on the
approaching Xaros swarm in seconds. The awesome heat
and raw plasma burst the drones apart like balloons,
destroying hundreds of thousands in seconds. None could
maneuver fast enough to escape the sun's fury as the
portal shifted and dragged the flare aside.

Torni felt the ground beneath her fuse to her feet and burning heat shot up her legs. Her omnium body was tough, but not strong enough to withstand the abuse seeping through the moon's crust. She had to direct the flare for only a few more seconds…

The ripples of light danced over the shield. The portal began shrinking and a strange oscillation coursed through the jump engine.

The engine exploded with a flash of red light, its energy trapped and slamming against the side of the shields, bursting through them like a levy finally giving way to a flood.

The portal vanished and the last of the solar flare stretched into space and faded away.

Where Torni had stood, only a small circle of blasted rock remained in a sea of black glass.

CHAPTER 27

Valdar lowered his hands from his helmet. The trailing edge of the flare that had erupted from the dark side of the moon continued through the void, dissipating to nothing within seconds.

The captain looked to his XO, who shrugged. The bridge crew glanced at each other, then turned their attention to Geller.

"Don't look at me!" the ensign squeaked. "I have no idea why…what's going on with the Crucible?"

A wormhole grew in the center of the great crown of thorns. Geller looked over his control panels, then to the Levin. The engineer just shook his head.

"Captain, a wormhole just formed…but our jump engines are in standby," Geller said.

"Then who's coming through?" Valdar tapped a

panel and entered a hushed conversation.

Geller tapped into a camera feed from one of the forward point defense batteries and zoomed in on the Crucible. Ships emerged from the wormhole, ships unlike any Geller had ever seen.

Sea-green warships shaped like mountain peaks and bristling with rail guns poured into real space. Geller counted two dozen before the last one appeared. Tiny arrow-shaped fighters poured out of the warships in orderly lines.

"I render appropriate greetings," came over the IR in toneless words. "This is Septon Jarilla of the Ruhaald. We are here to fight Xaros."

Geller didn't join the rest of the bridge as they erupted with cheers. He kept his eyes locked on the screen, and frowned as more ships emerged from the wormhole.

Silver ships, each several miles long, emerged behind the Ruhaald. Their hulls were corkscrew shaped, the edges burning with red light. Geller cocked his head to the side. *Why did this new arrival seem familiar?*

"The Naroosha arrive," a smooth voice said over an open channel. "Ambassador Ibarra sends her warm greetings."

"Geller," Valdar said.

The ensign wracked his brain, then reached down

next to his knee and pulled out a roughly bound photo album. He flipped through the pages, most filled with images of Toth cruisers, some with alien vessels, pictures taken from orbit around the world Nibiru.

"Geller!"

The book fell to the deck as the ensign sat bolt upright.

"Sir?"

"Set course to Japan," Valdar seethed with annoyance. "Take us over the North Pole. We'll rendezvous with the *Vorpal* there."

Geller took in a breath to voice a concern, but the twitch in Valdar's cheek told him to hold his thought until later.

"Captain, do we want to wait for these Naroosha and Ruhaald?" Ericcson asked.

"They'll catch up," Valdar said with a shake of his head.

At Geller's feet, the book had fallen open to a picture of a corkscrew-shaped silver vessel.

****

Durand rubbed her back against her Eagle's seat, trying and failing to scratch an itch between her shoulder blades. Dark storm clouds whipped past her canopy as she glanced at a clock on her HUD. She'd been in her flight suit for God knew how many hours and she didn't want to think about the combined funk of adrenaline, sweat and body odor waiting for her when this day ever ended.

"The storms on this planet are a joke," said Manfred, one of her Dotok pilots, over the IR. "The razor hail on Takeni, now that was an experience."

"The last time razor hail struck our village was when we were children." Lothar clicked his beak in annoyance. "Stop trying to impress our hosts."

Durand rolled her eyes and checked their distant waypoint as she and her squadron cut over storm driven waves.

"I remember watching it from the windows and surviving off tubers for months because all the crops died...not you," Manfred snapped.

Durand broke through the clouds and into a rainstorm raging over the Pacific Ocean.

She lowered her fighters to a dozen yards off the white-topped waves roiling across the water. A half-dozen Eagle fighters and two Condor bombers formed a formation behind her lead. She scanned the skies for drones and found nothing.

"All right, all of you, cut the chitchat." Durand

checked her inertial navigation system, then tapped a screen to add a new waypoint. She banked to the right and leveled out, streaks of rain washing over her canopy.

Her squadron had the curve of the Earth between them and the Xaros arch working its way across the southern Japanese island of Kyushu. The Xaros might have detected their descent so charging down the straight-line path from their arrival was a poor tactical choice.

"Fighters from the *Breitenfeld* and the *Vorpal* will launch a coordinated assault on the arch in…three minutes. Eagles, keep the Condors safe and tidy until their missiles hit home, we all understand?" Durand asked.

"I assume there's a valid reason why we can't just hit this thing from orbit with the ship's main gun?" asked Nag, one of the two Condor pilots.

"Have you ever seen what a rail cannon strike can do to a city?"

"We had to fly over what was left of Hong Kong during training. A lesson in loyalty…and punishment," said Glue, the weapons officer on Nag's Condor.

"One missed shot from orbit and the defenders holed up in the mountains will pay the price. Valdar won't risk that—yet—but he'll strike from orbit if we fail." Durand looked toward the sky and found nothing but the blue-gray cloud ceiling and more rain.

"Where is the Dotok squadron…" She tensed as dark objects appeared through the cloud layer.

"Those aren't our fighters. That's not them," Manfred said.

"Are you sure?" Glue asked.

"I've flown Gladius single-seaters since I've had feathers on my *clee'tik*. I know what they look like!"

"*Merde.*" Durand pulled her nose up and hit the afterburners. Pads around her core and thighs squeezed to keep the blood in her head as she accelerated to the storm.

A half-dozen Xaros drones dropped through the clouds. Durand opened fire with her gauss cannon and shattered a drone then cut her afterburners and rolled to the side as scarlet beams stabbed through the air around her.

She sped past a pair of drones and looped around to fall onto their tails.

A bolt of lightning exploded across the sky with a thunderclap. The sudden flash blinded Durand and sent her Eagle tumbling into a dive.

Durand blinked hard, fighting to clear her vision. Her ears rang like a bell. She felt the pull of her restrains shifting against her chest as her fighter flew out of control.

"Altitude. Altitude," sounded faintly in her ears.

The corner of Durand's vision came back and she

355

got a glimpse of her wild control panel. She pulled her stick back and to the left and opened the throttle. She flew for several seconds...and didn't slam into the ocean.

Soon after, her eyesight returned to almost normal and she looked around and saw her squadron below her. A dozen Dotok fighters formed three even lines stacked over the Condors.

"Gall? Can you hear me?" Glue asked.

"Gall here, returning to formation. Weather shook me up," she said.

"This is sword leader Bar'en. I remember this...Gall," said a voice with a heavy Dotok accent.

Of all the assholes in the galaxy, Durand shook her head. Durand had nearly killed Bar'en's wife by accident when the *Breitenfeld* first arrived to aid the Dotok on Takeni. The other pilot had not taken it well and nearly had his jaw broken by Glue when he assaulted Durand.

"We are nineteen seconds behind schedule," Bar'en said. "Accelerating to attack speed now." He said something in the whirrs and clicks of the Dotok language, then he and his fighters sped forward, pushed by blue flames from their engines.

"What did he say—at the end?" Durand took her place at the head of the formation and clicked her jaw to clear out her ears.

"A traditional Dotok saying for luck before battle," Lothar said quickly.

"No," Manfred clicked in annoyance, "it roughly translated to 'see if these hairless mammals can fly worth a damn.'"

"I know what he said, Manfred!"

The brothers switched to Dotok and engaged in a heated debate.

Durand rolled her eyes.

A dark shape rose over the horizon, nestled in red clouds. Yellow bursts of light echoed through the clouds. Durand made out drones and Dotok fighters in a massive scrum above the Xaros construct.

The spikes beneath the arch jabbed bloodred beams into the mountains beneath it. Durand remembered the video saved by Commander Albrecht, the *Breitenfeld*'s original wing commander, remembered watching the Xaros use the same tool to wipe out city after city the first time they invaded the Earth.

"I guess that's it," Nag said.

"Priority target is the ventral weapons," Gall said. "Eagles, charge rail guns and prepare to fire."

Durand cut her speed and flipped a switch on the side of her cockpit, charging the capacitor that powered the rail gun built into her fighter's fuselage. An icon blinked green seconds later.

"Target is the long spike, third from the right," Durand said. "Condors, go for missile launch."

Denethrite-tipped missiles streaked forward, each guided over IR beams.

Durand brought her targeting reticule over the spike and flipped the safety off her rail gun trigger. Her thumb tapped against the trigger, waiting for the missiles to get just close enough to the arch. The rail gun shells would travel significantly faster than the missiles…and if she timed the launch right, they could hit the Xaros with more incoming munitions than their point defense could handle.

"On my mark…fire!" Durand's Eagle rocked back as a snap of light exploded from the rail gun and staccato cracks of a dozen shells shattering the sound barrier echoed around her. Burning trails of air marked the shells' passing. The skies around the arch lit up as fighters and bombers surrounding the Xaros construct opened fire.

A sheet of red energy struck out from a spike tip and swept across the sky, obliterating two Dotok fighters. A pair of explosions erupted well short of their target.

"Contact lost. No hit!" Glue announced.

"Fire again. Fly them nap of the Earth and come in from below." Durand leaned forward as several spikes glowed red with cracks, then fell away from the arch. Three spikes bent their tips together, and a blazing ingot of light formed at the apex.

"Pull up! Pull up!" Durand raised her nose and fired her afterburners. She soared upward, evading a wave of murderous energy that lashed out from the arch. She strained against the acceleration to look over her shoulder and saw her entire squadron behind her.

"*Breitenfeld*, this is Gall." She leveled out and looked down on the Xaros killing machine. Explosions from dying fighters and disintegrating drones cut through the sky. "I don't know if we've got the firepower to kill this thing. We'll make another attack run from above, may have better luck."

"*Gall, this is Valdar. Stand by for the next assault wave.*"

"Say again? I thought we have every available asset on this attack."

"*You've got Ruhaald fighters coming in. Do not—I repeat—do not engage them.*"

A lightning-fast shape tore past Durand's cockpit. Another zipped past on her other side. She looked down and saw dozens of arrow-tipped fighters smaller than her Eagle closing on the arch.

The sky darkened around her. Hundreds of the

angular fighters filled the air, all arrayed in neat wedges of nine craft. The Ruhaald ships banked to their left and formed into a single line, all diving toward the arch.

They unleashed a torrent of thin laser beams against the arch's upper slope. The beams hit without any obvious effect at first...then the Xaros armor cracked and burst outward.

The lead Ruhaald fighter performed a precise attack on the Xaros, then pulled up and flew into the storm clouds. The next fighter in line repeated the same attack and maneuver.

"They must be drones," Manfred said. "Nothing natural can fly so perfectly."

"They're here. They're helping. I don't really care what they are," Durand said.

One side of the construct dipped to the ocean. The entire arch slid toward the sea as explosions peppered its surface. A spike broke against a mountaintop as the arch lost altitude.

Durand smiled as it fell into the dark waters and broke apart as the construct burned away.

"*Breitenfeld*...target destroyed. We're—" A drone tore past Durand's cockpit. Dozens more zoomed past, all heading to the southeast, and none showed any interest in killing her.

"This is Valdar. Return to the ship. Now!"

CHAPTER 28

Elias stuck his arm around a corner and blasted at a pack of drones. He looked the opposite direction and fired bursts of rounds from his rotary cannon and a drone diving down from the top of an apartment building. His rounds tore through the drone and the glass windows behind it.

Daggers of glass rained down on Bodel, who didn't seem to notice as he destroyed a drone picking through the lobby of the same apartment building.

Elias ducked away as a beam smashed through the corner where he'd been firing. He lowered a shoulder, dove through the window of a coffee shop and rolled to a knee, taking out the last three drones with aimed shots.

One drone skipped out of his line of fire. Its stalks twitched, then it shot around a corner.

"Did that one just retreat?" Bodel asked.

Elias touched the mask hanging from his neck.

"Think we got noticed?" Elias asked.

"I think *you* got noticed." Bodel lifted up his forearm cannon and fished out a malformed bullet that had jammed in a barrel.

A shadow passed overhead. Elias looked up and saw a swarm of Xaros drones passing across the sun. The drones spiraled into three tendrils reaching for the ground. One snaked toward Camelback Mountain, one angled away into the city, and the third came right toward the Iron Hearts.

"I ever tell you your plans suck?" Bodel asked. "Next time, *I* come up with the good ideas."

"You can try." Elias checked his battery charge. "I can't get a q-shell out, you?"

Bodel stomped his heel against the road and drilled his anchor through the concrete.

Elias bashed down the wall of the coffee shop and cleared a path to a wide service elevator. He ripped the doors away and found a quadrium-shielded hatch leading to the tunnels beneath the city streets.

A sonic boom from Bodel's rail cannon shattered every glass window of the surrounding buildings. Bodel raised his anchor and ran for Elias, charging through glass and sidestepping more than one disabled drone.

"That was my last one," Bodel said as he slid to a stop at the hatch and jumped down.

Elias followed and shut the hatch behind them. The aegis plating lining the tunnel and the hatch would slow the Xaros down for a few minutes, but it wouldn't keep the drones away.

"Last q-shell or last rail round?" Elias asked as they ran down the dimly lit tunnel.

"Both, what do you have left?"

"One rail shot, enough gauss to keep their attention." Elias went around a corner and tried to raise the city's defense command with no success. They turned a corner and found their path caved in.

"Shit," Bodel said.

"There's another way back to the hangar." Elias looked across a map of the tunnels and turned around. "It'll take longer."

A brief quake shook the tunnel. Then another.

"We've got a walker. Big one," Bodel said.

"Surface." Elias kept running until he came to a hatch in the ceiling. He pushed it up as a long quake shook through the tunnel. He peeked his helm over the edge as red light cast across his face.

"They're burning through the roads," Elias said.

"So much for taking the tunnels," Bodel said.

The roar of Eagles and the boom of cannons carried through the air. Quick red pulses played across Elias' face.

"Well?" Bodel asked.

"Mountain positions are fighting, got the walkers' attention. Come on." Elias crawled out of the hatch and into an Ibarra Corporation lobby. Plastic mock-ups of construction robots and 3-D printer foundries filled the room.

Elias felt tremors through his suit and saw the legs of the giant walker crush an abandoned car a block away. Elias pushed through the wrecked front doors and ran down the street, past a burning Eagle that ripped down the side of a building before it crashed to the road.

Elias pointed to an intersection. "I'll anchor there, hit the walker when it comes around."

A rail cannon shell shattered the side of the building, penetrated through another and ripped through the other side. The entire building collapsed in an avalanche of glass and pulverized concrete. Hunks of masonry showered down and a gray fog swept over the Iron Hearts.

They ducked into the broken remnants of a grocery store and waited for the building to collapse completely.

The shadow of the walker loomed through the fog.

"You're not going to get an anchor in that mess." Bodel pointed to the debris filling the streets.

"No, but there's another spot." Elias climbed up the broken remnants of the building to a broken metal beam that had once formed part of the building's frame.

Elias lifted his right foot and slammed the heel against a join between two beams of the frame. His anchor whirled as it drilled into the metal.

"You're crazy," Bodel said.

"Bring it here." Elias waved Bodel away. The other Iron Heart shook his head and made his way over the rubble as fast as his footing would allow.

Elias felt his anchor bite into the frame and his heel tightened against the frame. He reached up and grabbed the side of the frame, standing parallel to the ground.

"Carius would have my ass if he saw this," Elias said.

"Incoming!" Bodel ran by, firing over his shoulder.

Elias activated his rail cannon and brought it down next to his head. Electricity arced between the vanes as it charged. The walker's legs appeared beyond the edge of a building, then stopped.

Red light built up through the windows between Elias and the walker. Elias reared back as a beam burst through the structure and blasted a hole through the next several blocks. Elias felt intense heat against his legs and chest as the beam blazed just yards away from him.

The beam died away and Elias swung his body back up to face the walker. The Xaros was plainly visible through the neat hole it had blown through the building, its cannon pulsating. Elias aimed his rail gun right into the walker's core and fired.

The recoil ripped his anchor point out of the frame and sent Elias careening through the rubble filling the street below.

Bodel rushed over to his friend and found his feet sticking out from under the wide remnants of a wall, his anchor still embedded in a hunk of steel. Bodel grabbed Elias by the ankles and pulled him out of the rubble. His rail cannon was a twisted wreck, the rotary cannon broken loose from its mount.

"Elias? Elias!" Bodel shook his friend's armor.

Elias sat bolt upright, his rail cannon sparking and jerking from side to side.

"Did I hit it?" Elias asked.

The smoking remains of the walker lay in two neat pieces, one half crumbled over behind the building Elias and the walker had both shot through.

"Are you OK?" Bodel asked.

Elias kicked at the metal still attached to his anchor.

"That was a damn stupid idea," Elias said.

"If it's stupid but works…" Bodel grabbed Elias' anchor, gave it a twist to detach it and tossed it aside.

A light burned through the sky, like a fragment of the sun was coming to Earth.

"That's him," Elias said, "the General." He got to his feet and stumbled against Bodel.

"I'll tell the hangar we're coming." Bodel pointed Elias at Camelback Mountain and led him forward.

****

The mountain shook as another blast from the walkers hit. Hale stumbled against the tunnel wall. Dust showered down from the metal tracks bolted to the rock ceiling.

Hold together a little longer, Hale thought.

"Almost there." Cortaro ran past Hale and hopped onto a ladder against the wall leading down a rough circle cut through the floor. Steuben, Jacobs and Weiss followed Cortaro down the ladder.

Yarrow picked Hale off the wall. "Sure hope that shortcut works."

"You and me both." Hale got to the ladder, braced his hands and feet against the frame and slid down. He looked between his feet and saw the floor of the next lower level. He heard the crack of plasma fire before he cleared the ladder well. A Xaros beam cut through the air beneath his feet and ripped the ladder apart.

Hale released his grip and swung his rifle off his shoulder. He charged up the plasma coils and hit the deck solidly. A Xaros drone filled the hallway, stalks splayed out like a spider's legs. Hale fired from the hip, ripping a gash across the drone's side and breaking off a pair of stalks. The drone staggered backwards and thrust a stalk toward Hale.

He dove to the side, rolling out of the attack and onto one knee. He put two shots in the drone's shell and spilled its pyrite across the floor. Hale spun around, searching for the Marines that came down before him. Behind him was a partially collapsed hallway, the floor sloping downward.

Cortaro stuck his head over the edge.

"Nice shooting, sir," he said.

369

The rest of his team, covered from head to toe in dust, climbed over the edge.

"The drone hit something special," Jacobs said, jerking a thumb over her shoulder. "That happened."

Yarrow landed behind Hale.

"I miss something?" the corpsman asked.

"At least the drone didn't knock down the tunnel we need," Hale said. "Come on."

The tunnel curved, leading them to a rounded stone wall marked BATTERY 12. A hole the width of a coffee can ran through the wall.

"Drone came out of there." Hale pointed to the hole. "Cover the entrance." He grabbed a lever attached to a hydraulic rig and pulled it down. A blast door several feet thick swung open. Inside the battery, empty armor suits lay around the breach of a rail cannon. Smoking craters marked the impact of the drone's killing blows.

"See if she'll still fire," Hale said as he crept toward the open firing port. The rail cannon was smaller, the vanes stubbier than the *Breitenfeld*'s, not meant for long-range void combat. Outside the mountain, a Xaros walker like Hale'd faced on Takeni and Malal's vault pounded redoubts with its main gun.

"Got charge in the capacitor," Cortaro said, "but no round in the chamber."

Steuben grabbed a handle to a metal plate embedded in the floor and lifted it up. A matte-gray tapered dart twice the size of a Marine lay just below the floor.

"I will need help," the Karigole said.

"Sir, you aim. We'll load," Cortaro said. The Marines gathered around the shell and hefted it into the air, their power armor struggling with the weight.

Hale swung himself up into a chair bolted to the side of the breach and tapped a control panel. A cracked screen came to life, displaying garbled text.

"No help there," Hale said. He looked around and saw a pair of hand wheels on either side of the breach.

The Marines heaved the round into the breach, Cortaro cursing up a storm the entire time.

Steuben looked up at Hale. "Now would be appropriate to fire."

"Have to aim over open sites." Hale pointed to the hand wheels. "Move the declination right and elevation down."

"I don't know what a declination is but…" Weiss grabbed one of the handles and spun the wheel. The gun shifted to the left and Weiss changed direction.

Hale climbed onto the top of the rail cannon and looked down the barrel.

"Stop," Hale said as the weapon lined up on the walker. "Down…stop."

A shadow flit across the open port.

"Think we got something's attention," Jacobs said.

Red light cast through the gun chamber as the walker beat against the mountainside.

The walker moved closer, throwing off the shot.

"Lower another—" Someone grabbed Hale by the ankle and yanked him clear of the breach. A pencil-thin beam cut through the metal where Hale had been.

Marines fired on a stalk tip bent over the lip of the firing port, blasting it—and a generous portion of the façade—to smithereens.

Hale spun a hand wheel, trying to gauge the elevation correction he needed from the side of the weapon. He spied a lanyard connected to a metal handle against the breach, the analog firing system.

A beam hit the side of the cannon, boring through the electromagnets.

Hale lunged forward and grabbed the lanyard, pulling it down as he fell to the deck.

The cannon fired with a clap of thunder loud enough to pop Hale's ears. The buzz of a thousand insects filled his head as he struggled to his feet. He took his rifle off his back and stumbled to the open edge, his balance reeling from the disruption to his inner ears.

A stalk tip hooked over the edge. Hale batted it aside and leaned over the battlements. He found the drone and pounded it into oblivion with plasma bolts then he looked up. The walker lay on its side, its weapon's array shattered by the blow from the rail cannon. The walker burned beneath the setting sun.

"Well done," Steuben said as he lifted Hale up from the edge.

"What?" Hale asked, loudly.

"I believe you suffered some hearing damage." Steuben waved Yarrow over.

"Are you saying something?" Hale looked back to the crumbling walker. Two armor soldiers jumped over the construct, firing wildly behind them. A tear of light so bad it stung Hale's eyes came around a mountain spur.

Blinding light filled the gun port. Hale felt a tug on his shoulder and his feet lifted away from the floor.

He was falling. His eyes were flash blind, his ears still ringing, but his arms and legs swinging about without purchase convinced him he was falling. His body slammed against something and a vice grip closed around him.

"Steuben? Cortaro?" He fell against the ground and shook his head to clear it.

Hale's eyes recovered enough to see a pair of

giants standing over him. He fought to stand on wobbly legs. They were inside the mountain's main entrance, a mess of broken stone blocked the way to Phoenix. The rest of the hangar was empty but for broken machinery.

Steuben helped steady Hale.

"What happened?" Hale asked.

"The Xaros leader was about to fire on us," Steuben said. "I took immediate action to save our lives."

"Did you…did you *jump* off the mountain?"

"I did. The chance that I could cushion our fall with my grav-liners or that Elias would catch us seemed better than trying to stop a disintegration ray with my face," Steuben said. "I did not anticipate there being so many rocks coming down at the same time as us."

"Thank me later." Elias' hand retracted into the forearm housing and a crystalline blade with gold filigree came out. An aegis shield unfolded from his other arm. "Hope you two are up for a fight. This is as far as we go."

"I'll lower the blast door," Bodel said.

"Fight what?" Hale asked. An electric hum filled the hangar. The hair on the back of Hale's neck stood up as talons made of coherent light stabbed through the rocks blocking the exit.

The General tore his way into the hangar. The ground blistered and ignited into small fires beneath his

374

feet. The Xaros Master pointed to the faceplate hanging from Elias' chest.

+YOU+

Hale screamed in pain and fell as the word pounded through his head.

****

The General's word hit Elias like a spike through his mind. He backpedaled a step, fighting to focus. The Xaros Master was a wash of blazing light and heat through his optics.

Elias bashed the fist of his shield arm against his chest.

"Come on then." Elias held his blade in a high guard and charged. He slashed at the General and hit nothing but superheated air as the General jinxed aside in a flash of light. Elias ducked behind his shield and caught an energy blast against the aegis armor that knocked him off his feet.

Bodel leveled his cannon at the General and let loose on full automatic fire. Rounds exploded harmlessly a yard away from the General. The recoil pulled Bodel's shots up and to the side…and to the chain holding up the aegis blast door. Gauss rounds shattered the chain, sending the blast door down with a crash.

Bodel let out a war cry and charged, unsheathing his blade in a vicious slash to the General's neck.

The General caught Bodel's sword arm and slammed a punch against Bodel's shield. The Iron Heart flew back, bouncing off the floor like a stone across water. Bodel's arm, torn clean out of the socket, remained in the General's grip. The arm melted like wax against an inferno. The sword clattered to the ground.

An ammo case behind the General burst open. Ar'ri rushed out and lunged at the General with his sword. The tip cut across the General's hip, opening a gash across the chain-mail layer. Blue light burst from the wound.

The General slid aside and raised an arm overhead, the fingers turning to a scythe of hard light. He slashed at Ar'ri, who got his shield up and blocked the blow before it could slice him in half. The scythe bit into the edge of the shield…and stuck.

The General whipped around, slinging Ar'ri against the blast doors with a crash.

Caas burst out from a maintenance hatch and stabbed the General in the back of an arm. She twisted the blade and the General's arm fell limp against his side. The Xaros spun around and sent a blazing fist at her head.

Caas swayed back. The General extended a

hooked finger and ripped out the optics on her helm as his hand passed. Caas' hands went to her helm and she stumbled back.

There was a roar and Elias punched the pointed corner of his shield into the General's face, denting the faceplate. He arched his sword up and caught the General across the chest, cutting through a plate of red armor. Blue light shone out of the wound.

Elias brought his sword down for a return stroke. The General brought his arm up and the blade bounced off a force field coming off the General's armor. The Xaros' injured arm reknit and a blast of light slammed into Elias' hip, knocking him into the air.

Elias fell onto his back and skidded across the floor with a screech of metal. He brought his shield up and blocked the General's foot as it rammed down against his chest. The shield glowed red hot as intense heat coursed through the aegis, melting it from the inside out.

"Elias, hold on!" Hale yelled. The Marine had got to his feet, blood running from his ears and nose. He ripped an antiarmor grenade from his belt, twisted it twice and hurled it at the General.

The General didn't bother to react, confident in his kinetic shield until the grenade exploded and shot a lance of molted copper through his chest. The General floated back, one hand covering the wound.

He looked at Hale and his eyes flashed beneath the facemask.

"Ghul'Thul'Ghul!" Steuben ran at the General and buried his heirloom blade into the General's thigh. The intense heat from the General's being poured into the weapon and exploded in Steuben's face.

The General built up a ball of energy in his hand and punched toward Hale.

Caas rammed her shield into the General's fist. She looked at the General through the view port on her armor, hate in her eyes as she took the brunt of the General's blast against her shield.

Caas angled the shield to the side and slipped into the General's guard. She slammed her helm against the General's face and stabbed up. Her blade pierced just beneath the General's breastplate and came out just beneath his shoulder.

The General bashed her aside and rose into the air, one hand covering the wound. He backed into the aegis blast doors and tried to meld through...and bounced off. The General whirled around and pounded at the door, ripping at the aegis plate with long claws as he tried to find an escape.

Elias picked up Bodel's blade and hurled it at the

378

General.

The blade burst through the General's breastplate. He arched back and a wail filled the air. The General fell slowly to the ground.

Elias reached up and took the General by the neck. The Iron Heart's fingers burst into flames and fused together as he slammed the Master to the ground. Elias rammed his blade into the General's chest, pinning him to the ground.

"Let your end be in pain," Elias growled. "Let your end be in failure. This is for her. For us all!" Elias slammed his open hand down on the General's head and ripped it off. Elias held the severed head up and looked into the General's eyes as the light faded away.

Blue ooze poured out of the open neck and vanished in a cloud of steam. The General's armor went limp and collapsed against itself.

Elias tossed the General's empty mask and mail helmet away and fell onto his knees.

"Iron Hearts…who needs help…" Elias fell to his elbows.

Bodel, half-buried beneath a wrecked lifter, held up his remaining thumb.

"Ar'ri is unconscious," Caas said from her brother's side, "but he's stable." She shifted her body around to look at Steuben, who lay motionless on the ground.

"Steuben?" Hale got to the Karigole's side and rolled him to his back. Steuben's right hand was a mangled mass of blackened flesh, and a sliver of his blade was embedded in his face from the top of his right eye socket down across his jaw.

Steuben looked at Hale and gave the Marine a pat on the side of his head.

"Good fight," Steuben said.

CHAPTER 29

Valdar got out of his command chair and walked slowly across the bridge. There, in the skies high above Sri Lanka and barely visible from his ship's position high over the Pacific, a Xaros construct unlike any other he'd ever seen grew larger as more and more drones melded together.

The drones formed into a stretched pyramid, the tip pointing at the Earth.

"Ibarra, what is that?"

"Not…not something we've seen before," Ibarra said from a small screen on Valdar's faceplate. "The probe's picking up an impossible amount of energy in that thing. If the math is right…this new construct could cut through the Earth's crust and into the center of the planet. It'll heat up the planet's core. Drive the continental plates apart, volcanic eruptions everywhere. Worldwide devastation. This is impossible. The Xaros don't destroy worlds—ever!"

"I'll trust my lying eyes." Valdar snapped his head toward Geller. "Set a collision course. Full burn."

Geller nodded quickly.

"Valdar, the *Vorpal* will join you," Captain Go'ral said. "We will not let our final colony die before us. *Gott mit uns.*"

"Thank you, Go'ral. Ibarra, can the Naroosha and Ruhaald get their ships to Earth in time to help?"

"The Xaros will fire in…minutes, ten at the least. It'll take an hour for anything with firepower to get from the Crucible to you," Ibarra said.

"Minutes?" Valdar watched as the pyramid's surface glowed red. "We're not going to make it."

****

On the dark side of the moon, drones zipped across the surface as they raced to join the construct forming over India. Light from their stalks danced over the glass ocean scarring the Tsiolkovskiy crater and miles beyond its rim.

In the small circle where Torni had devastated the

Xaros swarm, the ground shifted.

An arm burst through the blackened ground. Long, skeletal fingers clawed the vacuum then slammed into the ground. Torni pulled herself out of the hasty grave the explosion made for her. Her body was a mess of heat-warped shell and gaps across her surface, resembling some horrific creature made from sea coral more than a human being.

+Join. Combine!+ The call was overwhelming, stronger than any urge she'd ever felt. The drone gestalt pulled her away from the moon and on the same path as the drones flying overhead.

+Together. Together.+ Torni grabbed a hunk of rock as big as her arm and transmuted it into omnium. The glowing material flowed down her arm, restoring it to her human form like a healing salve. She took in more of the dark rock and made herself whole.

She morphed into her drone form and took to the sky, falling in with a pack of drones.

The demands of the gestalt lessened as she came around the horizon and saw the Earth. Drones fed themselves into a growing mass. Data from the drones assaulted her mind like her head was inside a beehive.

Beneath all the noise, a still small voice remained.

What's happening…where am I going? Torni thought.

The drone mass shifted, transforming into a jagged spike pointed at the Earth's surface. The tip opened like a blooming flower and the spark of a disintegration beam lit up in the center.

We're going to…burn through. The image of the beam burning through the Earth's crust and into the mantle came to her: the Earth's core superheating and breaking the planet apart.

The fleet…impressions of human and other defenders came to her, all too weak and too spread out to have a hope of stopping the planet killer. She saw the *Breitenfeld,* her hull scarred, weapons broken, yet still attacking the Xaros without mercy as they went to join the construct. The words she'd put against the hull in gold lettering, *Gott Mit Uns,* shown in the sunlight.

Torni flew into the construct, her limbs melding with other drones as they added themselves to the weapon. More drones piled on top of her and she felt the entirety of the Xaros mass through the gestalt.

Deep inside her mind, she felt an itch. The kill command she'd received and carried since Malal's vault scratched at the back of her consciousness.

Will they know? If only…if only I could have seen Standish one last time.

Torni didn't fight the kill command, didn't banish

it away to the back of her mind like every other time before. She let it course through her…and into the rest of the drones. The command, designed to prevent the capture of a Xaros drone, was a fundamental piece of the drones' programming, written by the Xaros Master who designed them. The kill order overrode the General's last decree and the beam forming at the construct's tip faded away.

Torni felt a gentle warmth spread through her, then the sensation of pins and needles as her body began to burn away. The gestalt that had been hammering her mind faded away as the drones went off-line, leaving their bodies to disintegrate.

A ring of burning embers erupted from Torni and flashed through the construct. The spike broke apart and fell into the atmosphere. The Xaros became a rain of fire that would have covered all of Sri Lanka had any of their remains made it to the surface.

The last of the Xaros siege dissipated in the monsoon winds.

****

Valdar watched the Xaros pyramid crumble away. "Why?" he asked, the word hanging heavy over the bridge. "Why would it just...die?"

"No one's complaining, Captain," Ericcson said.

"Ibarra?" An error message popped up on Valdar's visor. He keyed the channel back to the Crucible and tried to hail the command center again. No response. He tried to open a new channel to Gor'al on the *Vorpal*, and got nothing.

"Comms, were the antennae arrays damaged?" Valdar asked.

"Negative, sir...looks like there's some kind of IR interference going through the atmosphere," the comms officer said.

A whine filled Valdar's earbud.

"This is Prefect Ordona of the Naroosha. The Crucible is ours. All Earth ships will take their weapons off-line immediately and set anchor in orbit around your larger moon. Noncompliance will be met with deadly force. Noncompliance will be punished with the nuclear destruction of a human settlement every twenty-two minutes, beginning with...Phoenix."

Valdar snapped to his feet. He went to Geller's station and saw the camera feed of the Crucible. The Naroosha and Ruhaald ships surrounded the jump gate. Shuttles from the silver vessels descended on the command center where the probe and Ibarra had taken up residence.

Broken human warships drifted away from the jump gate, bleeding atmosphere from wrecked tanks and trailing bodies. Valdar had left a small contingent behind to guard the Crucible…and they were gone, destroyed by the Ruhaald and Naroosha.

"They stabbed us in the back," Valdar said.

"The human fleet over the fourth planet will not leave orbit. Noncompliance will be met with deadly force. No human ship will travel between worlds. Noncompliance will be met with deadly force. You have ten minutes to obey."

Valdar felt the gaze of every man and woman on the bridge fall on him.

"Sir, what do we do?" Ericcson asked.

There were fewer than twenty warships still able to fight, all damaged and crewed by exhausted sailors. Even with the *Vorpal,* Valdar knew he didn't stand a chance against the newly arrived "allies."

"Get our fighters back aboard and get us into lunar orbit," Valdar said evenly.

"We're giving up?" Utrecht asked.

"No!" Valdar slammed a fist against Geller's chair. "This isn't over, you all understand me? I will be damned if we surrender to these bastards, but this isn't the time to fight. Not yet."

Valdar turned his eyes to the Crucible.

Ibarra, you crafty bastard, you'd better have something up your sleeve.

CHAPTER 30

An arrowhead fighter wobbled through the air, trailing smoke and steam. Standish winced as the craft skipped against the desert floor and bounced twice before grinding to a halt not far from one of the linked bunkers.

"There's no body in that one," Egan said. "It was abandoned the last time we pulled the lines back."

Standish zoomed his helmet's optics on the fallen alien ship. There was movement just beneath the canopy, but he couldn't make out what was in it.

"We need to go help," Bailey said.

"Now wait just a second." Standish held up a hand. "Are we sure it's even friendly?"

"Bloody things have been beating the piss out of the Xaros for half an hour and haven't tried to shoot us. They're mates." Bailey shoved a metal hatch out of the way and ducked into the tunnel. "Come on, you ratbag deros. It's the only decent thing we can do."

"Oro," Egan said, "stay with the doughboys. We'll call you over if we need help."

Egan stared at Standish until the Marine grumbled and followed Bailey into the tunnel.

He jogged to the empty bunker and found Bailey standing outside, her eyes to the sky. Columns of smoke rose from Phoenix. The sound of roaring engines and firing weapons that had filled the air for hours had fallen away to almost nothing.

"Maybe we won." She slung her carbine onto her back and walked toward the downed fighter. "Cover me."

Standish shouldered his weapon and sidestepped toward the front of the fighter, keeping Bailey out of the line of fire in case something horrible jumped out. Egan stood a few feet from him, his weapon ready.

The fighter was a bit smaller than an Eagle, with vectored engines and weapon pods built into the wings. The canopy was an angular dome, frosted over. Shadows moved within. Writing made of different-sized triangles flowed over the wings.

"I don't have the best track record when it comes to first encounters." Standish's toes ground into the dirt, ready for fight or flight.

"I'm pretty sure whatever's in there has no

intention of eating you," Egan said.

"So sure? Why don't you go over and rub your face all over it and see what happens."

Egan didn't move.

"Thought so," Standish said.

Bailey touched the fighter, running her hands along the canopy seem.

"You'd think there'd be an emergency release like our fighters," Bailey said. She shrugged and knocked on the canopy.

The canopy popped open on her side and green water poured out, splashing against Bailey's hips. She jumped back and drew her carbine in a hail of rapid-fire cursing. The canopy flipped over on a set of hinges and more water came splashing out.

The pilot wore a copper-colored, blocky space suit. Each hand bore a half-dozen tendrils twice as long as a human finger. Its helmet was a dome set against wide, thick shoulders. The alien had wide, squid-like eyes on either side of its head and a mass of feeder tentacles for its mouth.

"Nope. Nope!" Standish tried backing away but Egan grabbed him by the arm.

The pilot turned to Bailey, raised one hand and made a rough approximation of a wave.

"I extend culturally appropriate greetings," came from a voice box on the alien's armor.

Bailey lowered her carbine slowly. "You can speak English?"

"Bastion technology." The pilot's tentacles wafted over the voice box. The pilot pushed against the side of his cockpit, then fell back inside, splashing more water over the edges. "Assistance."

Bailey slung her rifle over her shoulder and approached slowly. The alien held out its arms and Bailey gingerly reached out to touch it. The tentacles wrapped around her upper arms several times.

"They've got stickers on them," Bailey said, her voice several octaves higher than usual, "like a damn octopus." She stepped back, pulling the pilot free from the cockpit. The pilot's lower body was a tail, covered in flexing scales that were part of its flight suit.

Bailey set it against the fighter's side. Brackish water spurted up from a crack over the pilot's tail.

"Leak. Leak." The pilot released Bailey and raised its hand next to its head, tentacles writhing. "Get the repair kit out of my tool chest."

Bailey put both hands over the crack. Water spurted through her fingers and hit her visor.

"What're you doing over there? Waiting for an

engraved invitation? Move your asses," Bailey snapped at the other two Marines.

Standish ran over to the cockpit, which was full of gray water he couldn't see through.

"What am I looking for?" Standish asked.

"Left. Front. Cylinder the size of my—" A burbling noise came from voice box. "Translation unavailable," chimed from a pleasant voice.

Standish turned his head to the side and plunged his arm into the murky water. He grouped around.

"Is it…is it supposed to be moving?" the Marine asked. He pulled out an object that looked like a piece of candy wrapped in seaweed.

"Give. Give!" The pilot reached tentacles to Standish. They stretched out and snatched the device away. The pilot pressed one end against the crack and thick red caulk came out with a bubbling noise. The pilot smeared the substance over the crack and the outflow of water ceased. It turned the tool over and jabbed the other end against a small ring inset against the suit.

The pilot sat back as its arms fell to the ground.

"Much better," it said. "I need…medical attention. Help is coming."

"Is there something we can do now?" Bailey asked.

A port opened on the side of the pilot's suit and dark red goo spat out.

"I will never complain about Steuben again," Standish said. "Ever."

A whine rose through the air. Standish looked up and saw a blocky ship descending toward them.

"I assume that's for you," Bailey said. "You got a name?"

Unintelligible babble came from the voice box followed by "—second class, Ruhaald expeditionary fleet. The Xaros are nearly purged from your planet. How did you destroy the leviathan forming over this land mass?"

Bailey and Standish traded a glance. "Thought that was you," she said.

The Ruhaald ship set down on landing skids a dozen yards away, blowing up a cloud of dirt that turned to mud against Standish's wet armor.

"Nothing like getting dusted to learn their pilots are just a bunch of dicks like human pilots," Standish said.

"...*are...stop them,*" Orozco said, the disturbance from the Ruhaald ship washing out his transmission.

"What was that, Oro?" Egan asked.

A ramp descended from the front of the shuttle. A force field held back a wall of water inside the craft. Several Ruhaald, all in the same armor as the pilot but walking on two legs, approached. Each held rifles made of tiny blocks stuck together seemingly at random.

A Ruhaald with a golden sunburst on its chest and shoulder armor stepped forward.

"I render culturally appropriate greetings," it said.

"Hello to you too." Bailey stepped away from the pilot. "I guess you're in charge."

The doughboys are coming! Orozco shouted through the IR. *Stop them! They think the aliens are hostile! Some got past me!*

"Why would they think that?" Egan turned around and saw three doughboys charging out of the bunker. Egan held his hands up and ran toward them.

"Hey, wait a minute." Egan stepped between a doughboy and the Ruhaald as the lead soldier leveled its weapon. The doughboy leaned to the side, then slammed his rifle against Egan, sending him flying through the air.

"Enemies!" the doughboy shouted.

The soldier's rifle fired and the high-ranked Ruhaald's torso blew apart. Dark slime and salt water splashed over Bailey and Standish.

"Stop! Stop!" Standish threw himself over the pilot.

Electricity crackled through the air as lightning burst from the Ruhaald rifles and struck the doughboys, burning them down to their skeletons within an instant.

Standish looked up from the pilot. The commanding Ruhaald's legs, topped by broken armor oozing whatever was left of the alien, wobbled for a moment and fell forward.

"I think we're in trouble," Standish said.

A shadow cast over him. He looked up and saw tentacles reaching for his face.

****

Orozco ran from the bunker, waving his arms to the Ruhaald craft as their soldiers forced Bailey, Standish and Egan up the ramp and into the watery interior.

"Wait! Wait! They didn't know!" He ran around the smoldering doughboys and watched as the ramp closed.

The shuttle lifted off the ground and blasted off into orbit.

Orozco slowed to a stop next to the dead Ruhaald and the crashed fighter. He looked back to the dead doughboys and felt his heart sink.

He touched his gauntlet screen and found an open IR channel to Camelback Mountain.

"Area command, this is Staff Sergeant Orozco out

at bunker Juliet-90. We've got a problem." He looked down at the lumps of blasted flesh that remained of the alien officer.

"A really…big problem."

CHAPTER 31

Malal sat in his cell, arms loose at his side, chin resting against his chest. His fingertips twitched with the sound of cracking bone.

The door to the brig opened and a silver box the size of a suitcase floated into the room. It stopped several feet from Malal's cell. A small cube floated off the box. It stopped in the air, then the rest of the box broke into cubes and formed into a pixelated shape of a hunched-back creature with a wide face.

"Malal, I am Ordona," the words came off the vibrating cubes.

Malal's head jerked up. His unblinking eyes stared ahead with a dead man's gaze.

"Are you?" Malal asked.

"I represent Bastion. Your bargain remains."

"Does it?"

"Your bargain remains…with some modification."

Malal rose to his feet and glided to the edge of the electric field of the cell wall.

"Tell me more." Malal's face pulled into a wicked smile.

TO BE CONTINUED…

With Earth occupied by traitorous allies, Captain Valdar and the crew of the *Breitenfeld* must find a way to liberate their home world without destroying it in the process.

The next chapter of the Ember War saga lies in **The Crucible**, coming September 2016!

ABOUT THE AUTHOR

Richard Fox is the author of The Ember War Saga, and several other military history, thriller and space opera novels.

He lives in fabulous Las Vegas with his incredible wife and two boys, amazing children bent on anarchy.

He graduated from the United States Military Academy (West Point) much to his surprise and spent ten years on active duty in the United States Army. He deployed on two combat tours to Iraq and received the Combat Action Badge, Bronze Star and Presidential Unit Citation.

Sign up for his mailing list over at www.richardfoxauthor.com to stay up to date on new releases and get exclusive Ember War short stories.

The Ember War Saga:

1.) The Ember War
2.) The Ruins of Anthalas
3.) Blood of Heroes
4.) Earth Defiant
5.) The Gardens of Nibiru
6.) Battle of the Void
7.) The Siege of Earth
8.) The Crucible (Coming September 2016)

Made in the USA
Lexington, KY
13 October 2018